Mr. Darcy's Debt
A Pride and Prejudice Variation Novel

April Floyd

Copyright © 2017 by APRIL FLOYD

All rights reserved.

No part of this book may be reproduced in any form or by any electronic or mechanical means, including information storage and retrieval systems, without written permission from the author, except for the use of brief quotations in a book review.

Several stanzas from the song Black Eyed Susan by John Gay were used in the text of this book. The song is in the public domain worldwide because John Gay died at least 100 years ago.

This book is for all my readers; those who inspire me, encourage me, and those who have always wanted me to give them just a little more. I hope this title gives you as much pleasure as it gave me in the writing. Would Elizabeth Bennet have ridden horses or even raced them? If her father still held a spark of his love for risk from his younger days, I cannot see why she would not have ridden with him to visit the tenants of Longbourn and then excelled as a horsewoman. I must also say this book would not have come full circle without the excellent guidance of Elizabeth Ann West. My best friend and sister from another mister who might also be my cousin since our roots are deep in Kentucky soil only a few counties apart. Also, the support and encouragement of Joy King (J. Dawn King), a fine and favorite JAFF author. Knowing that this novel gave her so much happiness as she read through the rough draft was a definite boost to my confidence. I wanted to rise to the occasion of impressing such an accomplished fellow author. And last, but certainly not least, my dear friend Beverly Farr, aka Jane Grix. Her phone calls come at just the right time and our kindred spirits share in a love of Shakespeare, paranormal tales, and all things Outlander.

Prologue

December 1786

Bertram Fitzwilliam, the Earl of Matlock, gathered his siblings and friends after the Winter Ball at Woodland Manor for a midnight revel on his sprawling estate that lay in the north of Derbyshire.

His sisters Anne and Catherine, along with his younger brother Reginald, waited by the door with Thomas Bennet and several other young people from their circle while the sleighs were readied for their jaunt. Anne Fitzwilliam took Thomas Bennet's arm as her sister, Catherine, raised one brow at the familiarity between the two.

"Will you skate with me first, Lady Anne, if the lake is frozen solid?" he asked with a twinkle in his eyes.

The earl's favorite sister listened as her friends dared her to take Bennet up on his offer. More and more her heart was preferring Thomas Bennet though he would never be seen as suitable match. "I gave you the first dance of the ball, Mr. Bennet. You must not be greedy!"

The tinkling laughter of young women carried across the entryway as Bertie clapped his friend on the back. "Come now, Bennet, let us save our bravado for the ice."

The group of young people moved through the front doors of Woodland Manor to the trio of sleighs now waiting in the front drive.

Anne and Catherine rode with the Abbot sisters and their cousin, Annabel Morely, while the gentlemen filled the other two sleighs. Annabel remarked on the few ladies present. "Are you certain we should go along? Father would not approve if he knew."

Catherine Fitzwilliam was as prim and proper as a young lady ought to be but even she enjoyed a bit of fun now and then. "Hush Annabel, your father would not approve of many things. It is likely why you are still at home instead of married as you ought to be."

The Abbot sisters covered their mouths though their shoulders shook with laughter. Poor Annabel was a beautiful girl with a strict father. Anne motioned for the Abbot sister seated next to Annabel to move over.

She left her seat by Catherine and sat with an arm about her young cousin. "Your father trusts Bertie implicitly Annabel. Besides, we have footmen and drivers as escorts."

Annabel Morely smiled at Anne before raising her chin at Catherine and the Abbot sisters in vindication. The horses pulled the sleighs away from the large house and down the lane to detour across the fields that led to the lake where the Fitzwilliam family skated during the winter months.

Bertram Fitzwilliam was a risk taker, a young man who loved the rush of living life on the edge. Thomas Bennet was cut from the same cloth and proved a great companion though their lives were soon to take drastically different turns. In their sleigh, joined by Reginald Fitzwilliam and the subdued brother of the Abbot sisters, Bertie teased Bennet about Anne's growing fondness.

Bennet was to marry for money while Bertram Fitzwilliam would be the most sought after bachelor of their group come the season in London. "Bennet, you must not lead Anne to believe she might have a future with you for I cannot allow it. Though I know you would be a fine husband, she must marry well."

Thomas Bennet sighed. He understood his friend's concerns regarding Lady Anne Fitzwilliam. She was a rare beauty with a tender heart. "Never fear, Bertie. My feelings for Anne are purely platonic. I would never wish to hurt her."

Silence descended as the sleighs approached the lake and the snowy fields sparkled in the light of a full moon. The winter night was chilly and the breath of the horses wreathed their heads in a bunting of frigid mist.

When the drivers came to a stop, Bertram set the footmen to work building a bonfire on the shore with the wood he'd had them bring along in the third sleigh. His friend sat beside Anne, their heads bent close together. "Bennet," he called, "hurry with those skates. I want to see how far out the lake is frozen."

Seeing that the ladies were happily situated near the small fire that was crackling merrily as the footmen tended it, Bennet turned and hurried to the lake, his skates over his shoulder. He called to his friend as he bent to lash the skates to his feet. "Go on ahead Bertie, I'm right behind you."

He could see that, near the shore, the ice was thick as they expected. Gaining his balance upon his blades, Thomas Bennet was soon gliding along beside his best friend. As they ventured toward the middle of the lake, Bennet was sure they ought to remain along the edges for the sake of the ladies. "I say, it ought to have been thicker here too. Let's go back, Bertie."

Bertram Fitzwilliam clapped his friend on the back and his laughter boomed across the semi-frozen lake. "You know well enough my ways of flirting with danger but yes, the ladies shall stay to the edge of the lake."

The two men returned to the shore and skated along the edge gliding effortlessly on the thickened ice. Bertram grew bored and struck out across the center while Bennet stayed to the edge making a circuit to meet his friend on the other side.

Anne stepped onto the lake and made a few figure eights before gliding out to the center to join Bertie on his way across. Bertie smiled and held out his arms. "Wait there Anne, let me come to you. The ice is thinner out here."

Instead, his sister continued for she always had followed Bertie in his stunts and merriment. Bennet continued his lazy circuit around the edge of the lake with only mild concern nagging at the edge of his mind.

Before her brother might advance more than a few feet, Anne reached Bertram's side and Catherine called to them from the shore, admonishing her siblings for skating on thin ice. "Bertie, bring Anne back this instant!"

Catherine would not skate without great encouragement and tonight she stayed near the bonfire chatting with the Abbot sisters who had never skated in their lives.

The next moment, Bennet watched in horror as the ice cracked under the weight of Anne and Bertram. The golden brother and sister of Woodland Manor seemed to be caught in time, stuck in its grasp as the ice gave way. They were suddenly plunged beneath the surface into water colder than the ice breaking around them.

Thomas Bennet thought for not a moment before racing to the center of the lake and jumping in after his friends. The shouts from the small crowd on the shore alerted the drivers and the footmen. The men raced onto the ice but were helpless in their aim to move closer to the center of the lake.

Bertie struggled to keep his sister afloat as his limbs grew heavy in the strength-sapping cold of the icy lake. Thomas Bennet grabbed his friend and began to tow him to safety. Bertie held tightly to his sister, his stamina beginning to fail.

The young Earl of Matlock freed himself from Thomas's grasp and pushed the now limp form of Anne Fitzwilliam into his friend's blue-tinged hands. "Take her, Thomas, she won't survive without your help. I'll come along."

Thomas Bennet bit his bottom lip hard enough to draw blood in order to keep himself moving forward. Anne was a much lighter burden than Bertie. He would get her to the nearest footman and go back for his friend. Bertie was making pitiful progress behind him and he prayed they might all come out of this foolhardy lark without suffering tragedy.

The terrified screams of Catherine Fitzwilliam, and the other ladies on the shore, rang in Thomas Bennet's ears keeping him alert as his legs began to slow beneath the water.

A footman and a driver hauled Anne from the chill waters and took her immediately to the bonfire hoping to mitigate the effects of the ice and frigid waters. Bennet turned, his own body protesting as he moved slowly back toward the center of the lake to retrieve Bertie. His friend waved him away, yelling with the last bit of energy he possessed but Bennet pressed on.

Bertie sank below the surface and Thomas Bennet pushed his body to the brink of exhaustion in order to reach his friend before all hope was lost.

Long minutes later, minutes that seemed like hours, Bennet held Bertie's limp form in one arm while making slow progress to the shore. He finally reached the drivers who'd come out as far as they might and waited while they hauled Bertie out and rushed him to the bonfire.

The three friends, soaked and chilled to the bone, were rushed in the first sleigh back to Woodland while the second sleigh was loaded with the terrified ladies and the young men who tried to comfort them.

The servants and family of Woodland Manor passed a terribly long night with the local doctor seeing to each patient in turn. By dawn's light, all three young people were in various stages of deterioration and the story of tragedy at Woodland spread even to London. It would be many months before Thomas Bennet was able to leave Woodland for Hertfordshire.

In the terrible weeks that followed the accident, Bertie rallied but once before pneumonia tightened its grasp on his weakened lungs.

One afternoon, he begged to see his dear friend. His fever was high but the doctor agreed that the young earl be granted a visit with the man who had saved him.

In the stifling heat and dim light of Bertram Fitzwilliam's bedchamber, Thomas Bennet sat and listened as his friend begged to know of Anne's condition. "Please Thomas, no one will say that she is recovered. The doubt is driving me mad with worry. Tell me whether the news is good or bad."

Bennet took his friend's hand and worried at the hotness of his skin. Bertie had seen Anne twice before his health had worsened but his fevered mind did not seem to recall those visits. He would not torture the man further. "She is well, Bertie. You were right to see her clear of the lake first."

Bennet held back tears as his friend cried out in relief and then struggled for each breath. He feared his young, strong friend would not be long for this world.

Bertie motioned for him to come close. "I shall see you well provided for as a thanks for saving my dear sister. You are never to worry over the entailment on Longbourn if you are not blessed with a son. Send Anne in please if she is able. I must see her before nightfall. I fear this is my last."

Thomas Bennet stayed by his friend's bedside for a time, talking low, telling jokes and amusing stories in an attempt to lift Bertie's spirits. He could not imagine losing his best friend in all the world. They were quite the unlikely pair to the passing acquaintance — a young earl who had taken on the mantle of guiding his family and a young gentleman burdened by the entail on his future inheritance, two more disparate situations could not have been found in one friendship.

Bennet was touched by Bertie's promise and hoped never to see the day when he might benefit from simply providing the duty of love and friendship to Bertie and his sister. When Bertie's insistence to see Anne could no longer be denied, Thomas Bennet rose and quit Bertie's bedchamber.

Anne Fitzwilliam hurried to her brother's room at Bennet's word, pleased that Bertie was eager to see her. She knew that he must be improving if he received visitors. Her joy became short-lived as she stepped into his room. The young man who had been her hero all through her younger years lay in his bed as pale as the sheets beneath him, sweat pouring off him as he shivered pitifully.

She went to her brother and took his hand, hoping he might be breaking his fever. "Bertie, dear sweet Bertie, you fool, I am here."

Bertie smiled the most beautiful smile and mouthed her name, his voice a broken whisper. "Anne, my lovely Anne," he whispered and she sat beside him.

Anne took a cloth and wet his lips, her tears at seeing Bertie so ravaged blurring her vision. "Here love, would you care for a sip of water? Or tea? I could have the maid bring tea."

Bertram gasped for breath, his head moving from side to side. "No, Anne, there isn't time, you must listen."

Anne Fitzwilliam would not believe her dearest brother was dying before her eyes. She had never known a moment's sorrow in her young life but there was no denying the truth. So she listened intently to Bertie as he told her his last wishes.

Promising him she would write down every word, she called his valet to witness. Anne took paper from his desk and did as he asked. Bertram Fitzwilliam's last act was to affix his signature to the paper his sister had made. When Anne laid aside the paper, Bertram begged her not to go. "Stay Anne, I do not wish to die alone."

She moved to sit next to him in bed and held him as tears coursed down her cheeks. Anne begged to call for their mother or father, Catherine or Reginald, even Thomas, but Bertie would not relent. "Please, Bertie, you must allow them to say their goodbyes."

He struggled for breath for a long moment before patting her hand, his body relaxing at the comfort she provided. "There is no time, poppet. Please, stay with me."

Chapter 1

November 1811

Elizabeth Bennet sat with her sister Jane in the parlor of Longbourn as their mother again peppered her eldest daughter with questions about her weeks at Netherfield. Jane Bennet had fallen ill after having tea with Miss Bingley, and her sister Mrs. Hurst, and Elizabeth had gone to Netherfield to tend her sister.

Mrs. Bennet's eyes were bright with anticipation as she moved to the edge of her seat eyeing Jane as though she had failed to impart some terribly important detail in her last retelling. "Tell me again what he said as you sat by the fire in the parlor!"

They had been home two days and yet Mrs. Bennet had not grown tired of imagining her eldest daughter as Mrs. Charles Bingley. "Mother, I've told you twice in as many days. It will not change with another telling," Jane protested looking to Elizabeth for assistance.

"Jane was ill, Mother, quite ill. Mr. Bingley was very kind and attentive but you cannot expect that a match be made under such conditions."

Mrs. Bennet ignored Elizabeth's assertion and turned expectantly to Jane. "Go on, Jane, tell me again how he looked when he spoke of the future. Were his eyes dreamy or were they cold like Mr. Darcy's?"

At her mother's mention of Mr. Darcy, Elizabeth allowed her mind to drift from the conversation and recalled her irritating attraction to one Fitzwilliam Darcy, the man who had seen fit to insult her terribly at the assembly in Meryton only a fortnight ago.

Her estimation of the man had gone from dislike to grudging respect in the two weeks spent at Netherfield. He had been the perfect gentleman while the Bingley sisters delighted in shaming Elizabeth at every turn.

Still, a tension remained between them though he had wished her well as she and Jane quit Netherfield. Mr. Bingley had asked if he might pay a call in a day or so to be sure Jane was truly well and Elizabeth wondered if Mr. Darcy might accompany the Bingley party on their visit to Longbourn.

Realizing that she hoped he might, Elizabeth rose from her seat and wandered to the window that overlooked their garden. She would love to walk about as the rains had kept her indoors all the days they'd tarried at Netherfield.

Mrs. Bennet's loud exclamations startled Elizabeth from her reverie and she turned to see her mother embracing Jane before bustling off to Mr. Bennet's study.

"Jane, whatever did you say to Mother?"

Jane sighed and shook her head at her favorite sister. "No more than I told her yesterday but Mother believes Mr. Bingley shall propose sooner rather than later. She is convinced he will seek an audience with father when next he comes to call."

Elizabeth had known her mother would draw such conclusions. Mrs. Bennet had paid a call to Netherfield herself during Jane's illness and had spoken quite rudely to Mr. Darcy.

Elizabeth had defended the man and thought now that his regard for her had only grown since that moment. Mrs. Bennet had advised her to ignore Mr. Darcy after his insult at the assembly and Elizabeth smiled to think her mother's insults given in the drawing room of Netherfield had made it difficult for her daughter to heed her earlier advice.

Happy to see bright rays of sunshine streaming through the parlor window at last, Elizabeth took Jane's hand. "Are you well enough for a small walk about the garden, dear sister?"

Jane nodded and followed Elizabeth to the parlor door as their mother's voice rang out in the hallway outside their father's study. Jane pulled Elizabeth towards the dining room instead with a plan to escape through the kitchen. "I'd rather risk another cold than listen to mother plan my future happiness without the benefit of an offer to warrant such action."

The eldest Bennet sisters were successful in their escape and Cook supplied them with a baked treat as she had done many a time over the years when the girls wandered into her domain.

While the sisters roamed the garden in the back of the home, a carriage arrived at the front of Longbourn. A stout man in the garb of a vicar stepped down and surveyed the house before him. A satisfied smile lifted the corners of his mouth and he turned to direct the driver to wait for the groom to come from the small stable to see to his horses. His mind corrected his mistake, *her ladyship's horses,* as he approached the front door.

His knock went unanswered for a long while and the man was ready to turn and wander the grounds of Longbourn for a sign of his cousin when Elizabeth and Jane appeared by the stone arch that separated the grounds from the lane.

"Here, young ladies, is your father at home?" he called in an inquisitive and irritated manner.

Elizabeth glanced to Jane for an explanation but there was none her sister could make. The Bennet girls approached the man to inquire as to his identity.

"Excuse me sir," Jane said as Elizabeth walked beside her, "why do you seek our father?"

The man seemed taken aback at Jane's question and stood dumbstruck for a moment. The door to Longbourn opened at last and Hill stepped outside. "Sir, what might I do for you this beautiful day?"

The man was a Mr. William Collins come from Kent to visit the family at Longbourn. Elizabeth and Jane were astonished that the man their mother had long bemoaned the existence of now stood at their doorstep.

Moving quickly, Jane thanked Hill and dismissed her as Elizabeth led their guest to the door. "Please forgive us sir, we were not aware that father expected a visitor. Won't you come in?"

Mr. Collins smiled at the two young ladies, for they were quite beautiful and the aim of his visit gladdened his heart. His patroness, Lady Catherine de Bourgh of Rosings in Kent, had sent him forth to find a wife from among his cousins. He followed Elizabeth and Jane to the parlor and sat to wait for an audience with Mr. Bennet.

Jane was the perfect hostess but Elizabeth was quiet and observant. Mr. Collins got the distinct impression that his cousin Elizabeth was not as obliging as she ought to be. That was a mark against her parents in his mind. Little did it matter, for if she accepted his proposal he would see to it that she exhibited the best social graces.

Mr. and Mrs. Bennet soon joined the party in the parlor. Mr. Collins stood as his cousin Thomas Bennet entered the room. "I trust my letter preceded me, cousin?"

The ladies of Longbourn turned their eyes to Mr. Bennet as one and he cleared his throat. "Why, yes Mr. Collins, it did. I hadn't the time to mention your visit to my wife."

Mrs. Bennet fluttered her handkerchief about and gave her husband a most disapproving look. "Do forgive my husband, Mr. Collins. He hasn't been himself lately. I shall have to send a maid upstairs to prepare your room, oh, and I shall have to advise Cook we have another for dinner."

Mrs. Bennet did not wait for Mr. Collins to give an answer as to the purpose of his visit and the man would not have in any case, not before speaking with Mr. Bennet. Instead, she hurried to the kitchen in search of Cook.

Jane and Elizabeth watched as their father led Mr. Collins out of the parlor to his study where they might converse without further interference.

Mr. Bennet closed the door of his study and, as the first order of business, went to his desk and poured two glasses of port. He tried never to conduct business without the aid of spirits and the practice had long served him well.

Mr. Collins accepted his glass with a happy smile and a nod of his head. Mr. Bennet waited until the first gulp of port cleared his throat before addressing his cousin. He suspected the man had made this trip in order to offer for one of the Bennet daughters for his letter had hinted broadly at such a motive.

"Mr. Collins, I am sure you would prefer to rest after your journey," Mr. Bennet began but his cousin interrupted him with much the same expediency as Mrs. Bennet always did and it was as though he was more likely related to her than, in fact, to Mr. Bennet.

"Oh, I say. The trip was quite unpleasant. Stuck on the side of the road for half a day with a broken wheel. The weather was most uncooperative, rain never ceasing..."

Mr. Bennet nodded his head and lifted his glass to halt the man's chatter. "Let us be thankful you've arrived in good health."

Mr. Collins lifted his glass in turn and found he quite liked his cousin, though the man had been much disliked by Collins's father. Finding his host had fallen silent and was now staring out the window by his desk, Mr. Collins cleared his throat.

"As you may have gathered from my letter, I am of a mind that I ought to marry one of my cousins. 'Tis a terrible thing to think of them cast out of their home should the conditions of the entail make it necessary."

Mr. Bennet felt a tickle in his throat and poured himself a bit more port. He had been uncommonly tired for a few days and thought he must retire after dinner instead of lingering in his study.

Smacking his lips as the familiar warmth from the port eased his aches and pains, Mr. Bennet eyed Mr. Collins for a moment before speaking. The man was much too happy by half. Drawing a breath and steeling himself for the conversation ahead, Mr. Bennet began to speak but found himself caught in a coughing fit instead.

After many long minutes, he regained control of himself and begged his guest's forgiveness. "I can't imagine where that came from, though I haven't been well these past few days."

Mr. Collins appeared displeased by the display and scooted his chair away from the desk. He dreaded illness of any sort and secretly hoped the man had only strangled on his drink. Thinking it best he leave the room for fresh air, Mr. Collins made to stand from his seat. "We may speak of the matter after dinner if you wish, cousin. Perhaps a period of rest might be in order?"

Mr. Bennet shook his head. He did not wish to be trapped in his study with the man after dinner. "We may speak of it now, after dinner I would prefer to retire to my rooms."

Mr. Collins sat again and laced his fingers together. "My patroness, I mentioned her in my letter, has said that I should make one of your daughters my wife. An olive branch, so to speak, to soften the loss of Longbourn."

Mr. Bennet nodded. He recalled that Lady Catherine of Rosings in Kent was the sister of his friend Bertie Fitzwilliam. Bertie had died many years ago after a terrible accident that Mr. Bennet still recalled from time to time in his nightmares. "How very kind of Lady Catherine to consider the welfare of my daughters. The Fitzwilliam family always did wish to manage the affairs of their friends."

Mr. Collins's mouth dropped open at this, the question he wished to ask stuck in his throat.

Mr. Bennet smiled and nodded. "Yes, indeed I am well acquainted with her family. I was a very good friend of the

Fitzwilliam siblings before I married Mrs. Bennet and settled at Longbourn to raise a family."

"My patroness did mention a debt that was owed, cousin, and I am happy to be of service to her in settling the matter."

Mr. Bennet narrowed his eyes at the man wondering at the repayment Lady Catherine believed he was owed. In his mind, there was no such matter between him and any member of the Fitzwilliam family. That time of his life was history and had long been buried.

He decided to move the discussion forward so that he might have time alone with the memories Collins had unwittingly brought to mind.

"If you wish to have my opinion on the matter of which daughter might be the best suited, I would say that you must seek the counsel of my dear wife. However, the girls are all of an age, save the youngest two. I doubt a parson would consider either silly girl. They only hold dreams of red coats and bonnets as their chief concern."

Mr. Bennet took up his drink and looked again out his window. His cousin took the move as a dismissal of sorts and rose to leave the man to his study. "I will see you at dinner, cousin, and shall take your advice into consideration."

Chapter 2

Mr. Collins returned to the parlor and was pleased to find Jane and Elizabeth still there, now sewing in quiet camaraderie. The laughter and noise from above stairs startled him but he sat with his cousins and smiled at them eagerly.

Elizabeth returned his silly smile and glanced at Jane. Mary Bennet entered the parlor then and Jane introduced her to Mr. Collins. "Mary, this is our cousin Mr. Collins. You'll remember that father has spoken of him many times."

Mary smiled shyly at their visitor before taking a seat near him. Mr. Collins was charmed by her quiet and retiring nature.

Mary Bennet was the middle child of the family and possessed a distinctly different demeanor than her younger sisters. Her chief happiness in life was reading the Good Book and playing the piano forte. Upon finding that Mr. Collins was a parson, Mary kept him occupied for nearly a half hour before Kitty and Lydia Bennet entered the parlor with an agenda.

"Elizabeth," Kitty whined as she snatched her bonnet from Lydia's hand, "mother has said you will walk with us into Meryton for ribbon."

Lydia caught hold of the edge of the bonnet and gave a fierce tug. Mr. Collins gasped as Kitty gave a piercing screech. Elizabeth jumped up and took Lydia by the hand. "I shall not reward either of you with a walk into Meryton until you stop this nonsense."

The youngest Bennet daughters were terribly spoiled by Mrs. Bennet. Whatever they desired, it was her happiness to indulge them while leaving Jane and Elizabeth to sort their horrible manners.

Mr. Collins was astonished at the foolishness of his youngest cousins and moved closer to Mary as she was the only sister besides Jane to be in possession of poise and grace.

Elizabeth held out her hand for the bonnet and Lydia stuck out her chin refusing her sister's demand. "Lydia Louise Bennet, do you wish to go into town and admire red coats or sit here with Mary and our cousin?"

Lydia placed the bonnet in Elizabeth's hand and stared at Mr. Collins. "I was not aware we had a visitor."

Elizabeth made the introductions and gave the bonnet to Jane. Kitty and Lydia were not the least bit mortified over their behavior and Mr. Collins now understood Mr. Bennet's warning about their lack of maturity.

Clearing her throat, Elizabeth moved to push her younger sisters out of the parlor before another spat began. "Jane, would you care to walk with us?"

Jane declined, pleading a headache. Elizabeth noted that the soft pink of her cheeks had faded and her complexion now seemed paler than it had only an hour ago. "Lizzy, I would not. Our turn about the garden earlier has tired me more than I thought."

Turning to Mr. Collins, Jane asked if he might like to join her sisters. Elizabeth glared at Jane but had to smile sweetly as Mr. Collins called her name. " Cousin Elizabeth, I am no great walker and am afraid my trip has left me wishing to remain here in the parlor."

Mary could see that Jane wished to be alone to rest and her face lit up with a wonderful idea. "Cousin Collins, I would enjoy walking to Meryton upon your arm, tis not far."

Mr. Collins did not wish to be subjected to the further tantrums and screeching of the younger girls but Mary now stood expectantly before him, her hand out. Delighted by her attention, he rose and placed her hand upon his arm and quit the parlor with the sisters.

Elizabeth sighed as she set off down the lane with Mr. Collins and Mary before her, chatting amiably, and her younger sisters skipping farther ahead.

While four of the Bennet sisters were away in Meryton with Mr. Collins, Longbourn received another guest. Charles Bingley had kept his promise to be certain that Jane was truly well. Mrs. Bennet was in high spirits and sent Hill for tea.

"Mr. Bingley! How lovely of you to come so soon after my Lizzy and Jane have come home. Mr. Bennet and I are most grateful for your attention to our Jane."

Mr. Bingley delighted in Mrs. Bennet's praise. He was quite pleased to be appreciated by his neighbors, especially the parents of the lovely Jane Bennet. "Think nothing of it, Mrs. Bennet. I am happy to have been of assistance. Miss Bennet was a most wonderful guest considering her ailment. And Miss Elizabeth showed such concern. I only wish my own sisters cared for each other so well."

Mr. Bennet entered the parlor and sat after giving Mr. Bingley his regards. Watching the man as stood near Jane, he now knew Mrs. Bennet had been correct in her estimation of the young man's interest.

It was not a surprising situation as his eldest daughter was quite lovely. Her agreeable nature matched Bingley's to perfection. Soon, he would have two of his five daughters married. The thought pleased him though he hoped his Lizzy would not be the one chosen by Mr. Collins.

His cousin was much too verbose and foolish to be a match for his quick-witted Lizzy. Feeling weak of a sudden, he thought to excuse himself to his study. He tried to stand but his legs would not obey.

Jane called to him from her seat on the sofa next to Mr. Bingley. "Father, are you unwell?"

Mr. Bennet gave a wave of his hand as if to dismiss her concern and tried to rise again. In a moment, he found himself pitching forward, his balance lost.

Mr. Bingley jumped up and caught the man before he fell to the floor. Mrs. Bennet began to fuss and cry over her husband's condition and Jane helped Mr. Bingley to move her father to the sofa.

Mrs. Bennet retreated behind the sofa where she might lean over her dear husband's weakened form. "Oh dear, he has not been well for several days. What shall we do? That awful Mr. Collins has come and brought such worry to my dear husband!"

Jane tried to calm her mother as Hill entered with the tea. The servant was shocked to find her master laying pale and lifeless on the sofa and Jane sent her to call for Mr. Jones, the apothecary. "Hurry Hill, send the stable boy."

Mr. Bingley went to Jane and took her hand. "I shall send for my physician from London. It will take time, but surely your father's condition warrants such concern."

Mrs. Bennet moved to sit by her husband in a chair Mr. Bingley had moved for her. "Oh Janie, he is so cold and pale. Why will he not wake up?"

Jane Bennet covered her mouth with one hand and turned away wishing desperately that her sister Elizabeth was home. Mr. Bingley turned to her, his eyes full of concern. "Miss Bennet, all will be well."

His countenance did not convey the conviction he tried to relay with an authoritative tone of voice. Mrs. Bennet continued to moan and sob beside her husband and finally the man came round. He gasped for a few breaths before his face went an awful shade of blue.

Mr. Bingley hurried to his side, pulling at his cravat and pounding the man on his back. His efforts were in vain and

Thomas Bennet breathed his last in his parlor at Longbourn with his wife gone limp in his eldest daughter's arms.

The funeral of Thomas Bennet was held three days after his death and Elizabeth Bennet had grown weary of the constant stream of visitors to Longbourn to pay their respects.

Mr. Bingley had spent many hours with Jane and Mrs. Bennet since he had been present when her father died and Elizabeth was glad that his sisters remained at Netherfield after their obligatory visit. Mr. Darcy had come twice and his presence had touched Elizabeth's heart.

The day after her father was buried in the cemetery in Meryton, Elizabeth roamed the fields and hills around Longbourn for hours until the cold chilled her to the bone. Mr. Jones had said her father had fallen ill suddenly, likely with the same malady that had kept Jane abed at Netherfield, but his heart had not been strong enough to survive the illness. Tears stung her eyes along with a biting wind that carried a hint of snow. With her cousin had come the loss of her father and in Elizabeth's mind the two would ever be connected.

When she returned to her home, all joy was gone from Elizabeth Bennet's heart. Her customary walk could not restore it and the task that lay before her assured there would only be more suffering.

Mr. Collins had barely waited until the service for her father was ended before pressing his case for marriage. She and her sisters, along with their mother, would be cast out of their home unless she, Jane, or Mary relented and married the man.

Her mind and heart refused to consider such a life bound to a man she could not love with her whole heart. His behavior since her father's death had been insufferable as he went about the estate with the steward making notes.

Surely now that Longbourn was his, he might have shown a modicum of restraint in asserting himself. But he had taken her father's favorite chair in the parlor and she'd found him in the study at one point with his feet up on her father's desk and the decanter of port nearly empty.

No, Elizabeth Bennet would not become Elizabeth Collins no matter how her mother might plead with her.

Leaving her bonnet and spencer by the door, Elizabeth entered the parlor to find her mother, Jane, and Mr. Collins at what appeared to be an impasse. Jane had done it then, denied him as well.

The sisters had spoken of it the morning of their father's funeral. How they neither one could honestly consider marrying their cousin. Jane planned that their mother and two younger sisters would stay with their Aunt Phillips in Meryton while she, Elizabeth, and Mary made their way to London to stay with the Gardiners, her mother's brother and his wife.

The older girls had spent many summers with the Gardiners and were welcome to the townhome on Gracechurch Street. But this time would be so different. Could the Gardiners afford to keep three of their nieces, at least until one of them was situated in an advantageous marriage? Mr. Gardiner was prosperous in trade but three unmarried young ladies would be quite a burden.

Elizabeth believed that Mr. Bingley had grown quite fond of Jane. The circumstance of their father's death had drawn out a protective side of the man that only strengthened his feelings for Jane. But they could scarcely hope to wait at Longbourn until Mr. Bingley offered for Jane with Mr. Collins eager to claim his right.

Mrs. Bennet rose and led Elizabeth to a seat beside Jane. The sisters held hands as Elizabeth looked to Mr. Collins. Mrs. Bennet sat again and addressed her second daughter.

"Lizzy, Mr. Collins spoke with your father about his plans to marry either you or Jane or Mary and Mr. Bennet was agreeable to the plan. Now that we are without my dear husband, and your father, we must accept Mr. Collins's gracious offer."

Her mother's smile was strained and Elizabeth could see that she would be in tears soon. Jane's refusal had likely been expected by their mother for Mrs. Bennet was set upon Mr. Bingley as the match for her beautiful Jane.

Elizabeth rose from her seat and went to stand by the fireplace. Mr. Collins was seated again in her father's chair and the sight of it angered her so until she was certain her heart burned as brightly as the coals in the fireplace.

Mr. Collins cleared his throat and Elizabeth glared at him, her grief and anger choking her until she wished she could dash from the room and take refuge in her father's study.

Instead, she drew herself up and stuck out her chin. She looked at her mother and Jane again before addressing Mr. Collins. Jane gave a small nod of her head but Mrs. Bennet had bowed her head and her shoulders shook with quiet sobs, the sound of which caused a tiny flare of guilt in Elizabeth's breast.

Gathering her courage for the fight ahead, Elizabeth turned to her cousin. "I will not marry you, Mr. Collins. I cannot."

Mr. Collins sat stunned, his mouth gaping open before turning to Mrs. Bennet. "It must be the grief speaking. I know cousin Elizabeth is not able to speak for herself at this moment. What say you, Mrs. Bennet?"

Elizabeth moved to stand beside her mother, placing a hand on her shoulder. "While we are shocked that father is gone, I assure you I am quite able to speak for myself. Mother and our younger sisters shall live with our Aunt Phillips while Jane and I, with Mary, go to London to stay with family there."

Mrs. Bennet raised her head as Jane kneeled before her. "Lizzy is right mother, she should not marry him. Mr. Bingley shall surely seek my hand and I will provide for you and my sisters once we are wed. Do not worry."

Mr. Collins rose from his seat and began to shout, his face red with rage. "This will not do! How have you managed to bring up such selfish, ungrateful daughters who would see you set out of your own home so soon after your husband's death? What of Cousin Mary, then? Is she set to refuse me as well?"

Mrs. Bennet struggled to stand and her daughters lent her their arms. She fixed Mr. Collins with her gaze and spoke clearly and without her customary display of emotion. "How dare you raise your voice to me in a house that never should have been yours? You call yourself generous and gracious, yet you have disgraced this family with your crass behavior since the moment of my dear husband's death. Longbourn is no longer our home and you shall not marry any of my daughters, not even Mary, though she might wish to accept you."

Mr. Collins rushed across the room but Jane and Elizabeth moved to stand in front of their mother. If the man wished to do harm, he would have to begin with the eldest daughter.

He drew up short and sputtered for what seemed an eternity before taking his leave of Longbourn. Elizabeth turned and embraced her mother, tears pouring unchecked down her cheeks.

In the parlor of a home no longer theirs, unsure of their future, the ladies of Longbourn held one another and cried again for the man who'd left them in such turmoil with his passing.

Chapter 3

Elizabeth Bennet sat with her hands clasped tightly in her lap as Mr. Collins introduced his patroness Lady Catherine de Bourgh of Rosings in Kent to all assembled.

There was, as yet, no explanation of the lady's presence at Longbourn save Mr. Collins's connection to the woman and still, it did seem odd that a peer should concern herself with the death of Thomas Bennet.

Mr. Collins had sent a letter to the woman upon Mr. Bennet's untimely demise to request that he might stay in Hertfordshire and settle the business of Longbourn since he had taken a wife in the person of one Charlotte Lucas two weeks to the day after Mrs. Bennet had declared her daughters would not marry him.

Charlotte, being a very dear friend of Elizabeth, had persuaded her new husband to allow the Bennets to remain at Longbourn until Mr. Bennet's will had been read.

An express had arrived not many days after the hasty wedding informing Mr. Collins that Lady Catherine would arrive in Hertfordshire as soon as she might.

Jane Bennet slipped a pale, trembling hand into Elizabeth's lap searching for the comfort of her dearest sister's grasp. Their mother sat on the other side of Elizabeth with her eyes on her husband's cousin.

Elizabeth recalled the series of events that had led to her father's untimely demise and her eyes stung again with hot tears she dared not indulge before their company.

Her odious cousin stared at them all in turn and Elizabeth glanced away from the man as Hill entered with tea.

Lady Catherine had been cordial to the sisters and their mother but had grown silent and pensive as her parson held court in Thomas Bennet's favorite chair. Elizabeth wished she had taken the chair up to her room but knew the puffed up he-goat would make her return it.

A quarter of an hour later, Hill entered the parlor again with their Uncle Phillips following close behind. The meeting at Longbourn was much more than a social call, it was the reading of Mr. Bennet's will. Lady Catherine de Bourgh cleared her throat after Mr. Phillips was introduced and Mr. Collins looked as though he wished to speak. Instead he remained quiet but his temper was rising.

His face looked as it had that day when Jane and Elizabeth had refused him and Elizabeth wondered if he might require Mr. Jones, the apothecary from Meryton, to be called to the home. Instead, he remained silent as Uncle Phillips arranged his papers upon the table by the window.

Nearly an hour later, with all the pronouncements made concerning Mr. Bennet's will, the party gathered in the parlor of Longbourn sat quietly as one. Mr. Bennet had left a sizable dowry for each daughter, and monies for Mrs. Bennet, all held by Mrs. Bennet's brother, Edward Gardiner — the tradesman in London. It seemed the ladies would not be left penniless.

As Uncle Phillips quit the parlor, Mr. Collins rose from his seat and began to bluster. "I say, my cousin has at the least provided a means to keep the lot of you from destitution but where shall you go? After this day, Longbourn will no longer be your home."

As her younger sisters began to cry anew over the loss of their home, Elizabeth eyed Mr. Collins with a cold fury. How dare he continue to cause such distress? She began to believe that their sadness gave him some degree of happiness.

Heartened by the revelations of her father's will, Elizabeth stood and eyed her cousin. "You hold in your hands the ability to ease our loss but you refuse. What is another week when Longbourn shall be yours forevermore?"

The parson sneered at Elizabeth Bennet while his patroness watched carefully. The man was most irritating but in honor of the memory of her brother Bertie, the mistress of Rosings had provided a living for him.

Thomas Bennet was the reason for his good fortune then and his death had blessed the man again with an estate. But fate had looked cruelly upon Thomas Bennet's wife and daughters and Lady Catherine's duty to her dearly departed siblings demanded she be present today to remedy the Bennet's sad situation.

Mrs. Bennet gathered the younger girls to her. "Go upstairs ladies and prepare your trunks, for we shall leave Longbourn before the sun sets on this day."

Jane called for Hill to assist the girls but stayed with her mother and Elizabeth to face their expulsion from the home with dignity. Mrs. Bennet stood between her eldest daughters, their arms about her to hold her up as they knew her nerves were strained from all that had passed these last few weeks.

Mr. Bennet had borne his wife's mercurial nature with a sense of humor and an unflagging devotion that inspired his daughters to seek a match made from love. Now that their mother was a widow and their sisters dependent upon them to make matches that would settle all their futures, the eldest Bennet sisters rose to the challenge.

Jane looked to Elizabeth, a nod passing between them, and spoke without a trace of the uncertainty that haunted them all. "Mr. Collins, we shall not tarry longer in your home but know this, all that you have gained came at a dear price. You might have truly shown generosity and kindness by allowing us a little more time."

Mr. Collins advanced upon the trio, his eyes narrowed and a palpable threat preceding him. Lady Catherine stood in one swift motion, for all that she did rely upon a cane, and moved to block his progress. "Enough Collins! I have seen quite enough. Go and wait for me in the carriage. It is on account of Mr. Bennet that you were given the living at Rosings."

The parson had drawn up short before the lady and, at her words, his face paled considerably. The man was shaken and in no mood to challenge the formidable peer. Not sparing a parting glance for his cousins, he hastened from the room with his hat in hand.

Once the man was gone, Lady Catherine de Bourgh sat and motioned for the stunned Bennet women to do the same. "I am sorry to have allowed him to berate you so at such a terrible time but I wished to see the spirit of the women my friend Thomas Bennet loved so dearly."

Elizabeth looked to her mother and Jane but they were equally confused. How had their father come to know Lady Catherine de Bourgh? The woman in question sat and retrieved a packet from the case at her feet.

She handed it to Elizabeth Bennet and rested her hand upon the confused young woman's for a moment. "These papers will explain in great detail the news that I have come to deliver. You may read them later if you wish, but I assure you each document is legal and binding."

Mrs. Bennet took the letter from Elizabeth but handed it back upon seeing her husband's name written boldly across the front. She turned her attention to Lady Catherine for an explanation of her most unusual visit. "Pray tell, your ladyship, whatever news could you have that pertains to my dear husband?"

Lady Catherine sipped her tea for a moment before returning the cup to the table. There was much to tell and she was eager to settle at Netherfield to rest for the night before returning to Rosings come morning. "Mrs. Bennet, your husband was a dear friend of the Fitzwilliam family. There was a time, long ago, when he was well known to our family through his friendship with my eldest brother. My sister, Lady Anne Darcy, and my brother, Bertram Laurence Fitzwilliam admired Thomas Bennet greatly."

Elizabeth flinched at the name Darcy and the three Bennet women voiced a flurry of questions all at once. Lady Catherine held up a heavily jeweled hand and smiled benevolently. "I do realize my news is shocking and quite unexpected. I shall answer three questions before I take my leave."

Elizabeth spoke first, her curiosity at the name Darcy compelling her to leave the question regarding her father to Mrs. Bennet. "You said the name Darcy, did you not? We met a Mr. Fitzwilliam Darcy at the assembly in Meryton before father fell ill. He is a guest at Netherfield, I believe."

Lady Catherine nodded and her eyes brightened at the mention of her favorite nephew. "Indeed, Mr. Darcy is my dear sister's only son. He shall wed my daughter Anne before I leave this earth. His friend, Mr. Bingley, was kind enough to offer rooms at Netherfield for my visit."

Elizabeth considered the woman's words regarding her nephew and his future. He was a handsome gentleman in possession of a great fortune, of course he would marry the daughter of a peer and his own cousin. It was likely the reason he remained aloof and distant that night when at the assembly when confronted by the gossip and rumors of her neighbors. Still, she had thought he might hold an admiration for her when she was at Netherfield with Jane, and then again when he came to pay his respects for her father.

Mrs. Bennet spoke and Elizabeth put thoughts of Fitzwilliam Darcy out of her head. "Your ladyship, I wonder at your declaration to Mr. Collins regarding owing his living to Mr. Bennet?"

The mistress of Rosings faltered for a moment as though lost in a terrible memory before answering. "Yes, Mrs. Bennet, Mr. Collins was recommended by my brother, the Earl of Matlock, because of his connection to Mr. Bennet. You see, our family owed a deep debt of gratitude to your husband for his brave actions on behalf of my eldest brother and sister. My family sought to enrich the lives of his relations as a means of repayment."

Mrs. Bennet's eyes brightened as she recalled the tale Mr. Bennet had told her all those years ago, the winter before they were married. She had wanted to skate on a pond near Longbourn and he refused her most vehemently. "Oh yes, I had forgotten after all this time. My dear Thomas was skating on a lake at Woodland Manor and nearly died himself after saving two of his friends who had fallen through the ice. That must have been your siblings."

Their esteemed guest nodded her head and Elizabeth saw the pain in the lines etched around her mouth. The parlor grew silent once more as the two older women were lost in their own memories.

Lady Catherine finally turned her gaze upon Jane and nodded for her to speak. The eldest Bennet daughter twisted her hands in her lap and dropped her eyes to the floor before speaking. "What shall we do Lady Catherine, in light of this surprising news?"

"You shall remain at Longbourn for as long as you wish, despite Collins's demand that you leave. I shall require that he and his wife return to Rosings with me in the morning to settle our business."

The three Bennet ladies released a collective sigh of relief before the grand lady of Rosings could continue.

"There is a country home provided for you in Derbyshire near Pemberley, the home of my nephew Fitzwilliam Darcy. The place is known as Somersal and Bertie made certain the home would be available to you should Mr. Bennet's death leave you in such a circumstance as your current situation."

All three of the Bennet ladies gasped aloud at this news, shocked at the enormous generosity of a man they had never known. Mr. Bennet had indeed been a particular friend of the

Fitzwilliam family for there to have been such arrangements made without the knowledge of his family.

Lady Catherine continued her speech before rising to leave the stunned ladies of Longbourn. "The estate belongs to my youngest brother Reginald. After the death of our dear Bertie, despite your father's best efforts to save him, it was left to Reginald with the stipulation that the home be kept aside for any heirs of Thomas Bennet who were left without a home due to the entailment."

Mrs. Bennet had one final question for the mistress of Rosings in Kent. "Pray tell, how did your brother know of the entailment?"

Lady Catherine smiled to recall it. "Bertie and Thomas were forever teasing one another over their fortunes in life. I am certain Bertie was moved to provide for any future heirs of his friend after Mr. Bennet had managed to save our dear sister. Anne and Bertie were very close, we all were."

Chapter 4

The brisk morning air stirred Elizabeth's eagerness to wander about the grounds of Somersal and she held tightly to the apple in her right hand. She'd had one for herself before leaving the kitchen for the stables. The shiny red prize in her hand was for Merrit, her favorite horse from the many residing in the stables of her new home.

Mr. Bennet had taught her to ride when she was a young girl and she had always enjoyed going with him to visit their tenants. Knowing how her skill on a horse pleased her father, Elizabeth had been happy to overcome her fear during those early lessons and press on. She was pleased she had done so as riding was an enjoyable pursuit that allowed her to see more of Somersal than she might on foot.

One of her treasured memories of her last day at Longbourn had been sitting in her father's study as Hill packed the books and papers Elizabeth selected from his overflowing shelves. She had taken custody of the sheaf of papers Lady Catherine had presented to her in the parlor after Uncle Phillips had gone and had sat at her father's desk going over each sentence carefully.

When she came to the paper that listed the assets of Somersal, she felt as though she were a princess in a fairytale. The home was situated upon a large parcel of land and was a popular hunting ground for their neighbors in Lambton and beyond. Being as she still enjoyed brisk walks twice a day, the rolling hills and grassy meadows would provide more than enough diversion.

There was the home, the stables, a greenhouse, two carriages, and a large garden with a maze and a lovely pavilion that overlooked a small lake. Never in his life would her father have believed the beauty of Somersal and Elizabeth reflected upon Lady Catherine's words about his relationship to her family.

Perhaps her father had visited Somersal in his youth? Her father's connection to the Fitzwilliam family fascinated Elizabeth. It was a mystery that had gnawed at her since the day Lady Catherine de Bourgh had appeared at Longbourn. Her father had never once mentioned the renowned family.

Mrs. Bennet had not written to Lady Catherine to find more of the story of her husband and his time spent with the Fitzwilliam family before he came to Hertfordshire though Elizabeth had gently suggested that she ought. She recalled her mother's words at their last conversation on the matter. "Lizzy, I cannot bear to ask. Perhaps Mr. Darcy might be of assistance? Surely there are tales in his family history regarding the loss of his mother's eldest brother. As accommodating as Lady Catherine was, the memory of her eldest brother seemed to diminish her in the telling."

Elizabeth shook the questions from her mind and hurried to the stables, her step light in the leather riding boots she'd found in London while they had visited with her Aunt and Uncle Gardiner before pressing on to Somersal before Christmas. Edward Gardiner had agreed to administer their dowries, and the monies left to Mrs. Bennet by her husband. There was still the question of how they might afford the staff and running of Somersal but Elizabeth had not thought more of the matter.

Upon their arrival at the country home, they had been greeted by a small army of servants and treated as though they were direct relations of the Darcy and Fitzwilliam families. There had been letters from Mr. Darcy and from the Earl of Matlock extending their condolences and offering aid should the need arise.

Elizabeth thought meeting Mr. Darcy again might be uncomfortable but had not considered the master of Pemberley might deign to pay a call. The stable doors were open when she arrived and she brightened at the thought of riding unfettered across the vast acreage of Somersal even with the chill of the December air pressing against the velvet of her coat.

Seeing Merrit toss his head upon her arrival, Elizabeth laughed and offered the horse his treat. He was a lovely thoroughbred with a coal black coat, a horse her father never would have been able to afford. "I see you are as eager as I to be off, Sir Merrit. Go on and have your treat and we shall go."

A handsome gentleman upon a beautiful bay stallion appeared near the stable door and Elizabeth turned as the groom called out to him. The shadow cast by the open door hid his face and she wondered who had come to call.

Their mother had made several acquaintances in Lambton and amongst their few neighbors but had not spoken of a young man. Mrs. Bennet would not miss the opportunity to speak of meeting handsome young men, not with five unmarried daughters in her care.

The gentleman dismounted seeming unsure of himself. Elizabeth waved him over and called out a welcome. The man left his horse with the groom for a moment to hurry and introduce himself again to Elizabeth Bennet.

Opening the stall for Merrit to join her, Elizabeth glanced at her visitor and struggled to maintain her composure when she recognized the man. Mr. Darcy stood before her as handsome as she remembered. "Mr. Darcy, what service may I be to you this fine morning? I was about to ride before I break my fast."

Mr. Darcy glanced about the stables recalling the years he'd spent riding with his mother and helping her choose the horses that had gone before. His eyes grew misty with the memory but he was pleased to find the current equine inhabitants being put to good use.

"I have come to offer my hand in friendship, Miss Bennet. I was intrigued to learn of your arrival at Somersal though I knew my Uncle Bertram had made such plans for the property, I did not know it was your family he had chosen. Our meeting in

Meryton was much too brief if you don't mind my saying," he said and bowed slightly to her.

Elizabeth could not hide her surprise at his declaration and stood speechless for a moment too long. Mr. Darcy lowered his gaze before inspecting his surroundings once more. "This stable holds many happy memories and I am happy to know you find pleasure in its use."

Leading Merrit, Elizabeth stepped away and glanced over her shoulder. "Would you care to ride along with me, sir? The morning is losing its shine the longer we stand about."

Mr. Darcy followed the young lady with the easy manner as she led her horse alongside his own. Before he might assist her in mounting Merrit, Elizabeth easily lifted herself into the saddle to sit as confidently as any man he'd ever known. His cheeks wore twin flames from the show her lovely form had provided.

She watched him with a twinkle of mischief in her eyes. Many men had made mention of her form and abilities as a horsewoman and she pursed her lips before speaking again. "I think I shall offer a challenge to you, sir."

Mr. Darcy chuckled at her impertinent speech. His brows rose in jest as he mounted his steed. "And what might that be Miss Bennet?"

Elizabeth graced him with the fullness of her smile before correcting him on the use of Miss Bennet as a moniker. "My sister Jane is Miss Bennet, you may simply call me Miss Elizabeth if it pleases you, sir."

Mr. Darcy tipped his hat and allowed the name of the lady before him to escape his parted lips. "Miss Elizabeth it is then. I find myself again regretting my refusal to dance at the assembly in Meryton."

Pulling on Merrit's reins, Elizabeth sent a saucy remark over her shoulder as she set off across the fields beyond the house. "If a gentleman does not find a lady handsome enough to tempt him, he should feel little remorse in rejecting her company."

Mr. Darcy sat in astonishment at her barb for a moment before urging his horse after her. A young stable hand struggled to mount a pony and follow along after the couple.

Mr. Darcy caught up to Elizabeth Bennet and rode along in silence for a time enjoying the cold bite of the air against his cheeks while wondering if the lady felt the cold. She rode expertly over the hills and showed a great love for the outdoors.

Most ladies he knew might ride in a hunt from time to time, but Miss Elizabeth appeared to be so at ease upon a horse that he thought she must ride far more often than was customary for her sex. Her seat and bearing upon Merrit convinced him she was more than capable.

He admired her riding habit and attempted to keep his eyes from roaming her feminine curves. She wore a black velvet coat cut expressly for her figure over a black silk shirt. Her breeches, again fashioned from a black cloth as she was mourning, complimented her slim but comely legs while sitting astride her mount. Again, the ladies of his circle would never have worn such a habit preferring to ride sidesaddle bedecked in voluminous skirts.

A thought occurred to him and so he struck up a conversation with the lovely lady. "Miss Elizabeth, I believe I deserved your jest back at the stable and I offer my most sincere apologies for the insult at the assembly. I must say, in my defense, I was not aware you had overheard my conversation with Bingley."

Elizabeth turned to face him as she slowed Merrit to a walk and again graced him with her most endearing smile. "Never fear, Mr. Darcy, for I did not take great offense at your slight. I made sport of you for the remainder of the evening if I recall."

The gentlemen feigned shock at her admission but was unable to hold back his laughter. "All is forgiven, then? Shall we yet be friends?"

His companion glanced back at the figure that lingered behind them before turning her gaze to his face once more. "I would like that Mr. Darcy. I have many questions about Somersal, my father, and how he came to be such a great friend of the Fitzwilliam family."

Mr. Darcy had heard the story of the man who had saved his mother's life though his own father had never cared for mention of the man. Lady Anne Darcy had not often spoken of Mr. Bennet in order to soothe her devoted husband's temperament. Thinking again of the loss his new friend had suffered recently, he halted the advance of his horse and turned to her.

"Miss Elizabeth, I would be pleased to answer any and all queries you might have regarding that particular history, but first I would like to offer my deepest condolences on the passing of your father. I did make his acquaintance when he came to pay a call to Bingley at Netherfield and I see much of his wit lives on in his favorite daughter."

Elizabeth shifted in her saddle, fighting the sudden tears that threatened to mar the moment. Breathing deeply, she looked away across the fields allowing herself a moment to regain her composure. Her effort was in vain and the tears came in a rush. She kicked her horse into a flat out run, the wind whipping her hair so that the pins holding up her curls fell away.

Mr. Darcy, horrified that he might have given offense, turned at the sound of the quickly approaching stable hand. The boy looked down at the ground as Mr. Darcy addressed him. "Young man, does your lady often ride so recklessly about the grounds?"

The boy nodded and raised his head. "The young miss races horses too, milord."

Darcy wasted not another moment before dashing off after Elizabeth. No wonder she was dressed in a habit that offered her the freedom to ride as she chose. He knew that ladies sometimes raced horses in smaller towns but never had he held an acquaintance with such a woman. He was intrigued and alarmed all at once.

His words of condolence had unsettled her and he knew the pain she must feel. Was that why the beautiful young lady of Somersal galloped across the fields? To escape the pain of losing her father?

His heart constricted in his chest as Fitzwilliam Darcy was no stranger to the capriciousness of grief. A person could be going about their day, emotions on an even keel, only to hear a familiar melody or catch a scent that reminded them of a loved one now gone and the pain was too much to bear.

He would catch her up and sweep her off her mount offering the comfort of his strong arms. Mr. Darcy wanted more than anything to hold her tightly and protect her from all pain. His rational mind knew it was an impossible task, for the mortal heart was never safe from the pain of loss.

It was also an impossibility that he might behave in such a manner with a woman he knew but had no claim upon. And yet, he wanted it more than anything he'd ever desired in his life. Her eyes, her smile, the wit and impertinence combined to tempt him far more than any man ought to be tempted.

Mr. Darcy's horse thundered behind her and Elizabeth slowed her flight. Her tears had long dried in the mad dash Merrit had so easily performed. He was a handsome horse and a fine racer. As Mr. Darcy rode alongside her, Elizabeth returned Merrit to a trot.

"I must apologize, Mr. Darcy. I was quite unprepared for the grief that overtook me."

Mr. Darcy shook his head, a tender look in his eyes causing Elizabeth to hold his gaze. "I am the one who must offer an apology, Miss Elizabeth. I well know the treacherous ways of grief. I ought to have been more considerate."

Elizabeth Bennet decided then and there that the Fitzwilliam Darcy she had met at the assembly was not an accurate representation of the man who rode beside her now and an odd flutter of her heart brought a demure pink blush to her cheeks. She had been correct in her musings that he had developed a fondness for her at Netherfield when Jane had been so ill.

Halting their progress, she slipped from her horse and gazed up at the handsome man who was now her nearest neighbor. He held the secrets of her father she most wished to know and he was so very kind upon closer acquaintance.

"Would you care to walk, kind sir?" she asked. Mr. Darcy dismounted and fought the urge to take her in his arms. Leaving his horse to follow behind, he walked easily with her admiring the loose curls that fell to her shoulders and bounced with each step.

He dared not mention the disarray as she had not yet become self-conscious of the state of her hair. Again, he'd known not a lady who might walk about with a gentleman while her hair was blousy and unkempt. Elizabeth Bennet endeared herself to him more and more as they went along.

Chapter 5

Resisting the urge to touch one of her cheeks, Mr. Darcy glanced to the sky noting the gray clouds that had gathered. Reluctantly, he turned for Somersal. Their walk had been made in companionable silence and he wondered why she did not pepper him with the questions he knew she wished to ask.

Clearing his throat, sad that they must soon part, Mr. Darcy asked if she would prefer to ride back to the country house she now called home. Elizabeth shook her head but moved closer to the man as her stable boy had turned when he saw them making their way back. He was a good few yards ahead of them.

Feeling her small hand upon his arm, Darcy glanced down and gave Elizabeth Bennet a wide grin before covering her hand with his own. He would walk in terrible blizzard for miles if it meant he could have her near to him.

She hummed a happy tune as they went along and Mr. Darcy wished he might take this wonderful morning and lock it away where he might relive it time and again whenever he wished. But the lovely lady did only live but a short ride from Pemberley, he reminded himself. Why should they not have many such occasions to know one another better?

When they could see the chimneys of Somersal, and the stable hand had returned to the stables, Elizabeth halted their progress and looked up into Mr. Darcy's eyes. "Would you care to visit with my mother and sisters, sir? Mother shall be most displeased to know I have kept you out in the cold and not invited you in for tea."

Mr. Darcy heard little of her words as his mind had gone on a journey of imagining what her full pink lips might feel like against his own. When she stepped away from him with a look of confusion, he ducked his head embarrassed at being caught out. "Forgive me, Miss Elizabeth, I was not attending."

Elizabeth noted the color rising in his cheeks and attempted to hide her mirth. The man was smitten! It was as clear as day but she did not wish to be so forward as to show him she knew of his predicament. Instead she pulled him along and gave Merrit to the groom. Mr. Darcy passed his horse to the man as well and followed Elizabeth inside Somersal.

Mrs. Bennet sat in the parlor with her daughters as they had finished breakfast not a half hour before Elizabeth entered with Mr. Darcy.

She rose and went to the couple, noting that they indeed appeared as a lovely couple, and welcomed Mr. Darcy to Somersal. "I declare, what a surprise it is to see you again Mr. Darcy! I was hoping you might grace us with your presence. Somersal is a lovely home and we are most fortunate to have commanded your uncle's concern and protection."

Mr. Darcy found himself speechless for a moment as the Mrs. Bennet before him seemed different from the woman he'd met at the assembly in Meryton, the parlor of Netherfield, and at Longbourn. Knowing the changes grief could work upon a person, he decided to take her at her word. "Mrs. Bennet, I have come to offer my condolences in person and to say I am well pleased to have your family safely arrived at Somersal. Your kind words are duly noted, madam."

He gave a slight bow and the girlish side of Francine Bennet emerged. She brought her fan to her chest and giggled as her younger daughters were wont to do upon meeting handsome young gentlemen. Her mother's opinion of the man had changed in the days since they had arrived at Somersal and found his letter of condolence. More than once she had mentioned that perhaps Elizabeth might rethink her feelings for Mr. Darcy.

Elizabeth placed her hands upon her mother's shoulders and guided the matron to her seat in the parlor while introducing Mr. Darcy to her sisters once more. "Ladies, I have had a most invigorating ride with Mr. Darcy across the fields this morning but knew I must bring him in for refreshments."

At this, Mary rose and went to see that tea was brought immediately. Mr. Darcy spoke to each sister in her turn before taking the seat Elizabeth offered him by the fireplace. His eyes roamed the parlor finding comfort in the familiar surroundings.

The walls were papered in a manner that suited the young ladies gathered and he wondered if his Georgiana might have enjoyed this visit. But then he would not have rode and walked alone with Miss Elizabeth and so was pleased he had come before his sister rose from bed.

As conversation swirled about him, he did mention his sister and offer an invitation to dine at Pemberley to his new neighbors. "Georgiana and I would be most pleased to have you as guests. In fact, I must insist upon it. Mr. Bennet was revered in my family for the friendship given to my mother's eldest brother and the valiant attempt to preserve his life. Though I did not know him by more than his first name, my mother always used his first name in the retelling of his daring rescue, my family on the Fitzwilliam side made certain to see that his family was always looked after from afar if they had the means to do so."

The ladies were enthralled by Mr. Darcy's mention of their father and Mrs. Bennet, though she wished to know more of her husband's friendship with the family, left it to Elizabeth to ask Mr. Darcy to share more of his intelligence on the matter.

Glancing to her mother and receiving a slight nod, Elizabeth placed her teacup on the table beside her. Fixing Mr. Darcy with a penetrating gaze, she asked the question she could not during their walk when her heart had been so full of memories of her father. "Mr. Darcy, is there much you know about that time in my father's life? Perhaps something your mother may have shared?"

Mr. Darcy placed his teacup next to hers and cleared his throat, taking his time to glance at each lady in the room before speaking. The warmth of the fire lent a cozy air to the room making it the perfect setting for remembrances.

"My uncle Bertram became an acquaintance of Mr. Bennet in their last year of school. Bertie, as we call him though he has long since passed, was a young man of an irrepressible nature. Though he was the Earl of Matlock, he was forever tempting fate and seeking thrills that most men would avoid. He always seemed to need a dose of danger to feel as though he was alive."

Mr. Darcy paused, the ladies fully under his spell, and thought of the story he must impart. They were keen to know of Mr. Bennet's early years that had led them to Derbyshire after his death.

"One night, after a ball at Woodland Manor, that is the Fitzwilliam country estate, my Uncle Bertie led a party of the young people that included Mr. Bennet and my mother, along with my Uncle Reginald and Aunt Catherine, to a lake on the property and there was much merriment as he flirted with the thin ice."

Elizabeth cringed at the thoughts that crossed her mind, for she knew now this was how his uncle must have died but waited for the man to finish his tale as chills chased down her spine.

"There were several small bonfires set about the edge of the lake as Bertie had nabbed two footmen to accompany the rowdy set on their rendezvous and Mr. Bennet sat before the smallest fire with my mother. There appeared to have been a budding romance between them but mother has always insisted that it was only an attraction that could never be pursued because of their stations in life."

Mrs. Bennet gasped and Mr. Darcy halted his tale to give her a moment to digest this fact. Thomas Bennet had never spoken of another woman to her, though his meeting and infatuation with Lady Anne would have been years before he met Francine Elise Gardiner. Still, the idea of her young, handsome husband losing his heart to another sobered the woman and she dabbed at her eyes with a handkerchief. Jane moved to sit closer to her mother and Elizabeth sighed to see her sister take her mother's hand in pity.

Mr. Darcy looked to Elizabeth before continuing his tale. "Not long after the party arrived at the lake, Bertie declared he would cross the middle from the far side. There were certainly flasks passed between the young men on the way to the lake and I believe he was well into his cups by this time. Halfway across the lake, my mother joined him but she and Bertie broke through the ice and nearly drowned before Thomas Bennet went into the lake after them. Uncle Bertie had my mother in his grasp and pushed her into Mr. Bennet's arms. She was hauled ashore by the footmen and though Mr. Bennet was worse for the wear, he turned back for Bertie. My uncle had sunk below the surface and was unconscious when Mr. Bennet hauled him up from the frozen depths of the lake. Your father stayed with him in the sleigh, rubbing his extremities and doing all that he might to rid Bertie of the icy waters he had swallowed."

Mr. Darcy's voice broke and he paused, the recounting almost painful. Though he had never known his Uncle Bertram, his mother had told him tales of her beloved brother on many occasions and Darcy never failed to recognize how exactly he favored his tragic uncle in the portrait that still hung in his mother's rooms at Pemberley. He resembled the man to such a great degree that his mother would often grow misty-eyed when she beheld her son.

Remembering where he was, Mr. Darcy finished his tale. "Bertie lingered for several weeks after the incident at the lake while mother and Mr. Bennet recovered. When Bertie took his last breath, my mother fled Woodland though a terrible storm raged outside. Mr. Bennet went after her and hauled her kicking and screaming back to Woodland and gave her over to grandmother who put her to bed. There is where the story ends for me. Mother would speak no more of it, but the retelling was always the same. It is said that Thomas Bennet saved my mother from the same fate as Bertie."

Quiet tears greeted him as the Bennet ladies each digested his story in her own time. Such loss and sadness was unknown to them in the happier days at Longbourn before Mr. Bennet had died. To know he had tried and failed to save a friend but had saved the friend's sister painted a deeper picture of their father. He was always leery of his girls seeking out bodies of water and avoided them at all cost himself.

Elizabeth dried her eyes and glanced at Mr. Darcy. The man seemed lost in his own thoughts from the retelling of a most personal story and she simply sat for a long moment studying the lines of his face. The strong, square jaw drew her eye and she followed its line to the dark curls that rested against the back of his cravat, her fingers itching to test one of the ringlets.

He turned, catching her gaze, and gave a small smile seeming to shake himself of the ghosts of the past. Elizabeth caught her breath as the look in his eyes pierced her. Here was a man she could love as surely as her father had loved her mother. Could a tender friendship bud into a romance that would unite a Bennet daughter with the son of her father's first love?

The idea thrilled her and she thought of the novels that rested by her bedside. She could not pretend nor be false with Mr. Darcy as the ladies in those pages did. She was in mourning and so could not attend events or consider courtship with a man but a friendship based on mutual habits would not be frowned upon.

As Mr. Darcy stood to take his leave, Elizabeth rose and saw him to the door of Somersal wishing he might join her again when next she rode the fields.

He turned after stepping through the door, and Elizabeth waited for him to speak. Mr. Darcy could not keep from allowing his gaze to sweep from the top of her head to the tips of the riding boots she still wore.

Elizabeth Bennet would become quite important to him as the days and months passed, he was certain of it, but he longed to keep a picture of her in his mind as she now stood before him. His mother would be pleased to know her only son now held an attraction for Thomas Bennet's favorite daughter.

The mercurial hand of fate seemed to push him towards her but Mr. Darcy held fast to his position. In his heart he wished to place a tender kiss upon her lips, but he knew he must take time to tend their new friendship before revealing the truth of his heart to the lady. She was a prize worth winning and Fitzwilliam Darcy knew he would do all that he might to win her hand.

Giving a nod of his head, he smiled at Elizabeth Bennet before turning to retrieve his horse from the stables.

Chapter 6

Elizabeth Bennet rode into Lambton with her sister Jane, her head filled with memories of riding across the fields with Mr. Darcy and his visit afterwards.

Her mother and sisters had discussed his tale many times since he left their parlor yesterday and Elizabeth had been hard pressed to bring their attention to the fact that she and Jane would seek out a governess for the younger girls. The young ladies had begun yet another argument over ribbon and bonnets while lamenting the dearth of redcoats in Lambton causing Elizabeth to speak plainly.

"If we are to dine at Pemberley, then there shall be an acquaintance with Miss Darcy to foster. I sincerely doubt she discusses red coats and frets over bonnets."

Mrs. Bennet's countenance had brightened at this declaration and she gave her blessing to Elizabeth's plan. "Oh my dear, you are quite right. Mrs. Alsop and I had discussed the same on our last visit. Young ladies must have proper instruction and teaching. Your father, rest his soul, never thought highly of having a governess but much has changed for our family."

Elizabeth had breathed a sigh of relief at her mother's words. With their father's death and the loss of Longbourn, the younger girls had been further coddled and had become quite bothersome.

"Mrs. Alsop will know of several young ladies well suited to the task. Do give her my regards and tell her she may expect a visit in the next day or so," Mrs. Bennet had said when Jane wondered where they might begin their search for a suitable companion for their sisters.

As the countryside rolled past, Elizabeth admired a particular white horse in a pasture alongside the road. "Isn't he perfect, Jane?" she exclaimed and her sister merely nodded. Jane did not understand Elizabeth's infatuation with horses but she had to admit the beast was quite lovely.

"Mother would not stand for you to bring another horse to Somersal, Lizzy, you must be satisfied with Merrit."

Elizabeth laughed at her sister. To think she might be so easily swayed from acquiring another horse was humorous but Jane was correct. The monies their father had left were sufficient to their needs but not to the running of such a home as Somersal and certainly not enough to purchase a horse when the stable stood full.

"A girl might dream, my dear sister, a girl might dream. Besides, when the races begin again in the spring I might win enough money to purchase him myself."

Jane gasped at Elizabeth's boast and fixed her sister with a withering gaze. "Mother shall have your hide if she finds out about these races. I wouldn't count upon participating without her knowledge."

Their father had never censured Elizabeth for her wish to race horses when he had been alive, but Mrs. Bennet simply abhorred the notion.

"What Mother does not know shall not hurt me." Elizabeth said and laughed at Jane's shocked expression.

Jane sighed and shook her head knowing there was no reasoning with her sister when it came to horses. Mr. Bennet had created a fine horsewoman in Elizabeth Bennet and Jane had come to admire her sister's bravery and tenacity in learning to ride well. Spring was months away and Elizabeth still might be persuaded to leave the racing to others.

Since arriving at Somersal, Elizabeth had made inquiries about racing and been assured that the ladies of Derbyshire did indeed participate, though the sport was still seen as being beneath ladies of a certain circle. Elizabeth was eager to race Merrit, knowing she and the horse had become one in the few short weeks she'd been at Somersal.

Jane began to speak of the dinner at Pemberley and Elizabeth forgot about horse racing for the time being. "Mother is eager to see the halls of Pemberley. I'm surprised she stayed at home today instead of spreading the news to all her new friends in Lambton."

Elizabeth smiled at the thought of sitting down to dinner with Mr. Darcy. Their walk in the fields of Somersal had been a welcome diversion after she'd recovered from the flood of emotions over her father. And his willingness to share what he knew of her father's life before Longbourn had endeared the man further.

Their carriage stopped before Mrs. Alsop's home and the two Bennet sisters were greeted by a tall, thin woman who must be their mother's friend. She led them inside and sent for tea.

"My dears, let me guess," she said as she inspected each sister for a moment. Showing Elizabeth to a seat and leaving a startled Jane standing by the parlor door, she smiled at the dark-haired sister. "You must be Elizabeth! Your mother has said that your eyes sparkle like the sun on a lovely summer day and she was not wrong."

Elizabeth was surprised by the woman's words. It was a compliment she would never have expected from her mother.

Mrs. Alsop returned to Jane and took her hand to guide her to a seat next to Elizabeth. "And of course, you are Jane Bennet. Your mother is quite proud of your looks my dear, and I must not chastise her for it. Why, it should be no time at all before you are sought by every eligible gentleman in the county."

Jane sat and cast her lashes to the floor thoroughly embarrassed at the woman's words. Elizabeth took up the conversation while her sister recovered. "Mrs. Alsop, our mother sends her kind regards and wished to assure you she may visit tomorrow or the day after. Of course, you are welcome at Somersal at any time of your choosing."

Mrs. Alsop beamed with good cheer and Elizabeth found herself drawn to the happy woman. "My dear, I should dearly love to visit your new home. My father worked the gardens there for many years before he passed, God rest his soul. I hear the flower beds are still impeccably kept."

Jane nodded her head as the tea arrived. "I am eager to see them come spring. Why, I'd be happy to walk with you there when you visit, as I'm sure you have much to tell regarding the history of Somersal."

Mrs. Alsop nodded at Jane, her smile widening. Elizabeth sipped her tea before addressing the reason for their visit. "Mother did say you might know of a young lady we could employ as a governess for our younger sisters."

Mrs. Alsop clapped her hands and a maid appeared immediately. "Bring Constance to the parlor, please."

Elizabeth looked to Jane in bewilderment and Mrs. Alsop reassured them. "Constance is my youngest daughter. She has never married and would make a wonderful companion for your sisters. My husband made certain she was given the very best lessons under the same tutors that saw to the education of the Darcy children at Pemberley."

Elizabeth turned as Constance entered the room and immediately saw why the woman may not have married. She moved with a slight limp and her left foot dragged a bit but her bearing was that of a queen.

Mrs. Alsop made the introductions and the Bennet sisters wasted no time in the quizzing of the shy woman.

"Miss Alsop, we have three younger sisters in dire need of instruction. They are all well read but do require a bit of polishing. Mary plays the piano forte and Kitty has a talent for painting. Lydia, well, her talent seems to be gossip."

Constance Alsop listened closely and thought for a moment. "Young ladies must be motivated to better themselves not by harsh criticism but rather by the patient application of praise. I shall see that the young mistresses dearly wish to rise to the station which they have entered, you may have my word upon it."

Jane found she quite liked Constance Alsop and continued the interview after glancing to Elizabeth. "I must warn you in all good faith that Kitty and Lydia are quite headstrong, and as much as I hate to admit it, spoiled terribly. Are you certain you are up to the task? Lizzy must be the one you report to for mother is too easy on the girls."

Mrs. Alsop sat her cup on the table and cleared her throat. "My daughter is accustomed to the rigors of managing young ladies for their betterment. There are several families in Derbyshire who are most grateful for her talents."

Elizabeth hurried to reassure their host. "Tis not Constance we doubt, Mrs. Alsop. Our younger sisters try our patience and sometimes Mother allows them their tantrums out of pity, I think, since the loss of father."

Constance leaned forward and took Elizabeth's hand. "I shall be all that is kind and proper while considering the recent upheaval in their lives. You may give me a few weeks with them and then review our progress if you wish."

Elizabeth breathed a sigh of relief. She wasn't yet sure of Constance, but only because the youngest Bennets could be terribly immature and foolish. "I believe your plan is most suitable, Miss Alsop. Will you come tomorrow and meet our sisters?"

Constance Alsop gave a beautiful smile that Elizabeth thought would make any man take notice did he look past her ailment. Perhaps, come spring, she might pursue a match between their quiet groom and Miss Alsop. Flirting with Mr. Darcy the day before had put romantic notions in her head. Thinking herself foolish to dream of love for another, Elizabeth stood and walked with Mrs. Alsop and Jane to the door to say her farewells.

In their carriage once more, the Bennet sisters decided to have luncheon at a local inn before returning to Somersal. As the footman handed the ladies down, Elizabeth glanced about and was surprised to find Mr. Darcy standing near the door of the Blue Goose Inn. He was speaking with another gentleman and when the man turned, Elizabeth saw that it was Charles Bingley.

Taking Jane's arm, Elizabeth nodded toward the entrance of the establishment. "It appears Mr. Darcy has come to Lambton with Mr. Bingley. What a lovely coincidence."

Jane covered her mouth with one gloved hand at the sight of Charles Bingley. While it was true that she had thought of him since their meeting in Hertfordshire, the death of her father and the move to Somersal had kept her mind too occupied to consider love. Now that he stood not a few steps away, her heart threatened to burst with joy.

As the sisters approached the Inn, Mr. Darcy turned and a smile spread across his handsome face at the sight of Elizabeth Bennet. He tipped his hat and took hold of Bingley's arm.

Charles Bingley's eyes met those of Jane Bennet and the man was returned again to the night they'd danced together at the assembly in Meryton.

Not waiting for Darcy, he addressed the Miss Bennets with a courtly bow before taking Jane's hand. "Miss Bennet, how wonderful it is to see you again. I have many times wished that I might have been of more assistance in your time of need."

Jane smiled demurely and was reluctant to release his hand. "Mr. Bingley, Mr. Darcy did not say you were visiting Derbyshire when he sat to tea with us yesterday but I am happy to find you here. Elizabeth and I stopped to take luncheon before returning to Somersal from our errands."

Mr. Darcy took Elizabeth's hand and asked if the gentlemen might join the ladies for their meal. Elizabeth looked to Jane and seeing her sister nod, accepted Mr. Darcy's invitation.

Once inside, Mr. Darcy ordered an elaborate meal and the Bennet sisters found themselves happy for the company.

Mr. Bingley explained that he and Miss Bingley were visiting for a time. "Darcy is so kind to invite us each winter to visit Pemberley but he did not mention you were in town. Did you say you must return to Somersal?"

Jane nodded. "Our family has connections to Mr. Darcy's family on the Fitzwilliam side. You must understand it came as quite a shock, but Somersal has become our home since father's death left us without one."

Mr. Bingley was surprised at the news. "I suppose Darcy would have told me sooner or later, but I am happy nonetheless. You ought to have told me of your family's predicament, Miss Bennet. I would have done all that I might to ease the burden."

Elizabeth smiled at Mr. Bingley, happy for Jane that he was at Pemberley. Perhaps they might resume their attraction in the coming weeks. "Neither of us would have thought to burden new friends with such terrible news, Mr. Bingley, but your kindness was evident from the moment we met. Let us be happy to meet again with better fortunes before us."

Mr. Darcy gazed at Elizabeth admiring her grace and intelligence. She and her family had suffered a great loss and yet she blossomed as the head of the ladies of Longbourn. It was clear to him from his visit yesterday, and her confidence today, that Mrs. Bennet had abdicated the position of authority to Elizabeth Bennet.

She caught him in his distraction and he shook his head to clear his thoughts. "I am sorry, Miss Elizabeth, I was not attending."

The object of his growing affection smiled and repeated her question. "Mr. Bingley has said he would like to pay a call at

Somersal. Would you bring him along one morning to ride? I am sure Jane would enjoy riding with us as well. She is as accomplished a horsewoman as I."

Jane shook her head. "Lizzy is mistaken, I am not nearly as good on a horse as she but I would not mind riding about Somersal with Mr. Bingley."

Mr. Darcy laughed and agreed to the plan. "Charles has business in Lambton the next few days but perhaps he may come before he is due to leave for London."

Mr. Bingley nodded. "I shall make time for the opportunity, I assure you."

After their meal was done, Jane and Elizabeth lingered at the door of the inn. Mr. Bingley, not wanting to part from Jane, expressed the desire to take a turn about town before the ladies might board their carriage to return home.

Mr. Darcy offered his arm, with Mr. Bingley following suit, and the party set off for a stroll around the heart of Lambton. There were many more shops than Meryton and the townsfolk went busily about their errands.

Elizabeth watched as Jane and Mr. Bingley bent their heads closer as her sister pointed to the fountain in the center of town. Mr. Darcy steered Elizabeth toward the stone structure, following her sister and his best friend.

"Do you believe in making wishes, Miss Elizabeth?" he asked as they sat on the edge of the lovely fountain.

Elizabeth considered his question for a moment before replying. "Once upon a time, I might have. But now? I dare not wish for more than has been given, sir. My family has nearly recovered from the loss of our home but the loss of father shall ever be present."

Mr. Darcy fished in his pockets and produced several shillings. He took Elizabeth's gloved hand and placed a coin there. "I think it is time you believe again, dear lady."

Elizabeth lifted her hand, glancing at the ripples in the fountain and trembled when Mr. Darcy took the coin from her and placed a kiss upon it. "For good luck," he whispered as he placed it in her hand again, closing her fingers around it.

Catching her breath as her heart raced at his intimate gesture and the idea that he would bless her wish with good luck, Elizabeth Bennet made the most outlandish wish she could imagine, one that included Fitzwilliam Darcy, and tossed the shilling into the water watching as it sank below the surface.

Mr. Darcy gave another of his happy smiles and Elizabeth thought how different he was now that she knew him a little better. She had been ready to dismiss him out of hand for his boorish behavior even after their truce at Netherfield but now, here in Derbyshire, she had come to see him without the insult holding any of its former weight.

Elizabeth sighed and waited as Mr. Darcy made his own wish. He held the coin out for her inspection and in a moment of recklessness, she took it and pressed her lips lightly against the metal surface. Mr. Darcy laughed and tossed his coin without hesitation, pleased that she wished him well.

"I wished for..." Elizabeth began but Mr. Darcy placed a finger against her lips before she might reveal her secret. "Tis bad luck to speak your wish aloud, Miss Elizabeth. Keep it close unto your heart."

Chapter 7

Several days later, Somersal was abuzz with the bustling of the Bennet ladies as they readied for a dinner at Pemberley. Kitty and Lydia fussed that they ought to be able to wear some adornment that was not gray or black but their mother refused their pleas.

"Your father is barely cold in the ground," she said, her voice cracking with emotion, "we shall observe a proper period of mourning for he was a good father and husband."

Jane embraced Mrs. Bennet and glanced to Elizabeth as she led the woman to her own rooms in the lovely country home. "There now, Mother. Elizabeth and Constance shall see to their compliance with your wishes."

Constance Alsop gathered the younger girls and took them downstairs to the parlor to wait until the carriage was brought round to deliver them all to Pemberley to dine with the Darcy family. The young woman from Lambton had quickly become a good influence on the girls.

Elizabeth sighed and retreated to her own room to attend the curls that had escaped their pins. Her hair almost always refused to be contained, the curls abundant and happy to be free rather than pinned up. But the Bingleys were present at Pemberley and Elizabeth would not give Miss Bingley reason to comment upon her appearance.

Knowing Jane would spend time with Charles Bingley made her smile and Elizabeth hoped that his attraction might grow deeper, for her favorite sister did deserve as much happiness as marriage to the man might afford. Watching them walk together in Lambton had convinced Elizabeth that Mr. Bingley had not forgotten her sister after all this time.

Jane appeared at her door and Elizabeth stood to walk with her to the parlor and join their three sisters. "In spite of our mourning dresses, you are most beautiful this evening, dear Jane."

Her sister tucked Elizabeth's arm in her own and remarked upon how lovely her hair was arranged. Elizabeth raised a brow and shook her head delicately. "Tis only a matter of time until a curl revolts and brings several more down with it."

Jane laughed merrily and paused before their mother's door. "And I shall eagerly return them all to their pins for you, though I don't think Mr. Darcy would mind to see them loose for they are so lovely. I often wish I had received such an abundance of curls."

Elizabeth shook her head in disagreement. "Your hair behaves so perfectly, Jane. Do not ever wish for such a thing!"

Mrs. Bennet joined her daughters in the hall, casting an approving eye to the dark silks they wore to honor their father. It pained her to take them to Pemberley dressed in such somber tones but she would not have tongues wagging about the decorum of her daughters.

The carriage was brought round and the ladies gathered in the entryway as Mrs. Bennet instructed the younger women to mind their manners or risk staying home come the next round of invitations from their neighbors. "As you well know, Mr. Darcy's family was so very kind to us without having made our acquaintance. I demand you behave as though your dear father was present and make him proud."

Constance Alsop gave a nod to support Mrs. Bennet and spoke her peace to the ladies who were now under her tutelage. "Do recall our talk yesterday, my dears. Pemberley is a grand home and you must make a wonderful first impression if you wish to become better acquainted with Miss Darcy."

Kitty, Lydia, and Mary mumbled their assent and followed their mother and elder sisters to the waiting carriage. Constance stood at the door watching as they were helped into the conveyance, her heart hopeful that the youngest Bennet ladies would make her proud. She had overhead the news that the Bingleys were visiting the estate for the winter and knew Caroline Bingley to be a most snobbish woman. Any misstep by her employer or her daughters would be talked about in the highest circles of the Ton once Miss Bingley spread the word.

As the carriage from Somersal approached Pemberley, Elizabeth bit her lip to keep from gasping aloud. The sweeping drive to the front door of the home revealed they had a way to go before they would arrive but the driver had stopped for a moment at the crest of a hill to allow the ladies a view of the estate.

A lake was situated in front of the home and what Elizabeth could see of the grounds in the fading light impressed her greatly. The wildness of nature was preferred in the appearance of the grounds over a more polished style, though the shrubbery nearer the house was immaculately shaped and groomed.

It did not seem in disharmony with the wilder aspects of the landscape though and Elizabeth wondered if she might one day walk the gardens of Pemberley on Mr. Darcy's arm. Perhaps she would suggest such an outing the next time they rode together.

When at last they arrived at the front door, Mr. Darcy appeared with his butler to welcome them to Pemberley. Each lady was handed down and delivered to Mr. Darcy for her welcome. Elizabeth watched as her younger sisters made the proper curtseys and spoke with much decorum. She was proud of them and hoped they would continue their good behavior through the dinner hour.

Watching her mother and sisters precede her inside the large double doors, she took in the grandeur of Pemberley's grounds once more before turning her attention to Mr. Darcy.

"Miss Elizabeth, do you find my home to be satisfactory?" he asked with a twinkle in his eyes, for he well knew she was smitten by the property. She could not have hidden the expression on her face and it gave him great happiness to know that the woman he found himself most drawn to admired his home.

"Indeed I do, Mr. Darcy. I was thinking that you must show me your gardens when spring comes."

The man could not hide his joy at her interest and tucked her hand safely into his arm. "What a lovely idea! I would be happy to give you a tour, but be advised that a full circuit can require the better part of an hour. With it being winter, you might prefer the hothouses if you desire to see blooms."

Mr. Darcy led her inside to the parlor where the Bingleys sat with her mother and sisters. Miss Darcy was also present and Mr. Darcy made the introductions. Miss Georgiana Darcy was nearly as tall as her brother though she was not more than sixteen years. Her hair resembled Jane's in color and she smiled more readily than Mr. Darcy.

Elizabeth sat beside her as Mr. Darcy moved to sit by Mrs. Bennet. Caroline Bingley's face held a sour expression and Elizabeth did not wish to engage the woman in conversation. Thankfully, Miss Bingley's attention was captured by her brother as he had taken a seat next to Jane.

Miss Darcy smiled at Elizabeth and exclaimed over the number of Bennet sisters. "My, it must be heaven at Somersal to have so much company."

Elizabeth bit her lip before answering. The young mistress of Pemberley must be quite lonely to think five sisters was a blessing. "Tis never a boring moment, Miss Darcy."

"Although William and I are quite close, I would dearly love to have had a sister." Her clear blue eyes conveyed such longing that Elizabeth found herself pitying the girl.

"Perhaps you might visit us at Somersal, with your brother's blessing of course."

Miss Darcy clapped her hands and rose to put the question to Mr. Darcy. She took two steps before returning to Elizabeth. "Forgive me, I am grateful for your invitation."

Elizabeth laughed as the young lady turned and went to stand by her brother's chair. She displayed such innocence that Elizabeth could not find fault with her flight.

Miss Bingley turned her attention to Elizabeth then and pretended at delight. "How lovely to see you again, Miss Eliza. Charles and I were greatly saddened by your father's death. I understand the loss as our own father has been gone for many years now."

Glancing down at her hands, Elizabeth quietly cleared her throat before replying. "Thank you, Miss Bingley. Our lives have changed most rapidly since last we met."

At this, Caroline Bingley revealed her true intentions. "Yes, I have heard. Mr. Darcy spoke of your situation at Somersal. How fortunate your father was acquainted with the Fitzwilliam family before he took up with your mother."

Elizabeth glanced to Mr. Darcy before replying to the horrid woman's insult. "My father's connection to the Fitzwilliam family has proven to be a matter of great good fortune. I cannot express the joy I have at meeting Mr. Darcy once more. Our mutual love for riding bodes well for our new friendship."

Caroline Bingley smirked as Mr. Darcy made his way to Elizabeth's side. "I was invited to tea with Lady Regina Morely just last week, their estate lies to the North of Pemberley, and she did mention that a young lady from Somersal has plans to race come spring. I was quite shocked."

Mr. Darcy cleared his throat and looked to Elizabeth. The color had risen in his cheeks at Miss Bingley's impertinence. "Miss Elizabeth is a fine horsewoman and did she wish to race I imagine she would be most successful. However, a lady of her circle would never engage in such vulgar behavior."

Elizabeth felt the heat rise in her face at Mr. Darcy's words. She would indeed engage in such behavior. "I find racing to be most exciting and not the least bit vulgar. Father allowed me to join the races in Hertfordshire whenever I wished and I have no intention of missing one in Derbyshire."

Caroline Bingley covered her mouth with one hand as her eyes widened in disbelief that the country chit now residing in an estate which belonged to Mr. Darcy's family would be so rude as to contradict the man. Her concern over his attention to the woman faded rapidly. Wishing to have Mr. Darcy think better of her, Caroline Bingley chose to pretend at concern for Elizabeth Bennet.

"Mr. Darcy," she said after recovering herself, "Miss Eliza is new to the community and has recently suffered such great loss. Perhaps she is not thinking clearly and will understand her place better before the races begin in the spring."

Mr. Darcy took Elizabeth's hand and led her to the fireplace, away from Miss Bingley. He wished to find whether she was serious about racing without prompting another reply from the conniving woman. "Miss Elizabeth, I saw for myself that you are a fine horsewoman and racing in Hertfordshire when you were a young girl is admirable, I admit it thrills me to think of it," here he paused as the color in his cheeks rose at his admission, "but ladies of Pemberley, and those connected to Pemberley as you surely are now, would never engage in such activity."

Elizabeth glanced about the room in an attempt to count to ten in her head. Mr. Darcy's words and Miss Bingley's false concern given after tattling of Elizabeth's spring plans lit the fuse on her temper. Her mother would be most displeased if Elizabeth caused a terrible scene, and Jane was sitting so very close to Mr. Bingley.

Instead of lashing out at Mr. Darcy, she thought of her dear father and what he would have said on the subject. *My Lizzy was never bound by what she ought to do. Pictures of perfection make her sick and wicked.*

The memory brought a smile to her face and she turned again to gaze at Mr. Darcy. He was the most handsome man, the devil in disguise who would tempt her to forget herself save for the fact that any attempt to intimidate Elizabeth Bennet only served to encourage her.

The butler arrived in that moment to announce dinner and instead of disabusing Fitzwilliam Darcy of his foolish notion regarding what she ought and ought not do, Elizabeth Bennet took his arm and allowed him to lead her into the dining room.

Chapter 8

Caroline Bingley managed to behave herself all during dinner where Elizabeth Bennet was concerned but could not hold her tongue from questioning Jane Bennet relentlessly. "How terrible it must have been to lose your only home so soon after losing your father. I cannot imagine."

Jane had smiled sweetly and looked to Charles Bingley before making an answer. His pointed gaze at his sister was meant to quell her poor manners but she merely shrugged her shoulders as though she had meant only sympathy for the woman.

"My family has endured a most terrible time, Miss Bingley, but the brave actions of our dear father secured a most fortunate home for us that was quite unexpected. It seems we are now much recovered from the loss of Longbourn."

Elizabeth gave her favorite sister a winning smile and nodded, raising her glass. "The Darcy and Fitzwilliam families have been most gracious indeed."

Caroline Bingley sniffed and cast her eyes to her plate. The country misses seated at Mr. Darcy's table were sorely mistaken if they believed their improved situation meant they might make a match with her brother and the man she meant to have for her own.

Georgiana Darcy turned to the younger Bennet sisters seated beside her and continued a lively conversation that was punctuated with quiet giggles while Elizabeth turned to Mr. Darcy.

His eyes were filled with merriment at the replies she and Jane had given Miss Bingley and he winked conspiratorially before whispering his approval. "Miss Bingley is not always so disagreeable. Well, I should say not usually. I fear she is concerned about her brother and Miss Bennet. She wishes him to marry some heiress in London."

Elizabeth waited until their last course was served before answering. "And what does Mr. Bingley wish? Or does that matter to his sister?"

Mr. Darcy laughed. "I can assure you that nothing matters to Miss Bingley more than joining the same circle as my family."

Elizabeth smiled and glanced at the woman in time to see the terrible face she made as Jane and Mr. Bingley shared a laugh. Returning her gaze to Mr. Darcy, Elizabeth thought for a moment knowing she must not antagonize Miss Bingley with Jane getting on so well with her brother. "Perhaps she worries that Charles might be tempted to spend his time in Derbyshire rather than return to Netherfield."

Mr. Darcy gazed a moment too long into Elizabeth Bennet's fine eyes before forgetting himself. "I imagine her fear is that he may not return to London where she wishes to remain. I can assure you she has no desire to return to Netherfield."

Elizabeth knew all too well that Miss Bingley despised the country and thought that she must feel the same about Pemberley save when Mr. Darcy was in residence. "I pity her then, for the country air is delightful when compared to London in my opinion. Although I have spent many summers in Town with my Aunt and Uncle Gardiner, I would never wish to live there."

Mr. Darcy was pleased to hear such a confession from the lady. He much preferred Pemberley to London though his business often took him to Town for longer than he wished each time.

When his guests rose to quit the dining room, Mr. Darcy parted company with Elizabeth Bennet and found for the first time in his life he wished to accompany the ladies into the parlor rather than follow Charles Bingley to the library.

In the parlor, Georgiana Darcy entertained the ladies with her musical prowess and drew the youngest Bennet sisters closer to her side. Mary turned the pages of music as the young Miss Darcy played while Kitty and Lydia danced with much gaiety.

Jane and Mrs. Bennet clapped in time with the music and Elizabeth roamed the parlor admiring the many paintings. Caroline Bingley attempted to keep a smile on her lips for Georgiana Darcy's sake but Elizabeth could see she was most uncomfortable.

She foolishly took pity on the woman and went to sit beside her. "Miss Bingley, have you any knowledge of the paintings in this room? They seem to be of the same style. I wondered if you might know the artist?"

Caroline Bingley eyed the impertinent miss she had come to dislike greatly at Netherfield. She stood, without a word, and approached the painting nearest the parlor door. Elizabeth followed wondering what had possessed her to be cordial to the ice queen.

"The paintings in this parlor were all done by Lady Anne Darcy. She was quite talented, wouldn't you agree?"

Elizabeth nodded, admiring the beautiful drawings of flowers and birds. "Indeed. I often wish that I held such talent."

Miss Bingley smirked. "Tis a pity not all ladies are as accomplished. Mr. Darcy was raised by a woman of exquisite taste and breeding. I'm sure he shall select as fine a woman to become mistress of Pemberley soon."

Elizabeth ignored the taunt and smiled at the petty woman. How terribly she must wish to be the woman Mr. Darcy would choose. "I believe he is to marry his cousin, Anne de Bourgh. Lady Catherine de Bourgh did mention that very fact when she came to pay a call at Longbourn."

Miss Bingley's mouth formed a perfect O and she sputtered for a moment before regaining her composure. "Lady Catherine de Bourgh paid a visit at Longbourn? I find that difficult to believe, Miss Eliza. Why ever would she do such a thing?"

"I would rather not bore you with the details, Miss Bingley, but she did and her words were that Mr. Darcy and her daughter would be wed." Elizabeth enjoyed the unpleasant look on Miss Bingley's face. Most women would not contort their features so but Caroline Bingley suffered no such restriction. The sheer array of dissatisfied expressions in her repertoire amazed Elizabeth Bennet.

"I do not believe Mr. Darcy agrees with his aunt but that is not my place to say." Caroline turned and hurried across the room just as the men entered the parlor.

Mr. Bingley went immediately to sit beside Jane and spoke charmingly to Mrs. Bennet. Never had Elizabeth seen her mother so happy since the death of their father. Even their arrival at Somersal had not pleased her as much as the attention Mr. Bingley gave to Jane.

Mr. Darcy had gone to stand beside Georgiana and watch the younger girls as they enjoyed his sister's talent. He seemed pleased with the behavior of the younger Bennet sisters and Elizabeth returned his smile when his eyes sought hers across the room.

She went to stand beside Mary when Miss Darcy finished a lively tune. Kitty and Lydia clapped fiercely for their new friend before finding their seats near their mother. Mary went to sit as well, leaving Elizabeth at the piano forte with Mr. Darcy and his sister.

The youngest Darcy shuffled her sheet music and smiled up at Elizabeth before turning her head to smile at her brother. "I would play one more song, brother, and ask that you and Miss Elizabeth sing a line or two."

Mr. Darcy meant to refuse but Elizabeth urged him to sing with her. Since they were in the company of close friends, he relented and waited while his sister began the strains of *Black-Eyed Susan*.

Elizabeth chose the first stanza of the song and Mr. Darcy knew immediately the stanza he would cite in reply. Their audience sat rapt with attention as Elizabeth's voice lifted across the room.

> All in the Downs the fleet was moor'd,
> The streamers waving in the wind,
> When black-eyed Susan came aboard;
> 'O! where shall I my true-love find?
> Tell me, ye jovial sailors, tell me true
> If my sweet William sails among the crew.'

Elizabeth reddened as she recalled that Mr. Darcy's Christian name was indeed William. She glanced to Miss Darcy but the young woman feigned innocence and continued playing happily. Mr. Darcy missed not a beat in his reply. The man would not sing his verse, for he was not a master of music. He only spoke it but with his eyes resting easily on her face.

> O Susan, Susan, lovely dear,
> My vows shall ever true remain;
> Let me kiss off that falling tear;
> We only part to meet again.
> Change as ye list, ye winds; my heart shall be
> The faithful compass that still points to thee.

Elizabeth's voice wavered only slightly as she chose another stanza and tried to ignore Mr. Darcy's gaze. When she looked at their audience, she knew their duet had pleased her mother. The woman's smile fairly beamed in the candlelight of the parlor. She made a motion to Elizabeth with her handkerchief, her right hand mimicking the beating of her heart above her breast.

Caroline Bingley rose and quit the room, so perturbed was she by the display. Elizabeth wished to feel some sort of sympathy for the woman but for goodness' sake it was only a song, not a declaration of their feelings.

Mr. Darcy did not notice the departure of Miss Bingley but finished another spoken stanza and bowed most charmingly to the room. He gave a sweep of his hand to Elizabeth and she performed a small curtsey to the clapping of her sisters.

The younger ladies joined Georgiana Darcy at a table on the other side of the room and Mr. Darcy led Elizabeth to the chairs before the fireplace.

"I did not know you possessed such a charming voice, Miss Elizabeth. It was a rare treat. Are there other talents you have hidden from me?" Mr. Darcy asked, his eyes resting on her flushed features.

Elizabeth felt the heat rising in her face and glanced about the room. She lowered her voice causing Mr. Darcy to lean forward in his seat. "I confess that the thing I love most in the world is the one where I am least capable."

Mr. Darcy was intrigued. "Do tell, Miss Elizabeth, for I am most curious now."

Smiling a devilish smile, Elizabeth licked her lips causing her admirer much discomfort as he imagined kissing them ardently. "I cannot skip stones to save my life. Oh, I have tried many times and the proper technique escapes me each time."

Mr. Darcy was charmed by her admission. What lady would sit in the parlor of Pemberley and share that she lacked prowess in such a common endeavor. He would be more than happy to teach her come the spring thaw. His eyes roamed her body in its dark silk and he imagined the warmth of her leaned against him as he helped her hold a skipping stone and release it to fly across the water.

Her laughter startled him and he cleared his throat. Elizabeth Bennet had a terrible effect upon him causing him to wander in his mind while she sat awaiting his reply.

He kept his eyes on her full lips as he spoke. "I might be persuaded to teach you the fine art of skipping stones, Miss Elizabeth, but you must never tell another soul for my reputation as a stern master might be dashed."

Elizabeth Bennet delighted in her ability to distract Mr. Darcy and bring forth the frivolity she knew resided in the man. "I would keep your secrets Mr. Darcy for I do love to know the heart of a man."

Their evening passed quickly then and Elizabeth was sad when the time came for her family to depart. Mr. Darcy saw his guests to the front door of Pemberley when their carriage arrived and waited with Elizabeth while her sisters and mother were handed into their conveyance. He turned and gazed into her eyes hoping she might accept his next invitation.

"Miss Elizabeth, I cannot recall a more enjoyable evening at Pemberley. You must come again for Christmas if your mother agrees. We do not have a party, but guests arrive throughout the day."

Elizabeth's eyes sparkled with the complete happiness his words brought. Though she stood before Pemberley dressed in the dark clothes of mourning, her heart felt as light as the snowflake that landed on Mr. Darcy's jacket.

Glancing up, she saw that more snowflakes had begun to fall. Unable to stop herself, she stuck out her tongue and caught one before dissolving into giggles. The younger girls waiting to enter the carriage had begun the same game.

Mr. Darcy laughed and stuck his own tongue out as he looked skyward. Being wholly unfamiliar with such a childish undertaking, he moved his head to and fro seeking just one snowflake.

Elizabeth laughed and took his arm, her hand going to his face. She held his jaw steady and turned his head a tiny bit. A snowflake landed on the tip of his nose and she giggled again but kept a her hand upon his handsome face.

Mr. Darcy's heart was racing at her touch, his hands itching to pull her close and kiss her smiling lips. Instead he breathed deeply as a snowflake landed on his tongue.

Elizabeth released him and stepped back, suddenly gone shy at her forward behavior. Mr. Darcy gazed into her eyes as Mrs. Bennet called her name.

"Miss Elizabeth..." he began and she took his hand giving it a squeeze.

"We shall come for Christmas, Mr. Darcy, Mother would not miss it. But we shall see one another before then? If the weather permits, you will find me in the stable each morning if you wish to have company."

Elizabeth Bennet dropped his hand and hurried to the carriage and her waiting family. When she turned to wave at him one last time, her cheeks were the color of the deep pink Damask roses that would bloom in the gardens of Somersal come spring.

Mr. Darcy stood with his sister, who even now was chasing snowflakes as the Bennet sisters had taught her, and watched until their carriage was out of sight. The pounding of his heart had slowed only a bit as he took his sister's hand and led her back inside Pemberley.

Elizabeth Bennet was finding her way into his heart and he found he welcomed her foray.

Chapter 9

Mr. Darcy arrived at Somersal the next morning in a carriage with a most disagreeable Caroline Bingley at his side. When she heard of his intent to ride with Miss Elizabeth the next morning, Miss Bingley had invited herself along though she detested riding and only did so once a year during the hunting season at Pemberley.

It was only done then to impress Mr. Darcy, though he never seemed to notice in his eagerness to be off with the hounds.

Though she had not considered Miss Elizabeth to be competition when the Bennets had arrived for dinner the evening before, she certainly did after her bold song of love and longing with Mr. Darcy afterwards in the parlor.

Charles had been quite angry with her after the Bennets had gone home to Somersal and Mr. Darcy had joined them in the parlor after seeing his guests to their carriage.

He had said not a word regarding her rude behavior towards his guests but his coolness penetrated her heart. She had made an apology and when he'd said he would go riding in the morning with Miss Elizabeth, her tongue had spoken before her mind might reconsider.

Now she sat in the carriage awaiting his hand to help her down, dressed in heavy skirts wishing she had not been quite so hasty in her speech the night before.

Elizabeth Bennet was standing in the stable yard with her horse and waved to them when she saw the pair approaching. If she was surprised at Miss Bingley's presence, she hid it well. Caroline Bingley gave the woman a tight smile and admired her horse.

"Why, what a lovely creature!" She said loudly and with much more feeling than she meant and stepped forward to touch the horse's nose. Merrit whinnied at Miss Bingley's screeching and tossed his head before prancing forward.

Caroline Bingley's face grew pale and she raised a hand to her mouth trying to catch the scream before it erupted. She was unable to do so and Merrit reared back, truly frightened at the continuing terrible noise the woman made.

Elizabeth stood in front of the horse as Miss Bingley clung to Mr. Darcy keeping him from helping to soothe the great beast. Miss Bingley had buried her face in his chest and now stood sobbing.

Merrit whinnied loudly and Elizabeth caught the reins and pulled hard. The horse settled and she walked him immediately into the stable and gave him to the groom. "See that he is calmed. I intend to ride him once our delicate visitor has been settled in the parlor with my mother."

Mr. Darcy had removed Miss Bingley's hands from his coat and was speaking to her in a gentle tone. Elizabeth stopped when she saw them standing thus and took several deep breaths before leaving the stable.

"Miss Bingley, are you quite all right? Merrit would not have harmed you, it's only that your tone of voice was most upsetting. He truly is a gentle soul."

Caroline Bingley looked to Mr. Darcy to find him nodding in agreement. She was deeply ashamed but instead of thanking Elizabeth for her expertise in controlling the horse, she stamped a foot and pointed an accusatory finger at her. "You cannot fool me. You must have some signal to cause that horse to misbehave. I have been shamed before a dear friend and it is all your fault."

Elizabeth bit her bottom lip to keep from laughing at such an outlandish display. It was several moments before she could speak without bursting into a fit of giggles. "Miss Bingley, I assure you I would never..."

Mr. Darcy moved to stand beside Elizabeth and Miss Bingley drew her hands up into fists at her side. "Mr. Darcy, you would believe such a lie from a woman who dearly loves racing horses? Why of course she controls them! Why else would a docile beast behave in such a manner when I simply went to touch him?"

Mr. Darcy smirked, for he was accustomed to Miss Bingley blaming others for her own shortcomings. He placed a hand on Elizabeth's shoulder and allowed his eyes to roam her fine form in its tailored habit. He meant to defend her against Miss Bingley's accusations but lost himself in the beauty of the accomplished woman before him.

Caroline Bingley became incensed at having to bear witness to his display and screeched at him again. "Take me home this instant, Mr. Darcy. I shall not stay and abide such mistreatment."

Mr. Darcy gave his attention to Caroline Bingley regretfully but he did not drop his hand from Elizabeth's shoulder. "Miss Elizabeth is a fine horsewoman, that much is true, but it was your voice that excited the horse into action. You must always speak in a soothing tone around horses, Miss Bingley, for they know when you are fearful. Merrit is a fine horse with an even temperament."

Caroline Bingley turned on her heel and stomped away. Mr. Darcy called to her, barely concealing the laughter that threatened to break free. "The carriage has returned to Pemberley. If you wish to go back, you shall have to walk or ride."

Miss Bingley spun and threw her hands in the air. "Surely you do not expect me to ride after such an upset. One of the Somersal carriages may return me to Pemberley."

Mr. Darcy shook his head. "You may wait in the parlor with Mrs. Bennet for our return if you do not wish to ride with us. I am certain she and Miss Bennet would appreciate breaking their fast with you this morning."

Elizabeth nodded and rushed to Caroline Bingley's side. "Indeed, mother and Jane were saying last evening how they must have you and Miss Darcy for tea soon, Miss Bingley."

Mr. Darcy retreated to the stable to choose a horse while Elizabeth towed a reluctant Miss Bingley through the front door of Somersal.

Miss Bingley removed her arm from Elizabeth's grasp and stood as a stone statue at the foot of the stairs across from the breakfast parlor. "I know your game, Miss Eliza," she taunted and raised her chin, "but Mr. Darcy will never be yours."

Elizabeth smiled at the bitter woman and turned to the breakfast parlor, calling for her mother. "Miss Bingley has come to call this morning."

Mrs. Bennet bustled into the hallway with the younger girls rushing out behind her. She took Caroline Bingley by the arm. "Miss Bingley, how lovely of you to come so early to visit. Jane was set to send an invitation to you and Miss Darcy but you must come and sit in the breakfast parlor with us."

Elizabeth smiled at her mother and bid Miss Bingley farewell before seeing herself out the front door. Able to freely laugh at the turn of events with poor Miss Bingley, Elizabeth skipped down the broad stone steps of Somersal and hurried to the stable to join Mr. Darcy in what she hoped would become their customary morning ride.

He stood waiting for her with Merrit's reins in one hand and the reins of a fine white stallion in the other. His horse was much larger than Merrit and Elizabeth had not had the courage to mount the beast even for a trot around the field beside the stable.

Perhaps with Mr. Darcy by her side she might at least attempt to sit in the saddle while they were out riding. At least for a little while. She smiled as she approached and he offered his assistance to help her mount Merrit. She thought of refusing but decided she quite liked his attentive nature.

Mr. Darcy held her hand and placed his other hand on the small of her back as she lifted her left foot into the stirrup. Elizabeth caught the scent of his cologne and breathed in deeply. The strength and maleness of the moment made her lightheaded and she paused a moment before swinging her right leg over Merrit's back.

Mr. Darcy leaned close to her, ready to assist and whispered encouragement. "Go on, my dear, the fields await."

Elizabeth smiled at him, their faces so close together that she could count his eyelashes. Turning before she might obey the wild command of her heart to kiss the man, she heaved herself up and sat trembling in her saddle. Merrit pranced a bit at her nervous energy but she quickly eased her favorite horse with quick rub to his strong neck.

Mr. Darcy stood gazing up at her for a moment, his expression one of wonder. Elizabeth blushed a bright pink and turned Merrit toward the field. Mr. Darcy startled and moved quickly to the white stallion's side. He mounted with ease and Elizabeth admired his broad shoulders and narrow hips as he turned to lead the way forward.

The cold of the winter morning turned the horses' breath to clouds of steam as the couple rode along in silence for a time. Mr. Darcy had led her along a circuit of Somersal that would show her the tenant farms of Pemberley as her new home bounded his land to the east.

They stopped at one particular cottage and Mr. Darcy dismounted and motioned for her to wait. The farmer and his wife appeared and the woman offered Mr. Darcy a small basket before curtseying to Elizabeth.

Having rode many times with her father to visit their tenants at Longbourn, Elizabeth smiled at the woman. The farmer's wife hurried back inside while Mr. Darcy stood speaking with her husband.

Elizabeth noticed the easy manner of the master of Pemberley as he addressed the man and was caught by surprise when their conversation ended and Mr. Darcy clapped the man on the back. The farmer gave a small wave in her direction and Elizabeth rewarded him with a nod of her head.

Mr. Darcy returned to his horse but gave the basket to Elizabeth. "Mrs. Drake makes the best scones in all of Derbyshire but you must not tell my Cook I said as much."

He winked and Elizabeth peeked inside the basket. There were four scones inside with what appeared to be a crock of jam. Steam rose from the basket and tickled her nose with the scent of freshly baked goods causing her mouth to water.

She closed the lid quickly, not wanting to allow the cold air to chill the heavenly offering and smiled at Mr. Darcy. "I'd love one now but we must ride away a bit first. I wouldn't want to appear greedy."

Mr. Darcy laughed as he mounted his horse and followed his lady as she spurred Merrit into a gallop towards a copse of trees. He would have to remember her love of small treats and play that to his advantage. Mrs. Drake might find herself busy in the preparation of extra scones in the mornings to come.

Elizabeth glanced over her shoulder as Merrit approached the trees and urged Mr. Darcy forward. "Come, kind sir. These scones shall not remain warm much longer."

He pushed the stallion into a gallop and passed Elizabeth and Merrit. He drew up and dismounted quickly leaving his horse to wander and crop at the stiff grass that lay covered in snow.

Elizabeth drew Merrit alongside the other horse and gave Mr. Darcy the basket and reins before dropping swiftly to the ground. She scouted a boulder nearby and perched atop the stone, shivering as the cold granite met her backside.

Mr. Darcy strolled to her side offering the basket before pulling it out of her reach as a tease. Elizabeth laughed and dared him to do it again. He took her dare and held the basket just out of reach once more.

Elizabeth sat still, her eyes twinkling with mirth before she finally lunged and snagged her prize. Mr. Darcy was caught off balance as she tugged the basket from his hand and went down hard on his backside.

His companion hastily forgot the scones and hurried to help him to his feet. Her expression was one of mortification as she dusted his jacket and breeches.

Mr. Darcy stilled her hands and Elizabeth stepped back with her mouth dropped open. She had just made contact with Mr. Darcy's posterior! With one hand over her mouth, she ran into the woods and hid behind a small tree.

Grabbing the basket of goodies, Mr. Darcy called out to her before following her into the copse. He allowed his eyes to adjust to the shadows and called her name again. "Miss Elizabeth, please, think nothing of your…err…concern on my behalf."

Elizabeth appeared from behind a tree three steps ahead of him and Mr. Darcy offered her the basket. "Shall we eat?"

Her face a much lighter shade of pink, she took the lovely gift and glanced at her feet. Mr. Darcy came to stand beside her, his warmth a welcome comfort in the shadows. "I believe we ought to head back to Somersal after we enjoy these scones, Miss Elizabeth, for it is quite cold this morning."

Elizabeth nodded and looked up. His eyes were the most lovely shade of dark green and she caught her breath as he moved closer. In her surprise at the nearness of the man, she took a step forward and stumbled causing Mr. Darcy to catch her in his arms. His lips grazed her forehead and lingered.

Mr. Darcy stepped away after a moment and suddenly became the one embarrassed. "I apologize, I shouldn't have…"

Elizabeth shook her head and gave his own words back with flutter in her heart. "Think nothing of your concern on my behalf, kind sir."

Chapter 10

The next day, the Matlocks arrived from London to spend a fortnight with the Darcy family. Colonel Richard Fitzwilliam handed his mother, Lady Margaret Fitzwilliam, down from the carriage while his father was greeted by his cousin Fitzwilliam Darcy.

His brother James escorted their mother to the front door of Pemberley and into the welcoming arms of Mr. Darcy. "Aunt Margaret, I am pleased you came. Georgiana is practicing her new sheet music in the salon."

Lady Margaret Fitzwilliam gave her nephew an adoring look and lightly kissed his cheek. "I shall be happy to listen while you entertain my fellows in the library. Reginald has moaned the last few miles about cigars."

Mr. Darcy laughed and led his favorite aunt inside Pemberley and to the salon. He was pleased to have his home full of friends and family during the holiday season. His mind wandered to the one friend he would most like to see and Mr. Darcy resolved to offer another dinner invitation to Miss Elizabeth and her family in the morning when they met for their customary ride.

After they'd returned to Somersal yesterday morning, he'd regained his composure and managed to keep his lips to himself though the lady made it quite difficult as they talked while she fed the horses apples and carrots.

Mr. Darcy would never have believed that he might find a lady as accomplished in the saddle as he, but Miss Elizabeth certainly came close. He admired her genuine love of Merrit and the graceful way she carried herself whether on horseback or dressed in a fine gown seated at his dinner table.

She reminded him very much of his dear mother. Though Lady Anne Darcy had been tall and lithe like Georgiana, the confidence she possessed and the way she always made him feel like he was the only person in the world was alive again in Elizabeth Bennet.

Striding to the library to sit with his uncle and cousins, Mr. Darcy felt a peaceful happiness that had eluded him for many years as the master of Pemberley. A certain young lady not many miles distant was solely responsible.

Reginald Henry Fitzwilliam, the Earl of Matlock, stood by the fireplace with smoke wreathing his head. His countenance was one of supreme satisfaction as he waved to his nephew.

"Darcy, my good man, how I have missed your selection of the finest cigars in the kingdom. Shall there come a day when you reveal your source?"

Fitzwilliam Darcy shook his head while pointing a finger at the man. "Now, Uncle Reginald, if I shared that bit of intelligence you would undoubtedly spread it far and wide and my supply would surely diminish. Some things are best enjoyed once in a great while, you know."

Mr. Darcy paused and selected his own smoke from the walnut humidor. "Would you be so happy to travel to Derbyshire in the chill of winter without one of these awaiting as your reward?"

The earl chuckled and took the empty seat by the fireplace allowing his large frame to relax into the sumptuous cushions. Pemberley was an oasis he enjoyed immensely and would never tire of visiting no matter the time of year.

Mr. Darcy clapped Richard Fitzwilliam on the back, genuinely happy to have his favorite cousin in his home. "I've missed you, cousin. How goes the war?"

Richard smiled and sipped from the glass in his hand. "Since I am presently standing in your library and not on some snowy parade field, I'd say quite well."

James left the earl's side and came to stand beside his brother. "Father says we must settle the matter of Somersal before we return to London but I cannot imagine putting a widow and her five daughters out in the cold at Christmas."

Richard nearly choked on his drink while the earl admonished his eldest son. "James, now is not the time for such discussion. The fate of Somersal is not your particular concern."

Mr. Darcy sighed heavily. He ought to have known the country estate near Pemberley would be a topic of great interest for the Fitzwilliam men. James would be the next Earl of Matlock but Richard was the one most in need of an estate to secure an advantageous marriage.

Taking the seat next to his uncle, Darcy controlled his tone of voice so that they might not argue. "Uncle, while I agree now is not the time to speak to you of Somersal, I cannot understand why James would think the Bennets would be put out in the streets."

The earl puffed on his cigar wishing his eldest son had held his tongue. Looking at the neatly rolled specimen in his hand, he decided he may as well get their business out of the way so that he might enjoy the peace and quiet of Pemberley. "By rights, Somersal is mine to do with as I please."

Mr. Darcy nodded his head. Indeed, as the Earl of Matlock, his uncle held rights to the charming land and home. Darcy had wished he might add it to his own holdings over the years but his father had said Reginald Fitzwilliam was a tight-fisted man and wouldn't part with it even for family.

Turning to his uncle and raising his voice, for he wished for James and Richard to hear their conversation, Mr. Darcy invoked the memory of the earl's deceased brother. "Uncle Bertie made a stipulation in his will, on his deathbed, which my own mother penned in her hand I might add. Does that mean nothing to you now?"

The earl made a derisive sound in his throat and placed his cigar in his mouth while he thought of how best to answer his nephew.

Richard was eager to make it abundantly clear that he was in no need of Somersal. He was a soldier with a long career ahead of him. Settling down was not part of his plans. "Darcy, father would like Somersal for my use when and if the day comes that I marry but that day is a long way off."

Reginald Fitzwilliam finished the ring of smoke he artfully blew out and stared at his youngest son. The man was ever a thorn in his side. He loved Richard but persuading him to leave her Majesty's finest had become the work of his life.

"When Richard shall settle at Somersal has little bearing on the matter. We have a sizable estate with a widow and five daughters in need of funding. I simply won't finance them until each is married and settled. As to my brother, Bertie would not have wished it so."

Mr. Darcy stood and paced before the fireplace. Had it not been for Thomas Bennet, the Fitzwilliam family would never have been joined to the Darcy family and their fortune would not have seen such growth without his skill though he had been quite young when his own father passed.

"Uncle Reginald, those ladies are not an added cost but a benefit. The home sits occupied and the servants are kept busy rather than idle. Had it not been for Thomas Bennet, as you well know, your fortune might have been a very different one than it is today. Had your brother been prudent and less inclined to risk, you might have never become the Earl of Matlock. Had my mother perished, the Fitzwilliam family would not have joined mine nor benefitted from the long years of excellent stewardship of my father and of myself. You cannot deny that."

The earl nodded his head, for he had thought as much through many a sleepless night as head of his family. "Be that as it may, I will not fund the running of Somersal. Paying for the upkeep has been an investment but adding to the cost for a family that is not mine, well, I just will not continue."

Darcy eyed his uncle and knew that money was not the issue. "You were jealous of Bertie and Bennet, weren't you?"

Reginald Fitzwilliam stood quickly from his seat, his face flushed a deep red. He held his cigar in one hand and poked a finger at his nephew with the other. "You have no business stirring up memories of the past! If you wish the Bennets to remain at Somersal, you pay the bills!"

Before his uncle could quit the library, Mr. Darcy sought to make peace. "Uncle Reginald, I am sorry, I had no right to speak on your personal feelings. You are right, the past is the past but my mother spoke of Thomas Bennet with much admiration. He saved her life. You cannot expect that I would allow his widow and daughters to be left without a home."

Though James had broached the subject, he and Richard remained silent knowing the battle was between their father and Darcy. Neither man would now appreciate comments from either Fitzwilliam brother.

The earl resumed his seat by the fire as he was loath to leave the comfort of his favorite room in all of Pemberley. "If you find it in your heart to finance this family for years to come, I shall not interfere. As for Bertie and Bennet, theirs was an uncommon friendship the like of which I have not seen since. I may have chafed at their connection in my youth but I would never disrespect my brother's dying wish of allowing Bennet's ladies the use of Somersal."

Fitzwilliam Darcy thought of saying more on the matter but decided his uncle had suffered enough for one day. The topic of Somersal was finished as far as he was concerned. The earl would not support the ladies but he would not remove them from the estate either. Darcy moved to sit with his cousins and leave the earl to his cigar and his memories.

At Somersal, Elizabeth sat with her sister Jane in the parlor and winced at the discordant strains of a piano forte being brutally misused in the salon. She made a mental note to address the deficiency with Constance. "I swear, Kitty has sublime skill when it comes to painting but her abuse of the piano forte must stop for the sake of my health. My head is pounding."

Jane shook her head and concentrated on her embroidery. "I believe dear Constance shall be most relieved if your wishes are made known for her suffering is of a magnitude much greater than our own."

After another five minutes more of the terrible noise, Elizabeth rang for a maid. When the young lady arrived, she sent her to the salon with a message for Constance. "Please tell her that Kitty must stop this instant. I cannot bear the nuisance a moment longer."

The maid struggled to hide the laughter that shook her shoulders and gave a quick curtsey as she hastened from the room.

Jane sighed and placed her embroidery aside. "Miss Darcy and Miss Bingley ought to arrive soon for tea. Your poor head shall receive no reprieve, I fear."

Elizabeth quite agreed with Jane and rose to quit the parlor. "Perhaps a bit of fresh air will make all the difference."

Once out of doors, Elizabeth Bennet hurried to the stable to see Merrit and give him a treat. Her ride with Mr. Darcy the morning before played repeatedly in her mind. The man who had found her lacking at the assembly in Meryton and then seemed to soften where she was concerned during her stay at Netherfield with Jane, had now come to show feelings that were an order above friendship.

As she rubbed Merrit's nose, she imagined she could still feel the tingling on her forehead where his lips had rested, though it was clearly a matter of her own clumsiness rather than any forward behavior on his part.

They had sat and shared the scones, speaking of their favorite childhood treats provided by various cooks over the years. Mr. Darcy had admitted to a passion for Black Butter and Elizabeth agreed. The hearty apple flavor had been her own favorite.

After their modest repast was done, Mr. Darcy had stood and helped her from the granite boulder where his coat had been spread to shield her backside from the cold. Elizabeth had taken the garment and held it for him as a valet might.

Mr. Darcy had laughed and remarked on her skill. "I've not had the pleasure of such a lovely valet, Miss Elizabeth. You spoil me."

Elizabeth lowered her lashes as he straightened the coat on his broad shoulders. She wished she might run her hands across his back and smooth the fabric. Instead, she clasped them together and brought them to her face to secretly inhale the lingering scent of his cologne.

Mr. Darcy had turned and held out an arm. "Shall we return to Somersal?"

Elizabeth had laid her hand on his arm and smiled up at him. "I would rather ride for another hour, sir. But Mother shall wonder where I have gone and my sisters expect a trip into Lambton when I return."

They had ridden in companionable silence across the frozen fields, one with the certainty that he was in love and the other with the certainty that she wished to always start her day by his side.

The clatter of horse's hooves outside the stable roused Elizabeth from her memories and she glanced up in time to see a carriage from Pemberley had arrived. How had she passed the better part of an hour daydreaming of Mr. Darcy in the stable?

Shaking her head at behavior that would better suit her youngest sisters, Elizabeth stood and shook out her skirts. She smiled at the warmth in her heart and the distinct lack of pain in her head. She was certain spending the afternoon in the company of Caroline Bingley would alter her mood.

Chapter 11

Upon entering the parlor, Elizabeth noticed there were two ladies sitting with her mother and Jane while Miss Darcy had moved to the large table by the windows that overlooked the gardens to join her younger sisters in the making of paper flowers.

One was Miss Bingley, of course, and Elizabeth knew she would accompany Miss Darcy to tea in order to needle the Bennet sisters, but the other lady was much older and quite regal in her bearing.

Mrs. Bennet turned and called for her to join them. Caroline Bingley wrinkled her nose when Elizabeth neared as though she was offended. Knowing she had just left the stables, Elizabeth smiled and surreptitiously sniffed herself in the course of taking her seat.

"Lady Matlock, this is my second eldest daughter Elizabeth Bennet," Mrs. Bennet said and made the introduction.

The grand lady gave a tight smile before addressing the late arrival. "I am pleased to make your acquaintance Miss Elizabeth. Georgianna has spoken highly of your family."

Elizabeth wondered if the woman was indeed pleased to have accompanied her niece and Miss Bingley as the Bennet family now resided in a home that belonged to her family.

"What a lovely surprise to have you at Somersal, Lady Matlock. We are most grateful to the Fitzwilliam family for their generosity."

Caroline Bingley frowned and made a small noise in her throat which she quickly pretended was a cough as Lady Matlock fixed her with a severe stare.

A maid entered with the tea cart and a strained silence ensued as the maid poured out for the ladies seated together before moving to the young ladies at the table.

When all were settled again, Caroline Bingley remarked upon the selection of finger sandwiches, seed cake, scones, and fairly cake. "My, my, Mrs. Bennet, I would not have thought to expect such bounty from a widow with five daughters."

Elizabeth brought her teacup to her lips to keep from delivering an insult to their guest. Mrs. Bennet suffered no such restraint and smiled sweetly at the rude woman. "While I appreciate your concern, Miss Bingley, Mr. Bennet did not leave us destitute. As this is yet another instance of misdirected sympathy where my family is concerned, perhaps it would be for the best if you simply understood that my daughters and I do not struggle to entertain our guests."

Lady Matlock gave an approving glance to Mrs. Bennet, for the woman's high spirits displayed when they had first arrived gave the mistaken impression that she might possess more sentimentality than sense.

Miss Bingley, now mortified that her barb had fallen far short of its aim, rose from her seat and pretended interest in the activities of the younger ladies.

Elizabeth glanced to Jane before setting her cup on the table before her. "Lady Matlock, do tell us about your trip to Pemberley. Were the roads kind?"

Mrs. Bennet nodded at the turn in conversation and remarked upon the weather. "I cannot imagine traveling from London in this cold. Going to Lambton is trial enough these past few days."

Lady Matlock clucked her tongue in agreement. "Twas a wearisome journey, but the Earl and I would never miss a Christmas at Pemberley. Our sons, Richard and James, would never allow it even did we wish to remain in London. 'Tis a grand tradition stretching back many years we are loath to dismiss."

Mrs. Bennet was happy to hear it. The arrival of several more young men would only prove beneficial to the prospects of her daughters. "Mr. Darcy is a most wonderful host. Why, he had us to dinner not long ago and Pemberley is indeed the loveliest estate I have ever seen."

Elizabeth wondered at the mention of the Matlock's sons and steered the conversation in their direction. Thinking of an acquaintance for Jane who did not suffer the misfortune of having Miss Bingley as a sister was her chief aim. "Do your sons live in London the year round, Lady Matlock?"

"Certainly," the woman said with great affection in her voice, "Richard is a soldier and so may be called away from time to time, but James will be the next Earl of Matlock. He is very close to his father. I expect he shall be engaged by our next Christmas visit to Pemberley."

Mrs. Bennet fluttered her handkerchief and praised the Fitzwilliam family once more. "How lovely it is to think of one's children well matched and settled. With five daughters, I certainly do hope for the same."

Elizabeth and Jane glanced at their mother hoping her words were not seen by their visitor as grasping. Situated as they now were at Somersal, it should not prove difficult for any of the Bennet sisters to marry well. Lambton was a larger community with many well-to-do families situated as their neighbors.

Lady Matlock did not seem upset but quite the opposite. "Mrs. Bennet, I must confess that I hold an envy for those blessed with daughters. I do love my sons, do not misunderstand me, but a woman does wish to lead a young woman successfully through her first season. Oh, in London alone, the fitting for gowns and shopping for necessary accessories is thrilling. I try to bring Georgiana to town as often as Darcy will allow."

Mrs. Bennet glanced to the table where the young mistress of Pemberley sat happily with her daughters. "Miss Darcy is the loveliest girl, and her manners are impeccable. I am certain she will have a lovely season when her time comes. We are hopeful her grace and elegance will inspire our younger girls."

Lady Matlock and Mrs. Bennet chatted for the remainder of the visit and Elizabeth breathed a sigh of relief. She had hoped to impress the wife of their benefactor so that she would not regret their presence at Somersal.

Elizabeth knew that the Matlocks must wish for the estate to be clear for one of their sons and with three sisters behind her, and years before they might marry, it stood to reason that time might not be on the Bennet's side.

Still, they were settled for the time being. If she might race in the spring and win, Elizabeth could send the money to her Uncle Gardiner in London against the day her family might find themselves again without a home.

Lady Matlock called Miss Darcy to her side and the ladies made their farewells. Mr. Darcy's sister was not happy to be leaving. Lady Matlock placed an arm about her niece's shoulders. "We must not wear out our welcome dear. The Bennet sisters are welcome to visit at Pemberley whenever they wish, your brother said as much this morning over breakfast."

The youngest Bennet sisters joined hands with Georgiana Darcy and promised they would come the next day when Constance released them from their studies.

Elizabeth stood with her family as their guests boarded the Darcy carriage. Fortunes were changing for the Bennet girls but in her heart, Mr. Bennet's favorite daughter could not rest easy. She felt the weight of responsibility for her mother and sisters. Elizabeth Bennet could not dismiss thoughts of a future where they might be put out of a home again.

Mr. Darcy sat in the study with his cousin Richard and Charles Bingley as they discussed the spring season ahead. "Georgie would love to spend it in London with Aunt Margaret but I am not settled on those plans just yet."

Charles Bingley sighed with a trace of melancholy. "I would stay in Derbyshire if it was at all possible, but business will keep me in London. I must decide on the lease to Netherfield as well."

Richard Fitzwilliam listened to the two gentlemen and was glad in his heart that he was not subject to the same concerns. He only went where he was told for as long as he was told and nothing more. Having been born the second son was a blessing he would cherish to his dying day. Being an earl and moving in the circles his family frequented did not appeal to the rough-and-ready mind and body of a soldier.

Still, he would not mind living out his days at Somersal when the time came for him to give up his commission. The country suited him well and he could never imagine remaining in London when he had no need to do so.

Darcy had grown silent for a moment but then put a serious question to his best friend. "Charles, your business is in town and your sister despises the country. What possible use is Netherfield when considering those two facts?"

Charles Bingley stood and paced before his friend and the Colonel. "Honestly, I keep it with the hope that Miss Bennet might one day wish to marry me. It is my intent to court her and win her hand. Her family could return to Hertfordshire once more and dwell at Netherfield."

Mr. Darcy thought on this plan for a moment. He did not wish to see Miss Elizabeth gone from Somersal and he had settled the problem of financing the family with his uncle. "I would not think the ladies would wish to be uprooted again, Bingley. And there is the matter of having to see their cousin every day, the one who behaved so terribly after their father died. No, I don't believe they would wish to recover in the shadow of Longbourn."

Mr. Bingley sighed, for he knew his friend was right. "I had thought of that and I realize the idea was to serve my own selfish desire to have Miss Bennet think of me as a savior of her family. I must see her every chance before Caroline and I return to London and hope that she will know my heart."

Richard chuckled at the two men. They were both smitten by love and arranging the lives of others to achieve their aim of winning hearts. "When shall I meet these lovely ladies who have been the cause of such concern for so many years?"

Darcy rose and went to the window overlooking the frozen gardens of Pemberley. "If you are up to an early morning ride, you may meet Miss Elizabeth on the morrow. She and I have a custom of riding the fields of Somersal each day."

Charles Bingley volunteered himself to accompany his two friends. "I would go and then pay a visit to Miss Bennet afterwards. They did invite me, if you recall, when we dined with them at The Blue Goose in Lambton."

Darcy regretted his decision to share his time with Miss Elizabeth but with his best friend and cousin along perhaps he would be less tempted to take her into his arms and declare himself.

Not that the idea did not appeal to him. But he must wait, for he wished Elizabeth Bennet to say the words he longed to hear. He wanted to win her heart by being the man she needed him to be instead of the man she'd met in Meryton at the assembly.

The sound of Georgiana's happy voice in the entryway carried to the study and the gentlemen went out to greet the ladies upon their return from Somersal. Mr. Darcy was eager to know what his Aunt Margaret thought of the Bennet family but would not ask pointed questions in front of his sister and Miss Bingley.

Instead, he would sit with them all in the parlor as Georgiana was certain to regale them with details about their visit. And he knew for certain that Miss Bingley would share some unflattering detail about either Miss Bennet or Miss Elizabeth to counter his sister's praise.

Chapter 12

Mr. Darcy arrived at the Somersal stables with Mr. Bingley and Richard Fitzwilliam just as Elizabeth was leading Merrit outside. Surprised to see the two men with Mr. Darcy, she shaded her eyes for a better vantage of her visitors. One was of course Mr. Bingley, and she determined the other must be one of Mr. Darcy's Fitzwilliam cousins.

The man sat with ease upon his horse and so Elizabeth believed he might be Colonel Fitzwilliam. The men dismounted and Mr. Darcy made the introduction. "Miss Elizabeth, these gentlemen heard that we would ride this morning and begged to come along. I hope you do not object."

Elizabeth did object, quite strongly, but she smiled in welcome. She would rather ride alone with Mr. Darcy but he was entertaining family and friends and so it was only natural the men would wish to ride with them. Charles gave her his genuine greetings. "Good morning, Miss Elizabeth. Darcy has said you are a fine horsewoman and I insisted on seeing for myself when I recalled the invitation you gave at The Blue Goose."

Admiring Mr. Bingley's smiling face and dancing eyes, Elizabeth felt a twinge of guilt at wishing Jane might find a match with anyone else. 'Twas not the fault of the man that his sister was Caroline Bingley. "Mr. Bingley, I am happy you came. Perhaps we might race?"

Mr. Darcy cleared his throat at the mention of racing and took the opportunity to introduce his cousin. "Miss Elizabeth, this is my cousin Colonel Richard Fitzwilliam. He is a soldier in His Majesty's finest."

Richard Fitzwilliam was a dashingly handsome man, taller and broader than his cousin and with an impish smile that made Elizabeth think of what a handful he must have been when but a young boy. "Colonel," she said and made a small curtsey, "tis a pleasure to make your acquaintance. I did think you must be a soldier as you rode up with such easy grace."

The soldier gave a smart salute to the lady and remarked in kind. "Miss Elizabeth, I could say the same. The way you handle Merrit is admirable. He is a gentle beast but he never cared for ladies upon his back before."

Elizabeth's eyes grew round and she looked to Mr. Darcy, who nodded, before returning her gaze to the colonel. "I am astonished. Merrit and I have been the best of friends since the day of my arrival at Somersal. Perhaps the other ladies simply did not appreciate his beauty."

Richard Fitzwilliam's booming laughter startled their mounts. "I say Darcy, this one is surely your match. I don't recall having seen you upon Merrit's back before, either."

Darcy shrugged, his cheeks red from more than just the cold air of an early December morning. "I admit I was surprised the first morning I came to visit. But Miss Elizabeth paid him such devoted attention I could not find fault with the beast for preferring her."

Now Elizabeth was the one to blush furiously and so she mounted Merrit and leaned forward to whisper to her favorite horse, "Why you scoundrel you! We are a match the two of us. They'll never understand our love."

Merrit whinnied and tossed his proud head before setting off at a brisk trot. Mr. Darcy stood watching Elizabeth Bennet ride off with his heart before turning to mount his horse. Richard and Charles had been quicker than he and were now gaining on Merrit and Miss Elizabeth.

Darcy thought of her words to Charles about racing and shook his head. She was a spirited young lady with talent to spare when it came to horseback riding. But he worried so when he thought of her racing Merrit in the spring.

He had avoided the topic after their first dinner at Pemberley when Miss Bingley had delivered her gossip, for there were other more interesting topics of discussion when he was alone with his Elizabeth.

His Elizabeth

Mr. Darcy braced himself and spurred his horse to action. The lady was not yet his but in time he hoped she would be. Certainly his heart believed it so.

He rode along behind the happy trio watching as Richard pointed out landmarks and Charles relayed tales of younger days spent at Somersal.

Darcy yearned to be alone with the young lady he'd come to admire and esteem, but he did enjoy watching her from afar. The tilt of her chin, the sound of her laughter floating back to him on a chill breeze, the way she sat easy in the saddle yet ready to dash off as one with Merrit.

He'd only seen one other lady as confident and assured, his mother. Her daring on a frozen lake so many years ago had brought the Bennet family as close to his front door as possible and delivered the woman he knew he would love for an eternity whether she chose to love him back or break his heart.

A shout from Richard brought Darcy out of his memories and he watched as all three riders ahead of him took off in a thunder of hooves across the field. Elizabeth must have dared them to race and being foolish, both Charles and Richard had taken her up on her lark.

Mr. Darcy watched with great interest as Miss Elizabeth held the lead throughout even into the turn beside a stone wall that marked the edge of his property. He could see that her hair had come loose from its pins waving in a dark, silken banner behind her, and that Charles had not a chance to catch her.

Richard was giving his best effort and Darcy would tease him mercilessly later that a lady had bested an old soldier. Merrit's hooves churned up the frozen ground and Elizabeth turned to glance over her shoulder. Richard was leaning forward low in the saddle and giving his horse a terrible time. The beast was winded but gave a good show.

In the blink of an eye, as Darcy returned his attention to Elizabeth, Richard's horse stumbled and went down hard. Charles was behind him and pulled his horse to the right just in time to avoid the rolling mess that was half horse half man.

Elizabeth screamed and Merrit became frightened. Mr. Darcy saw the vision of his love being crushed under the frightened beast and drove his horse into action. He caught Merrit's reins and led the horse along using the body of his steed to slow Merrit's frightened pace.

Charles had dismounted and ran to Richard who lay deathly still upon the cold ground, his body twisted in unnatural angles. Elizabeth had jumped off Merrit once Darcy had control of the poor beast and ran to Richard's horse, weeping and calling for help as she pulled with all her might on the poor beast's reins. The injured animal attempted to rise and Charles pulled Richard away from the horse.

Mr. Darcy was amazed by Miss Elizabeth's quick thinking that likely saved Richard from worse injury. He could not have been certain he would have approached the gravely injured and terribly frightened horse so readily himself.

He stayed on his horse and with Merrit in tow, though he wished to go to Richard's side, raced to Somersal to send the stable boy into Lambton for help.

Thankfully, he kept a skilled surgeon near Pemberley for fear of something happening to Georgiana. They were much too far from London to risk only having an apothecary to hand.

Jane Bennet had come outside to find whether her sister had returned and Mr. Darcy told her of the accident. Jane gave him only a few words before dashing back inside the home. "Bring him here if you can. I shall have the servants bring a bed down to the parlor for him now."

Mr. Darcy didn't have time to argue that Richard would be taken to Pemberley. The groom came out of the stable with a horse, a cart, and several stable hands. They followed the master of Pemberley to the field where his cousin lay injured.

Mr. Bingley held a sobbing Elizabeth in his arms and tried to console her. "Twas not your fault Miss Elizabeth. The colonel has done every foolhardy stunt a man might do. It was an accident, nothing more."

In a terrible moment that brought agonizing moans from Colonel Richard Fitzwilliam, the men picked him up and loaded him on the cart. One man remained beside the fallen horse that was now struggling for breath.

Mr. Darcy directed the men to take Richard to Somersal as even he could see the slow bumpy ride in a cart to Pemberley might be more than his cousin could bear in his current state. He held up a hand to the man that waited with pistol in hand beside the fallen horse. Elizabeth could not possibly endure the destruction of the horse.

He turned and went to her, his arms out to console her. She looked past him for Richard, stricken with a consuming grief. His heart broke for the poor, sweet girl. For that was what she truly was still, a reckless, happy girl who'd only just found joy at Somersal after losing her father.

Elizabeth hugged herself tightly wishing to disappear. But Mr. Darcy stood before her while his dearest cousin was trundled away broken at her hand.

She ran when he tried to speak to her, ran like her life depended upon it. Tears blurred her vision and Elizabeth stumbled, scrabbling against the frozen ground and rising to her feet again as Mr. Bingley and Mr. Darcy chased behind her.

The crack of a pistol broke through Elizabeth's grief stricken mind and she fell on her knees brought low by the tragedy her foolish risk had brought. There was no going back, no saving the beautiful horse. Elizabeth Bennet was broken as well.

Charles Bingley went to her side and helped Elizabeth to stand. Mr. Darcy followed behind hoping the surgeon was well on his way. He would not return to Pemberley until he was apprised of Richard's condition. Delivering the news to the Matlocks would be difficult even were his cousin to survive the accident.

In the parlor of Somersal, Richard Fitzwilliam lay in agonizing pain. Jane Bennet had dashed inside after Mr. Darcy's arrival and set the servants to work. Her sisters had been sent to the salon and the parlor declared off limits for the foreseeable future.

Water was boiling in the fireplace and maids were tearing strips of clean cotton for the surgeon's use. Jane had assembled the ready supply of herbals and medicaments the household possessed and resolved to go into Lambton to replenish the lot once the surgeon had seen to the Colonel.

Checking that her preparations were plentiful once more, she made a circuit of the room before returning to the broken man's side. His face was quite pale and his breathing labored. He moaned with every other breath and she wished she might do something to aid him.

Sending the butler for whiskey, for her father had often used the spirit when one or the other of his stable hands or tenants had been mildly injured, Jane waited patiently while speaking soothing words to Richard Fitzwilliam.

The butler returned with the best whiskey the house possessed and waited to assist his mistress. Jane took the glass and the butler poured. He placed the decanter on the table by the sofa and went to place his arms gently beneath the colonel's head to lift the man so that Jane might bring the glass to his lips.

The colonel made a terrible noise but Jane continued her mission. "Colonel Fitzwilliam, you have been badly injured and you must drink for me. The surgeon is on his way from Lambton. This whiskey should help for a time."

Richard Fitzwilliam blinked several times, the pain in his body a mighty force that threatened to deliver him to a blessed darkness that hovered just beyond his reach. He focused on the fair lady before him and the scent of whiskey burned his nostrils.

Heeding the good lady's words, he pursed his lips as she held the glass for him. He took several draughts before resting, the fiery liquid giving him pleasure if not relief.

Another few sips and his head was placed gently back on the bed. He was in a parlor, that much he could tell by the roaming of his eyes, and there was a lovely fair-haired maiden tending his needs. *Perhaps this was what heaven looked like*, the old soldier thought and chuckled before regretting that decision. His lungs informed him it would be a good long while before he might laugh without terrible pain.

He whispered to the fair lady who had taken pity on him so that she might not remove the whiskey. "Come closer, dear, and help me with another round. You are far too lovely and kind to be a demon and so I must be in heaven though the pain would mean our heavenly Father would punish me just a bit for my transgressions."

Chapter 13

The surgeon arrived from Lambton as Elizabeth Bennet sat with Colonel Fitzwilliam in the parlor. Mr. Darcy stood on the opposite side of the bed Jane Bennet had demanded be brought down for the injured man.

Charles Bingley had escorted Jane from the room so that the surgeon might make his exam without delay. Standing by the parlor door, Jane called to Elizabeth and waited as her poor, despondent sister drifted across the room. She bumped into several pieces of furniture on her journey as though she had never stepped foot in Somersal and did not know the room.

Jane took Elizabeth in her arms and with Charles's assistance walked with her to the breakfast parlor. Mrs. Bennet remained in the salon with the younger girls though she had been kept abreast of the situation by the maids that had assisted Jane with the setting up of the colonel's sickroom.

Somersal was quiet now, the bustle and activity reduced for the moment. The whole of the house seemed to wait with a great breath held in expectation of the worst.

Mr. Darcy remained in the parlor with his cousin and the surgeon while the man made his assessment of Richard's many injuries. The grunts that accompanied his careful inventory pained Mr. Darcy but he held his tongue until the surgeon signaled his exam was complete.

"Tis a wonderful turn Miss Bennet has done your cousin, sir. The whiskey must be of the best quality to have given him such relief. I must say, I believe he shall live. He has broken bones and cracked ribs, but no internal injuries I can find wonder that it is.

He will walk again under his own power after a tedious recovery but he certainly shall never be a soldier again."

Mr. Darcy released a breath and collapsed on the sofa. God willing, his dearest cousin would live but what kind of life might it be? Shaking his head, he stood again forcing the pity from his voice. "Fix him doctor, do all that you must and spare nothing. The staff of Somersal stands ready to aid you as needed. I shall send to Pemberley to notify his mother and father. Can you wait until they have arrived to begin?"

The surgeon shook his head. "I would rather not, sir. Every moment we lose, his body shall become accustomed to the injuries and resist my best efforts. I must begin now."

Removing his coat and opening his bag, the surgeon requested his burliest footmen and several maids to aid him in the hours to come. "I must have the strongest footmen available and maids who do not faint at the sight of blood."

Mr. Darcy left the man in the parlor and gave instruction to the butler to assemble the staff required and see they were present in the parlor as quickly as possible.

Wanting desperately to go to Miss Elizabeth, Mr. Darcy forced himself to direct his feet to the front door, down the wide stone steps of Somersal, and around the house to the stable once more. The horses he and Charles had ridden from Pemberley were in stalls kept for visitors and he wished with all his being that he could go back to his arrival that morning and change the fate of his cousin.

Instead, he asked for Miss Elizabeth's stable boy and sent him to Pemberley with a message for the Earl of Matlock. "Speak only to him, young man, for the ladies must not hear of such terrible news from a servant. Hurry back and stand at the ready to be my courier when the need arises."

The young lad nodded gravely and repeated Mr. Darcy's instructions to show he understood the master's commands.

Turning to make his way back inside the home where his cousin lay in peril, Mr. Darcy stopped and breathed deeply. He must go to Miss Elizabeth and make her understand she was not to blame for Richard's plight. But did he believe it himself or was he only eager to absolve her of blame because of his tender feelings for the lady?

It could not be so. His cousin was as dear to him as his own sister. The thought of Georgiana lying in that parlor instead of Richard shook him to his core and he bit back bitter tears as he realized there was a small, insistent part of his heart that indeed blamed Elizabeth Bennet.

A Bennet had been the salvation of his mother on a dark dreadful night many decades past but now a young lady from that man's house may have visited great harm on his family.

He could not bear to condemn her with his words for he knew when he looked into her lovely eyes he might forget all that had happened. And yet, Richard lay in her home, the home his family had provided, broken and forever removed from any hope of a future in his beloved profession.

At Pemberley, the young stable hand went first to the stables and was taken to the kitchens to speak with the housekeeper, Mrs. Kensington, and the butler.

"Here boy," said Kathleen Kensington as she stood beside the butler forming an impervious wall in front of the small servant, "what is this about? You cannot speak with the Earl of Matlock as an equal. Tell us your news and we shall deliver it."

The boy shook his head furiously. "Mr. Darcy himself said I must deliver the news to the earl my own self, mum. I will not fail him."

Mrs. Kensington shook her finger at the lad. "It won't do you any good to be telling tales in this house, young man. Now out with it and hurry, for if my master has sent an urgent message we must make haste."

Again the stable boy shook his head. "If you do not allow me to see the earl I shall return to Somersal and the master will be most displeased. I tell you, this is a matter most urgent. A life hangs in the balance."

The butler took the boy by the arm and marched him up the stairs to the parlor. "Wait here while I bring the earl. Do not sit nor touch a thing. You are right filthy and smell strongly of the stable."

Sticking his tongue out only after the butler had turned his back, the lad moved to the warmth of the fireplace but did mind his manners. While he was not one to be easily dismissed when on an errand for the master of Pemberley, neither was he foolish enough to muck about the room leaving fingerprints and smudges on the lovely bright silks of the chairs and sofa.

Not many moments later, the butler returned with a rotund gentleman who inspected the stable boy from head to toe. Never had the halls of Pemberley greeted such a dirty little ruffian from the stables, but apparently the boy had been sent in haste. His nephew ought to have sent a footman instead.

"Speak up boy, what have you come to tell?"

The earl waited with the butler by his side but the boy held his tongue. Reginald Henry Fitzwilliam was short on patience at having been brought from the warmth and enjoyment of the library to stand before a stable boy who remained as silent as a corpse before him.

He turned on his heel to quit the parlor but the boy finally spoke. "I must give you a most urgent message from Mr. Darcy, sir, but I cannot speak it with the butler present."

The earl turned back, though he wished to be done with the brash young servant and instructed the butler to leave them. The man was not the least bit happy about the situation, for he wished to know what news there was from Somersal that demanded a lowly stable boy to speak only with the Earl of Matlock.

After a stern look from the earl, the butler left and closed the door with much fervor, so peeved was he to be commanded by the whim of a child.

The earl moved to the fireplace and stood before his messenger. "We are alone, son. Pray tell what is so vitally important that you have upset the entire household, and my blessedly peaceful morning, to have us know?"

Becoming suddenly shy before the earl, the stable boy bowed his head and mumbled his answer. "Your son, sir, he has been injured and you must come at once with me to Somersal."

The great man before him kneeled suddenly before the lad. "Say that again boy, for I cannot have heard correctly."

Again the words were spoken and the earl was stricken to know he had not misunderstood the simple lad from the stable of Somersal. Clearing his throat and rising to gather his wife and eldest son, the earl pulled the bell cord to call for a carriage.

He left the stable boy standing by the fireplace and hurried to make haste to Somersal. How he might break the terrible news to his wife he did not know and to young Georgiana, truly they must not see Richard in such a state.

The butler sent a maid upstairs for Lady Matlock and her eldest son. "Say that they must come down immediately for the earl has a carriage waiting."

The young maid shook her head and dashed up the stairs stopping on the third one to turn and seek guidance from the butler. "What shall I tell her Ladyship is the matter?"

He shook his head. "There is nothing we might say as even I am not privy to the news. The earl's orders were to bring them down, even Miss Darcy, and to do it quickly."

The young maid gulped, a feeling of dread in her chest, and turned to continue her flight up the stairs to search out the Darcy and Fitzwilliam family members without delay.

When, long moments later, the Lady Matlock descended the staircase with her eldest son, Georgiana Darcy, and a complaining Caroline Bingley, she looked to her husband and saw that his expression was most severe.

"Reginald, what has happened? Why are we to Somersal without delay?"

He shook his head and turned to the parlor addressing the young stable hand. "Come boy, we must be off. You may ride on the back of the carriage with the footman."

The earl sent his son ahead with Georgiana Darcy and Miss Bingley, who was still prattling on about the inconvenience, with promises that they would hear the news on the way to Somersal. "I must speak with your mother, James. See to your cousin and Miss Bingley."

James Fitzwilliam escorted his cousin and Bingley's sister to the carriage and helped them inside. His father was rarely so serious and he began to worry when he thought of Richard. Surely Darcy would not have sent for them to come without delay to the home where the Bennet family resided at such an hour without terrible news to share.

He placed an arm around Miss Darcy and listened as she partially spoke his own concerns aloud. "James, there must be some terrible thing for brother to send for us. I do hope the Bennet sisters are well. I have truly come to enjoy their company."

"I would not think Darcy would send for us were one of the sisters ill, it would make no sense for us to burden them with company in a time of illness. I fear we must wait for father, my dear."

Miss Bingley became agitated at their conversation and placed a hand to her throat. "Surely you cannot think that Charles or the colonel might be injured?"

James Fitzwilliam regretted the inclusion of Caroline Bingley to their party but there was nothing they might do to leave her at

Pemberley. For all he knew, her brother might well be the cause for alarm. But in his heart, he knew it must be Richard. There was no other reason to involve his parents in the situation. "Miss Bingley, please do not make such assumptions. We shall have the facts when Father and Mother join us."

Reginald Henry Fitzwilliam held his wife in his arms as she struggled to escape. Her bitter cries echoed in the empty halls of Pemberley as the news of Richard Fitzwilliam's injuries moved throughout the great house.

"Come, Margaret, we must go to him now. Darcy has sent for a surgeon and 'tis very likely the man has come."

Lady Matlock gave herself a moment more to indulge in her shock and grief before bracing herself in her husband's arms. "Richard shall need me to be strong if he is to survive this terrible accident. Let us go and hope he is in capable hands. Darcy would not have it otherwise."

The earl swallowed the solid lump in his throat and escorted his lady to the waiting carriage. He would see that Richard was removed to Pemberley as soon as arrangements could be made so that his wife might not be kept from her son.

Chapter 14

Jane Bennet greeted the Fitzwilliam family and escorted them to the breakfast parlor where cold meats and cheese had been assembled on the sideboard behind the table for the long day ahead. Lady Matlock startled as she took her seat when the screams of her son began again in the parlor across the hallway.

"Perhaps we ought to move to the library further down the hall," Jane suggested and was met with a cold stare from the earl.

"If Richard must suffer alone with none of his family present, then we will remain here as close as we might in case...," here the earl's voice broke and Mr. Darcy went to stand behind his chair.

"Richard was in good spirits when I left his side to give the surgeon room to work. It gave me hope to speak with him. He knows of his injuries and what must be done. He wishes for everyone to know that Miss Elizabeth is not to blame." Jane held her gaze steady on the earl's face as she spoke.

Charles Bingley sat near the head of the table with Jane on one side and his sister on the other. Miss Bingley had made a terrible fuss over him when the Matlocks arrived at Somersal.

At the mention of Elizabeth Bennet's name she gasped aloud. "Poor Colonel Fitzwilliam lies broken in the parlor because of Miss Elizabeth! She raced him didn't she? I told her that night at dinner that racing was a vulgar sport and see where it has led? How scandalous she would do such a thing!"

Mr. Darcy's voice thundered throughout the breakfast parlor. "Miss Bingley! You will not speak so of Miss Elizabeth in this home or in my presence. Her part in this tragedy is coincidental. Richard and I have raced over the fields of Pemberley more times than I can recall. This was an accident and nothing more."

The earl shook his head and stood. He shoved his chair aside and demanded to speak with Miss Elizabeth. "She shall answer for her reckless behavior, nephew. You need not protect her from the repercussions of her choices. Bring her to me!"

Lady Matlock attempted to calm Miss Darcy as arguments broke out around the room. Her husband and son engaged Darcy and Bingley in strident tones while Jane Bennet had words for Miss Bingley.

It was to the ladies her attention turned and she stood to move around the table to better hear their exchange. Miss Bennet was defending her sister in a most calm fashion given Miss Bingley's tantrum.

"Elizabeth would never wish to bring anyone to harm, Miss Bingley, and you are quite wrong to say otherwise. She does love to race but even Mr. Bingley has said he was the one who challenged the colonel. My sister simply joined in the merriment."

Drawing up to her full height, the Lady Matlock placed her fingers in her mouth and gave a shrill whistle. Little did the occupants of the breakfast parlor know of her tomboy tricks from childhood but they served her well in this moment of mayhem. The room fell silent at the unexpected noise and Richard's moans once more filled the room. Waiting until her son's piteous cries subsided, Lady Matlock demanded they all be seated.

She moved to Mr. Bingley's chair and took his hand as he stood. "Miss Bennet has said that you claim to have begun the race. Is that a fact, young man?"

Charles Bingley's face paled considerably and he thought to give a long speech concerning his part in the terrible turn of events but instead he simply gave an affirmative declaration.

Having Elizabeth Bennet bear the responsibility for the accident would only harm her family and he could not bear that. Watching her in the field after Richard was taken away, he knew he must rewrite the truth and have Miss Elizabeth believe her shock, instead of the truth, caused her to take responsibility. "Tis true, your ladyship, and I am most sorry for it."

Mr. Darcy's face went from stern to disbelieving in the space of a moment. His earlier assertion that she was not responsible for the accident had been borne from his wish that it was indeed true. He could not allow his uncle to have cause to remove the Bennets from Somersal. "Charles, Miss Elizabeth mentioned racing not moments after we arrived. Are you certain she was not the one to instigate the event?"

Charles Bingley began to answer when Elizabeth Bennet entered the room. "He is lying, Mr. Darcy. It was I who challenged them both and drove Merrit into a gallop before either might answer."

Mr. Darcy looked from his friend to Miss Elizabeth and went to stand beside Bingley. "Tell the truth, Charles."

Elizabeth Bennet trembled as the Fitzwilliam family beheld her in the riding habit that was stained with Richard's blood. In their mind she was to blame and she would do all that she might to make amends. "I shall spend every waking hour dedicated to his care and if he shall never walk again, then I shall be his legs."

Lady Matlock gasped and covered her mouth with one hand. The young lady before her had come to Somersal through a promise made by her husband's eldest brother on his deathbed and now her own son lay broken in the home he would one day inherit did he survive.

Charles Bingley went to Elizabeth's side ignoring the hands of his best friend on his shoulders. "Miss Elizabeth, you are mistaken. Your mind has taken on this burden because of the terrible shock at seeing Richard injured and hearing the gunshot that spared his poor horse further suffering. I instigated the race and it is true you galloped away first on Merrit, but you did not deliver a challenge to either myself or the colonel."

Caroline Bingley stood and went to her brother. "Charles, you must not take on the burden she must bear. I know you admire Miss Bennet, but the Bennet family has ever been trouble since we have known them."

Charles Bingley took his sister in hand and removed her from the breakfast parlor. He called for a carriage from Somersal to return her to Pemberley. "You have spoken out of turn and have embarrassed Miss Bennet, her entire family, and our own. I expect you to take our carriage at Pemberley and leave for London come morning."

Angry that her brother would not listen and leave Somersal with her, Caroline Bingley refused his advice. "I shall wait at Pemberley for you to regain your senses and then we shall return to London together."

Shaking his head and turning his sister toward the front door of Somersal, Charles Bingley gave her one last piece of advice. "You will leave come morning or you shall find yourself at the mercy of our sister and Mr. Hurst. I shall not keep you when you refuse to obey my wishes."

Left without a retort at this threat, Miss Bingley gave a shrill cry and flounced out the front door of Somersal. Mr. Bingley gave a great sigh of relief and rejoined the gathering in the breakfast parlor. He made his apologies for his sister's rude behavior and went to sit again beside Miss Bennet.

Georgiana Darcy had risen from her seat and requested to wait with the younger Bennet sisters in the salon as she had become quite upset by Miss Bingley's accusations toward Miss Elizabeth. "Brother, I cannot bear to hear Richard's cries any longer and I will not listen to the blame being placed upon poor Miss Elizabeth. She is suffering terribly with guilt and it is not fair."

Lady Matlock went to her niece and led the young lady from the room. Before stepping into the hallway, she turned and spoke quietly to Elizabeth Bennet. "Your offer of assistance is admirable

Miss Elizabeth. He shall have the best of care but if you wish to tend him, you may. I do not believe you are responsible, but I do believe caring for him shall ease your burden."

Elizabeth bowed her head, tears coursing down her cheeks, and noticed the blood stained clothing. She began to tremble and call her sister's name. "Jane...oh Jane..."

Jane Bennet rose swiftly and went to her sister's side. She took Elizabeth's hands, which shook terribly, and led her from the room. "Come Lizzy, I shall have a bath drawn and see you to bed."

The Fitzwilliam family remained in the breakfast parlor with Mr. Darcy and Mr. Bingley awaiting news from the surgeon. The earl began to speak of his plans to move Richard to Pemberley. "It may be a day or so before he is able but we ought to send word for a room to be made ready. We must also send a servant into Lambton in search of a capable woman to provide his care. Several footmen shall be required as well, aside from their duties at Pemberley."

Mr. Darcy shook his head. "We shall seek Richard's thoughts on the matter when he is able to speak with us. For now, Somersal is well staffed and Miss Bennet has provided an admirable sickroom on a moment's notice. Let us not add to our worry this day."

The earl shook his head and would not be consoled. "Though Pemberley is your home, Richard is my son and I shall decide where he recovers. He needs to be near to his mother as he mends."

Lady Matlock entered the breakfast parlor at her husband's words and went to sit beside him. "We must worry about the particulars later, Reginald. Jane Bennet has proven her mettle with quick thinking and provisions before the surgeon arrived. I will not tolerate further argument nor harsh words while my son suffers across the hallway."

The Earl of Matlock gave a deep sigh and rose from his seat. "I would wait in the library if it is all the same. I need time to think on what shall be done now that Richard may need Somersal as his own home."

Lady Matlock shot him a withering glance and the earl hastened from the room. Mr. Darcy rose to follow him, for his words regarding Richard and Somersal gave him some measure of concern.

Charles Bingley stood and offered to make a plate for Lady Matlock while James remained in his seat, his face pale and his expression one of great worry. "Mother, is there something I could do? I cannot bear to sit here and listen to Richard and not be able to go to his side."

Lady Matlock touched the face of her eldest son and swallowed the tears that threatened. Now was not the time to indulge her grief. "Perhaps you and Mr. Bingley might go to Pemberley and bring some of Richard's things. It might cheer him to wake to some familiar book or blanket."

James leaned over and kissed his mother softly on the cheek. "I shall not be long, Mother. Thank you."

Charles Bingley delivered the plate he'd made for the lady and clapped James on the back. "Richard will be fine, you know. He's a tough old soldier with a strong constitution. Come, let us go to Pemberley so that we might have something familiar by his hand when he is able to sit up."

Lady Matlock picked at the food on her plate and wondered how a lovely holiday visit to Pemberley had ended so terribly. Her son's future as a soldier was most certainly ended and she did not agree with her husband that Somersal was a pressing concern. She would see that Richard came to stay with them in London instead of living alone in the countryside.

Allowing her tears to fall unchecked, Lady Matlock pushed her plate away and left the breakfast parlor as the voice of her son lifted again in a weary, broken moan. Working the handkerchief in her hands into knots, she called for a footman and had him move a chair to a place beside the closed door of the parlor.

Sitting carefully and motioning for the footman to leave her, Margaret Fitzwilliam began to petition her heavenly Father. "Oh Lord, let this cup pass from my boy, my youngest child. He is a good and kind man, so full of life and such a gallant and happy soul. Bring him healing, Father, and relieve his pain. Hold him in your hands and give him strength. Help me to leave my grief at this door when I enter to give him only hope and the balm of my presence. Amen."

Chapter 15

Elizabeth Bennet listened to the words her sister Jane spoke convincingly while a maid helped her bathe. "Lizzy, Charles is certain of the facts. You did not challenge Colonel Fitzwilliam to a race. I think you are in such shock that you have made yourself remember that which you did not do. Mr. Darcy has said you mentioned racing upon their arrival. Perhaps that is what you recall."

Looking up to the ceiling while the maid poured a warm pitcher of water down her back, Elizabeth thought perhaps Jane was right after all. She closed her eyes and remembered speaking to the men when they first arrived, but soon the image of Colonel Fitzwilliam rolling and tumbling in a heap with his horse crowded her mind and she brought a hand to her mouth to catch the loud sob that escaped her lips.

Jane dismissed the maid to wait for them in Elizabeth's room and finished bathing her sister. Holding out a sheet, she urged Elizabeth to step out of the tub. "Come, my dear, I shall put you to bed and bring your dinner later. You must rest. The terrible events of the morning have worn on you so."

Elizabeth allowed Jane to help her with a nightgown and sat with tears slowly rolling down her cheeks as Jane brushed and plaited her hair. "Jane," she whispered, her voice a trembling, fragile thing, "what shall Mr. Darcy think of me now? I know it is terrible to entertain a selfish thought at a time such as this, but surely he will forgive me?"

Pulling back the counterpane, Jane helped her sister into bed and then sent the maid for a pot of tea and two cups.

"Mr. Darcy has nothing to forgive, my dear. You must accept that you bear no fault in the matter and be thankful you were not the one injured. A man as strong and stout as the colonel shall recover in time but a lady such as yourself, even though you are accomplished in the saddle and used to walking about for miles, would not have survived the mishap."

The maid returned long minutes later with the tea and Jane thanked her before closing the door. Alone with Elizabeth, she poured their tea and continued her reassurances as she removed a vial of laudanum from her skirt pocket. She'd asked the surgeon for it knowing her dear sister might be inconsolable after witnessing the terrible accident.

Taking time, she poured a small dose into Elizabeth's tea cup and stirred gently. Picking it up, she turned and approached the bed. "Here, my darling, have a sip of tea to calm your nerves."

Elizabeth for once did not argue with her beloved sister nor again insist upon her guilt in the accident. She sipped steadily from the cup and murmured her thanks.

Jane took up her own cup and drained half the contents before retrieving a novel from the bedside table. She read several pages until Elizabeth's breath became even and steady and her eyes drooped.

Placing the book on the bed, she rose and went downstairs to the salon. For there to be four young ladies and Mrs. Bennet situated inside the room, the silence that greeted her when she opened the door was quite surprising.

The girls rose as one when she entered and Jane motioned for them to sit. "I have come for Mary, ladies. In a moment, I shall have Constance take the rest of you into Lambton for a bit. Mary," she called and waited while her middle sister made her way across the room.

"I would like for you to sit with Lizzy for an hour or so. She is sleeping, and should not awaken before I return."

Mary hugged Jane and whispered her concern. "Is it true that Lizzy was the cause of the accident?"

Jane looked at Mary for a long moment and sighed. Turning her sister to face the rest of the party gathered in the room she cleared her throat and placed an arm around Mary's trembling shoulders. "Mr. Bingley has said that he was the one to challenge the colonel to a race this morning. Elizabeth is in a state of shock and believes with all her heart that she is responsible. We may have to help her over the next few days until she is recovered. And we must pray for the colonel."

Georgiana Darcy sat up straighter in her chair and nodded her head. "See? I did know that Miss Elizabeth would not have done such a thing. Mr. Bingley took the blame, I was there in the breakfast parlor and heard it myself."

Constance called the girls to her and ushered them to the door of the salon.

Before her sisters might quit the room, Jane reminded them all that they were not to gossip in Lambton about the accident. "If anyone makes an inquiry, you must simply say you are not at liberty to discuss the colonel's health. Do I make myself clear, ladies?"

The girls gave their immediate agreement and Constance reassured Jane. "Do not worry, mistress, I shall mind them all and speak for the Bennet family in their stead if it pleases you."

Jane took Constance's hand and gave a gentle squeeze. "Indeed, that would be most prudent."

Miss Darcy left with the Bennet girls and Jane turned to Mrs. Bennet. At last she might sit for a moment and not think of what to do next. Her limbs grew heavy as she sat and a great sigh of relief left her lungs. "Mother, 'tis been a terrible day. What shall we do now that the colonel lies injured in the parlor?"

Mrs. Bennet had been uncommonly quiet and Jane wondered what thoughts she had entertained as the day progressed.

"Lady Matlock did say, when she came to bring Miss Darcy to sit with us, that I was not to worry over Somersal as her son would be a long time in recovering from his injuries."

Jane blinked several times and thought on Lady Matlock's words. In the midst of her son's cries of pain, she had taken the time to reassure Mrs. Bennet. "Mother, did you ask her directly about Somersal?"

Mrs. Bennet shook her head most urgently. "I most certainly did not, Jane Bennet! Why, that would have been a terrible thing to do while her youngest son lay injured and in pain."

Jane breathed a sigh of relief. Thinking she might speak with Mr. Darcy, she rose to quit the salon. Mrs. Bennet spoke before she reached the door. "Do you think I might sit with Lady Matlock for a time? I would not wish to burden her, rather lend my support while we wait."

Jane smiled at her mother. "I do not think she would mind, Mother."

Jane Bennet quit the salon and stepped into the hallway. Her aim was the library, to see if Mr. Darcy was waiting there, but she glanced down the hallway to the parlor first. Seeing Lady Matlock waiting by the door in her chair, Jane's heart broke at her bowed head. She approached slowly and called out, her voice a little above a whisper. "Your ladyship, is there anything I might do?"

"Just pray Miss Bennet, if you please. Richard's cries have ceased for over a half hour now and I am terribly worried."

Jane called for a footman and had him bring another chair so that she might sit with Richard's mother. Forgetting custom and strictures, she took Lady Matlock's hand and prayed quietly with the woman. When she was done, she lifted her head and her heart broke again upon seeing the fresh tears that stained the woman's face.

Thinking to give her a bit of hope, Jane spoke of the colonel's words when she had given him whiskey before the surgeon came.

"He took the whiskey I offered without complaint. As a matter of fact, he made a remark about heaven and hell and regretted an attempt at laughter. He was in good spirits, your ladyship, truly he was. He is such a strong man."

Lady Matlock embraced Jane and thanked her for her support. "He always could find humor in the darkest times. Knowing that eases my mind."

Jane rose as her mother approached. "The girls are going into Lambton with Constance, Lady Matlock. Miss Darcy wishes to accompany them if you do not mind?"

Thinking of her niece again, Lady Matlock nodded. "Certainly, we cannot expect them to stay locked up in the salon all day. I hope you cautioned them not to speak of Richard's condition?"

Jane nodded her head. "Yes, they have been warned. And Constance shall pay heed and reply for them should anyone inquire."

Mrs. Bennet sat with Lady Matlock then and soon the two mothers were discussing matters to do with headstrong children and memories of past childhood misfortunes they had needed to attend or kiss away.

Jane turned and walked quickly to the library where she knew Mr. Darcy and the earl must be awaiting news of Richard's condition. The door was ajar and she stopped when the voices of both men drifted into the hallway.

Mr. Darcy was quite angry and he nearly shouted at his uncle. "There is no reason to discuss the future of the Bennet family at this time. I've told you that I shall provide the staff and bear all manner of expense until they have no need of the home, which will likely be many years hence."

The earl's voice boomed near the door and Jane took several steps back and pressed her body against the wall. "That is not my concern at present, though I understand why you feel you must bear the cost. However, Richard shall never be a soldier again and shall have need of Somersal as his home once he is truly recovered."

Mr. Darcy's voice faded and Jane imagined he must be pacing the room. "Still, we must wait until that time comes. Richard may have other plans that you are not aware of at this time. And what of Aunt Margaret's opinion in the matter? She may wish for Richard to remain in London until she is certain he is well and ready to live alone here in the country."

The earl began to argue again in earnest and Jane found her her feet. Moving quickly but quietly away from the door she scooted down the hallway. Her mother and Lady Matlock were oblivious to her appearance and so she turned and made her way upstairs to sit with Elizabeth.

Her mind turned the words of Mr. Darcy over and over as she made her way to Elizabeth's room. The colonel would never be a soldier again, even she knew that much by having seen his injuries before the surgeon arrived. She'd feared he would not survive another hour at the amount of blood that had soaked his tattered clothing.

Yet, he might very well recover in time and as the earl had said, he would need a home. Somersal was his home, the earl had said so in his argument with Mr. Darcy. As she approached her sister's door, Jane Bennet resolved not to worry about tomorrow or the days and years to come.

Elizabeth would find a way to keep a roof over their heads and she could help. They would plan and save and maybe write to their Uncle Gardiner in London. No matter what the future held, the elder Bennet sisters would prepare their family in case yet another home was taken from them.

When she entered Elizabeth's room, she found Mary praying quietly for the colonel and for Lizzy. She gently tapped her shoulder and then dismissed Mary thanking her for staying by their sister's side. "Twas a kindness Lizzy would dearly appreciate, Mary. You are indeed the sweetest of all of us."

"I was growing bored with all the chatter in the salon. I can stay a little longer if you need me."

Jane smiled at the sister who was hardest to figure out of all her siblings. "I may take you up on that after the surgeon has gone. I cannot sit with the colonel and with Lizzy at the same time."

Chapter 16

Elizabeth Bennet awoke some hours later to find her sister Jane dozing in a chair beside her bed. In an instant, the memory of Colonel Fitzwilliam's accident returned to her mind as vivid and real as if she were in the field watching it happen again.

She gave a cry and startled her sister. Jane rose from her chair and settled herself on Elizabeth's bed. "Tis alright, dear Lizzy, I am here and I have excellent news. The colonel is resting peacefully downstairs and the surgeon has said he will recover. You must not worry now."

Elizabeth sat up slowly, her head a bit fuzzy. She was truly grateful to know of Richard Fitzwilliam's condition but still the agony of having caused his plight pained her heart. "Jane, I have ruined everything. Mr. Darcy shall never forgive me, nor the Matlocks."

"Lizzy, I know you've had a terrible shock this morning, but you must understand you are not to blame. Mr. Bingley is the one who wished to race. He said it himself in the breakfast parlor this morning."

Elizabeth shook her head. "It can't be. Why would Mr. Bingley do such a thing? I was the one who spoke of racing."

Jane leaned closer to her sister and spoke softly. "Lizzy, you must accept that you are not to blame. Richard will need our help to recover and the Matlocks will be staying here for the foreseeable future. The time for blame and recrimination is past. It was an accident and we must focus on the colonel's health."

Elizabeth knew Jane was right, it truly made no difference why the trio had begun to race but in her heart she worried that Mr. Darcy would see her differently now. "I will do all that I might to assist the colonel in regaining his health. Perhaps in time, I shall come to feel less guilt than I do now."

Not wishing to further upset her sister, Jane did not mention the conversation she overheard between Mr. Darcy and the earl. There would be time for that discussion later. For now, she meant to have Elizabeth dine with the family and see the colonel.

"Come, let me do your hair and help you dress. We must be brave and strong. If there is any one thing to be done now, it is to attend the colonel as best we can."

In the parlor, Lady Matlock and the earl sat with their son and listened as he spoke of his injuries. "Mother, it was truly an accident. Who could have imagined one of us might be hurt? I am only thankful it was not Miss Elizabeth."

The earl grunted at this and rose to pace the room. "Charles Bingley has said he is the responsible party."

Richard tried to hide the pain that was creeping back but his gasp sent Lady Matlock into action. "Let us stop this nonsense. What difference does it make now? Richard is a grown man and is, or was, fully capable of riding or racing a horse. We must put our energies to better use."

The colonel sighed as the pain lessened but he was weary from the ordeal. While he had been under the care of the surgeon, Charles Bingley had protected Miss Elizabeth from the wrath of his family. "As usual, Mother knows best. Father, it was Bingley who wished to race but still, my fate is not a matter of blame. I chose to do what I did."

The earl turned to his son, his face splotched a bright red in places. "I simply wish to have a point on which to focus my anger, son. Mr. Bingley shall have to do if you insist upon it."

Lady Matlock silenced further discussion before her son might struggle to argue with his father. "Richard's care is all that matters to me. I will not hear of revenge visited on Mr. Bingley, for he did not act out of malice. It was a simple folly that ended badly."

The earl knew his time had passed to press the matter. "I shall be in the library until dinner, Margaret."

Richard gave a small sigh of relief when left alone with his mother. "Father shall overcome his anger in time but why is he bent on blaming anyone? What good shall that bring?"

Lady Matlock shook her head. "You know how he feels about the Bennets and Somersal. It is on his mind that you shall need this estate sooner than any of us imagined after today's events. Darcy has tried to reason with him but you know your father."

Richard's eyelids drooped and he did not speak for several long minutes. "I have need of Somersal at present to heal and recover, but only when I am married and ready to begin a family may I choose to live here."

The colonel succumbed to sleep after this declaration and Lady Matlock called for a maid. "Come for me when he awakens. He is not to suffer and I fear the pain was nagging him moments before he fell asleep."

The maid curtseyed and took the seat beside the injured man. "I shall do my best, your ladyship."

Stepping outside the parlor, Lady Matlock decided to retire to the room Mrs. Bennet had afforded her and the earl. They would remain at Somersal until Richard was truly recovered.

Elizabeth had accompanied Jane to the salon and now sat quietly by the fireplace. As the flames danced before her, she knew now more than ever her family's security at Somersal was at risk. The colonel would require many months of care to recover and would not be leaving the home soon.

Mrs. Bennet called to her and Elizabeth turned. "Lizzy, dear, you must leave the horses alone for a time. I fear your days of riding about the grounds are at an end."

Jane watched her sister's reaction carefully. "Mother, I had not given another thought to riding. I believe I must do what I might to aid the colonel in his recovery."

Pleased to find that her most headstrong daughter gave no argument on the point, Mrs. Bennet turned to Jane. "Mr. Bingley has returned to Pemberley but Lady Matlock did say he was quite adamant about his part in the unfortunate accident. Do you think he shall leave now?"

Jane had not thought of the Bingleys plans for she had been worried for her sister and the colonel. "I would imagine the Bingley's plans have changed as Mr. Darcy will not wish to entertain now that the colonel has been injured."

Mrs. Bennet shook her head in regret. "Tis a pity. I had hoped there would be time for the two of you to become better acquainted. Perhaps you might visit the Gardiners in London come the spring and pay a call at Hurst House?"

The idea had crossed Jane's mind. Mr. Bingley could not be always at Pemberley with his business in London and the lease on Netherfield. "I shall send a letter to Miss Bingley come morning and inquire about their plans. I may make mention of visiting her in the future since I cannot say such to her brother."

Pleased by Jane's thoughtful decision, Mrs. Bennet beamed at her favorite daughter. "Tis every mother's wish to have such a beautiful, sensible child. Though we are not in peril at the moment, as Lady Matlock did assure me about Somersal, it would be wise to see you well matched, Janie."

Elizabeth's ears perked up at the mention of Lady Matlock. "What is this about assurances from the Matlocks?"

Jane noticed the agitation in her sister's tone. "Somersal is to be the colonel's home one day, Lizzy. Since he shall have to give up his commission now, it only makes sense to think he will retire to Somersal earlier than he may have hoped."

Rising to cross the room and look out upon the grounds of Somersal, Elizabeth drew in a breath at the great, unsettled feeling in her chest. Her mother had just said she must not ride again for some time and yet she must now race come the spring, though not for enjoyment so much as necessity.

If she had felt the threat of losing their place at Somersal before, that worry only grew larger in her mind now that she had been made to consider the repercussions of the colonel's accident.

As the younger Bennet sisters and Miss Darcy returned to the salon from their trip into Lambton, Mrs. Bennet turned her attention to Kitty and Lydia as they spoke to her of seeing Mrs. Alsop. Constance had taken the girls there for tea before returning to Somersal.

Jane joined Elizabeth at the window and took her hand. "Come, Lizzy, there is much we must discuss out of earshot of Mother and our sisters."

Elizabeth followed Jane from the room wondering what other news she might have about their situation. When at last they were alone in Jane's room, Elizabeth paced before the fireplace. "You know more than you shared with Mother, Jane."

Taking a seat and motioning for Elizabeth to do the same, Jane sighed. "Indeed, and I would not tell Mother of it unless I am made to do so."

Elizabeth sat when she realized Jane would not speak further until she ceased her pacing. She wished she could escape the home and recover in the quiet, cold beauty of this winter day but that bit of comfort would have to wait.

Jane gazed into the fire as she spoke not trusting herself to meet her sister's eyes. "While you were sleeping, I went to see to mother and the girls in the salon. After Constance had ushered them upstairs to prepare for a trip into Lambton, Mother informed me that Lady Matlock had assured her there was no cause for worry where Somersal was concerned. I thought I might speak with Mr. Darcy on the matter but when I got to the library I overheard a conversation, more of an argument actually, between the earl and Mr. Darcy. It seems he is our benefactor when it comes to the cost of running Somersal. Of course, we knew mother did not have the means to afford all that we enjoy here."

Elizabeth blinked in confusion. "But I thought the Matlocks were responsible for the upkeep of Somersal, even with the stipulation that we remain here. Why has Mr. Darcy taken on the expense?"

Jane remained quiet for a moment before giving the answer she had worked out. "I believe Mr. Darcy must feel a great debt to Father. His mother could have well been the one to die from pneumonia after that accident except that father and his Uncle Bertram managed to get her to safety first. And, if I am honest, I believe he feels a great deal for you Lizzy."

Jane's revelation shocked Elizabeth into action. Rising from her seat and standing by the fireplace, she gave herself a moment to think. "I must race Jane, there is no other way. The colonel shall surely settle here after he is recovered and all the money Mr. Darcy possesses will not stay the earl's hand in removing us. I will not see my family without a home."

Much to Elizabeth's surprise, Jane agreed. "That is why I told mother I shall write to Miss Bingley. I can go to London after the colonel has made a turn for the better and seek to establish a relationship with Charles. If he has gone to Netherfield instead, perhaps I shall pay a visit to Charlotte on the pretense of mending fences. I would never be so forward as to chase after Mr. Bingley otherwise, but if he does care for me, then it shall not hurt for me to marry a man of means given our situation."

Elizabeth pulled Jane to her feet and hugged her tightly. "Do you truly care for him Jane? You must not pursue a man simply for the benefit of our family."

Jane thought on Elizabeth's words. "I do, Lizzy. He is most kind and the regard he held for me in Hertfordshire has grown though we have been apart for some time."

Knowing her sister would never seek a man she did not love, Elizabeth felt the tension of the day leave her body. "I shall spend as much time as possible caring for the colonel and the rest shall be spent riding Merrit over the fields without Mother's knowledge. I must arise each day earlier than before and prepare for the races."

Chapter 17

Richard Fitzwilliam was the first person Elizabeth Bennet saw the morning she had ridden Merrit for the first time after the accident. It had taken her a week to work up the nerve to move freely about Somersal with the Matlocks in residence, but the wait had been worth the trouble.

Being careful to stay far from the boundaries of Pemberley on her early morning circuit, Elizabeth had avoided Mr. Darcy entirely. So when she entered the parlor to relieve the maid who sat with Richard upon his waking, it was quite the shock to find Mr. Darcy seated beside his cousin.

Since the day of the accident, she had not spoken with him nor been alone in his presence. Her heart had ached to recall their time spent riding across the fields but there was nothing to be done about it now. So much had changed, she was certain he felt differently for her now.

Mr. Darcy turned as she entered and offered a greeting. "Miss Elizabeth, good morning. Have you come to sit with Richard?"

Elizabeth approached the other side of the colonel's bed and glanced at Mr. Darcy. "Good morning, sir. I have come to read to him if he wishes."

Richard felt as though he was intruding upon a private meeting as the two gazed at one another for a moment too long. "Miss Elizabeth, I would dearly love to have you read to me but a beautiful young lady such as yourself ought to be more happily employed."

Mr. Darcy shook his head in agreement. "My cousin is correct. There are maids aplenty here to sit with him and read should the need arise."

When Elizabeth smiled at Richard, Mr. Darcy felt his heart twist. She was simply concerned for his cousin and nothing more, but he could not deny she had been distant and aloof in his presence. When she leaned over Richard to smooth his covers and check his head for fever, Darcy caught the unmistakable scent of the stables and the outdoors.

"Miss Elizabeth," he said, hoping to draw her out, "do you still ride each morning?"

Elizabeth seemed startled by this question and retrieved a book from the table beside his cousin's bed. Bingley and James had brought the book from Pemberley, along with several other personal items from Richard's room there. "I should not think of riding so soon after the accident, Mr. Darcy, if ever again."

Richard attempted to hold up a hand as his cousin began to speak again. The wince he gave did not escape either of his visitors. "Miss Elizabeth, what a pity! You must ride. Merrit shall become a terrible bother for the groom if you do not. A woman as accomplished cannot give up that which she loves and does so well."

Biting her bottom lip to keep the tears that threatened at bay, Elizabeth gazed at the colonel. "Sir, you cannot think that I would enjoy riding ever again after what has happened. It would be terrible to be so unkind."

Richard's weak laughter sounded almost like a gasp and he winced in pain as his ribs protested. Lydia Bennet had been eavesdropping at the door of the parlor and now stepped inside. "Lizzy, perhaps the colonel is right. Papa always said if you fall off the horse, you must simply get back on."

Lydia crossed the room and stood beside Elizabeth, her bubbly demeanor causing the colonel to keep the smile he'd meant for Elizabeth plastered on his face. Elizabeth was mortified at Lydia's flippant remark in light of the colonel's terrible accident. She took her youngest sister by the arm. "Such a terrible thing to say, Lydia! Certainly Constance is waiting for your in the salon."

Mr. Darcy watched as Lydia Bennet removed her arm from her sister's grasp and leaned closer to the colonel, her voice a conspiratorial whisper, "You must forgive Lizzy, she says that I am the overly dramatic sister. Yet, I would rather laugh and live than frown and fret."

The colonel struggled to contain his mirth. "I quite enjoy your optimism Miss Lydia. 'Tis much more encouraging than the sad, worrisome looks and dour conversation everyone else gives upon entering this room. Besides, now that we are better acquainted due to my unfortunate accident, I find myself hoping you might visit in the morning more often."

Lydia blushed a lovely shade of pink before giggling. "I am happy to know it, sir, for I have thought of nothing more than helping distract you from the pain of your injuries. The rest of the house only worries for you but I know you are a soldier and do not think you are beaten yet."

Elizabeth was accustomed to her youngest sister's forward behavior but deeply embarrassed as she carried on so in front of Mr. Darcy. "Lydia, you must return to the salon with the other girls."

Mr. Darcy nodded his approval at this and Elizabeth felt perhaps they could mend their friendship on their mutual feelings regarding Lydia. Richard Fitzwilliam, however, was not happy to have his new friend dismissed so quickly. "Surely this Constance might make an exception again for the good of an ailing man?"

Lydia giggled and took the book from Elizabeth's hand. "Constance is aware of how I spend my mornings now, Lizzy," Lydia fibbed boldly, "and I shall sit and read to the colonel for a time. He needs a bit of humor as you can see. Take Mr. Darcy and go riding or something."

Elizabeth rose as Richard gave a small nod. "Yes, please do. There is no reason you ought to sit by my bedside serving penance when there is life to live. I will not be the reason for further suffering and maudlin thoughts. Besides, Miss Lydia has read to me for several mornings now and I quite enjoy her company."

Mr. Darcy began to speak again but his cousin shot him a look that brooked no disagreement. Standing and turning to Elizabeth, he took her hand and led her from the parlor. "He is right, you know. You are paying dues you do not owe. If you wish to tend my cousin, you should only act from kindness and concern, not from a sense of debt."

His mention of debt cut through Elizabeth's confusion at the appearance of Lydia and her apparent ease with the colonel. When had sitting with Colonel Fitzwilliam become a normal part of her youngest sister's routine? Returning her attention to Mr. Darcy, Elizabeth spoke of her feelings about the situation with their houseguests. "There is much my family owes the Darcy and Fitzwilliam families, sir, the least of which is my dedication to the recovery of your cousin."

Mr. Darcy could see that she would not be moved but held hope in his heart that she would listen to the wise words of his cousin. Tinkling laughter from the parlor, followed by the rich, bass tone of Richard's voice, caused the pair to move further from the door.

"While it is admirable that you wish to aid Richard in his time of need, it is not necessary to spend every waking moment with him. My aunt will likely wish to sit with him a great portion of each day in the weeks to come and it seems Miss Lydia has found a better use for her time than trimming bonnets. Perhaps you ought to consider returning to your habits as well. There is no harm in walking the fields if you wish to avoid the horses."

Mr. Darcy knew she had not avoided Merrit or he would not have caught the scent of the stables on her person nor noticed the glow in her cheeks from riding in the chill winds of the early morning."

Elizabeth thought she saw a flicker of hope in Mr. Darcy's eyes as he spoke. If he wished to persuade her to reveal her secret, she would not give in so easily. "I have walked each morning, sir, after visiting Merrit in the stables. I find it helps me sort the worries that haunt me."

Mr. Darcy took her hand wishing he might place a gentle kiss upon the soft skin of her wrist. He was lost without their morning meetings and wondered why she was taking pains to keep her distance, addressing him as sir as though they had never been friends. "I should love to walk with you, Miss Elizabeth, for I have dearly missed our morning habit of riding together. Perhaps I might join you tomorrow morning?"

Pulling her hand away, Elizabeth lowered her lashes. "I am up much earlier to begin the day. I find the time alone refreshing and would not wish to give it up."

A pained silence stretched between them and Mr. Darcy gave a sigh. He could not force the lady to endure his company. But if she came upon him as he was riding surely she would walk with him for a time.

"I see," he said thinking it best not to press the issue but rather use patience as his ally.

Elizabeth turned and bid him a good day before disappearing down the hallway towards the salon. She tried to smother the hope that crept into her heart at his words. He did not hate her nor hold her responsible for the colonel's injuries. He wished to walk with her each morning now that he thought she no longer rode about on Merrit.

But he had never mentioned his part in the running of Somersal, not in the many days of the renewal of their acquaintance nor mere moments ago.

Thinking to broach the subject with him when next they were alone, Elizabeth stopped outside the salon and drew in a breath.

She could not fault Mr. Darcy for keeping his secret when she had just told him she could not think of riding again.

Entering the salon, she was pleased to find Jane alone. "Where have the girls gone with Constance? Have they not begun their studies?"

"Mother wished to visit Mrs. Alsop and Kitty has gone with her. Mary is in her room, I believe. I am not certain where Lydia may be, but I imagine she shall be cross to have missed another trip into Lambton."

Elizabeth sighed and went to sit with Jane. "Lydia is in the parlor with the colonel."

Jane raised a brow at this bit of information. "Whatever for? I cannot imagine the colonel would be pleased to entertain a silly girl in his condition."

"He certainly seemed pleased with her. You know she flirted shamelessly with him though I did try to intervene and it seems this is not her first such visit. How has she been able to do such without our knowing?"

Thinking her sister was having a bit of fun at her expense, Jane shook her head. "I cannot believe it, Lizzy. You must be playing some sort of joke. Lady Matlock would not be pleased, I do not think, to have Lydia capering about in the colonel's sickroom. And Constance surely would have told us."

Elizabeth agreed. "I would think so, but the colonel was adamant that Lydia stay and read to him regardless of what I had to say about it since she had done so previously. I was summarily dismissed and left to speak with Mr. Darcy alone in the entryway."

Jane forgot about Lydia and the colonel at the mention of Mr. Darcy. "He did bring a letter from Miss Bingley this morning. It seems she and Mr. Bingley are to leave for London soon. Though her letter did say she was not quite certain whether they might remain there come spring. I do not think she wishes for me to know where they might be."

Elizabeth was not surprised by the news of Miss Bingley's letter. There was never any doubt as to her feelings concerning Jane and her brother. "I do not think that Mr. Bingley cares very much for his sister's opinion when it comes to you, Jane. You must pay a call as a courtesy when you arrive in London and he shall surely not leave for Netherfield then."

Jane smiled at her sister's thoughts for they had been her own once she had finished reading Miss Bingley's letter. "I spoke with mother earlier about going to London for a time. I would take Mary along and perhaps the younger girls, for it is too crowded at Somersal at the moment."

A knock sounded on the salon door and Lady Matlock appeared. "Good morning ladies," she said as she entered the room.

Jane and Elizabeth rose to greet her but she waved for them to remain seated. "Please do not trouble yourselves. I simply wished to establish a routine of sorts when it comes to caring for Richard."

Elizabeth swallowed the guilt that rose in her breast and gave the woman a small smile. "Of course. It would seem there are plenty of hands available and we must think of the colonel's preferences in our planning. I saw him this morning and he was in excellent spirits."

Lady Matlock was pleased with Elizabeth's agreement. "He is much stronger than I gave him credit for being. As a mother, it is difficult to match the memory of the child with the reality of the adult your offspring becomes. So, let us compare our schedules that we might best tend Richard and go about our lives."

Jane spoke up to inform the woman of her plans. "As much as I would dearly love to be included, it seems that I shall soon leave for London. Before I go, I would be happy to sit with the colonel as needed. Being newly arrived to Somersal, and still in mourning, there are not so many demands upon our time."

Elizabeth nodded her head in agreement. "Yes, we have kept closer to home than we might have in Hertfordshire. I would suggest that you determine the schedule, your ladyship, and we will be happy to oblige."

Lady Matlock thought for a moment before speaking. "I am grateful to you both. As much as I love my son, I cannot sit with him all day. He will not stand for it as he has already complained over all the fuss. Perhaps we ought to speak with him to find his desires before we commit to a schedule?"

The eldest Bennet sisters agreed and the trio quit the salon to descend upon Colonel Fitzwilliam and find his thoughts on the matter.

Lydia's laughter greeted them at the parlor door and Lady Matlock glanced at Jane and Elizabeth before entering the room. The sisters were mortified by Lydia's immaturity at times but now, upon hearing the camaraderie between the silly girl and the colonel, they simply gave a shrug of their shoulders.

Colonel Richard Fitzwilliam had eaten most of his breakfast and seemed quite well considering his injuries. His eyes were bright and his voice steady though his face registered the fatigue of pain.

Lady Matlock went to him and sat, her eyes flicking to Lydia who now stood on the other side of the colonel's bed. Elizabeth called to her and she reluctantly joined her sisters as they stood near the parlor door.

The colonel called after her, his tone genuine. "Miss Lydia, thank you for your kindness this morning. While I would enjoy your company whenever you wish to sit with me, you must be terribly bored by now. And Constance shall wonder where you've been."

Lydia blushed and gave a curtsey. Jane and Elizabeth were surprised that no giggles escaped their lighthearted sister and watched in amazement as she addressed the colonel with much more decorum than they had ever seen her display. "Colonel

Fitzwilliam, your company is the most engaging I have ever kept. I would never consider your company boring. As for Constance, I'm afraid I have told her that I have a headache whenever I wished to come sit with you, otherwise she would have told me to leave you be."

Jane took her youngest sister by the arm leaving Elizabeth in the parlor with Lady Matlock and the colonel. He was quite amused by the scene as his mother shook her head in disbelief.

Chapter 18

Turning her attention to her son, Lady Matlock explained their presence. "Richard, we have come to discuss a schedule of sorts and wanted your opinion since you shall be the one bound to endure our company."

Colonel Fitzwilliam glanced at Elizabeth as she approached his bed. "Mother, I am not ill and do not require a sitter. I am simply injured and will recover fully in time. I would not like to become a burden."

Elizabeth sat in the chair Lydia had vacated and shook her head at the colonel. "The last thing you could ever be is a burden, Colonel Fitzwilliam."

Richard sighed, a most painful endeavor for the man with his ribs broken. "I am afraid you are mistaken, Miss Elizabeth. If I allow you and mother to manage my recovery then I am indeed a burden. The maids have done a fine job in seeing I want for nothing. I only request your company from time to time, but not from pity nor duty. If I am to have a dedicated sitter, then I would choose Miss Lydia. She is the only person to enter this room with a happy smile. I find myself in better spirits in her company."

The two women sat speechless as the colonel grew silent. They would not deny him Lydia's company if he truly wished to have her sit with him. He was in the parlor after all and so there was no impropriety to his request.

Elizabeth thought for a moment before hitting upon a solution that would keep her sister from spending an inordinate amount of time with the colonel. "Perhaps you would rather have your own rooms for privacy, it cannot be comfortable to recover in the parlor."

Richard had already thought of such a thing himself and refused outright. "I believe if I am locked away upstairs I shall never wish to see anyone and fall into despair. If it is not too great of an imposition, I would rather remain here where you all may come and go as you please and where I might see Miss Lydia for a time each day."

Knowing she would not press the issue, Elizabeth smiled at the colonel. "Of course it is no imposition. We have little company from Lambton and if we have a need to entertain, the salon is only a few steps past the parlor."

The colonel smiled and turned to his mother. "It is settled then. The maids and footmen shall assist me when needed and my family and friends shall only spend time with me as their schedules allow."

Lady Matlock did not seem pleased but as her son was the injured party, she did not argue with him. "Tis only your complete recovery that concerns me, Richard. If at any time you wish to amend your choices you have only to say so."

Elizabeth left the colonel and his mother in the parlor and returned to the salon. Jane was there in a chair by the windows while Lydia sat at the table on the far side of the room flipping the pages of a large book. Jane's brow was furrowed as Elizabeth approached and she motioned for her sister to sit before casting her voice low in a conspiratorial whisper. "Lizzy, do you think we ought to have a talk with Lydia? I think the colonel may expect more than she is able to deliver in the way of conversation and companionship."

Elizabeth knew he likely would be disappointed once the novelty of Lydia's company gave way to irritation but that was a lesson the good man must learn in his own time. "Of course we must tell her not to make a nuisance of herself as he is not well and will not be for some time. I would ask Mother to speak to her, but I fear she would only encourage Lydia to seek more than a friendship where the colonel is concerned."

Settled now that tea had been brought to the salon, the eldest Bennet sisters fell to discussing Jane's plans in London and Elizabeth's plan to race Merrit. Jane worried that her sister would not be able to hide her secretive early morning ritual for the few months until spring. "What will you say if Mother finds you are still riding Merrit?"

"I had not thought so far ahead, Jane. We must not burden Mother with our concerns over Somersal, for she will not believe it since Lady Matlock assured her of our place here. I would not tell her of Mr. Darcy's involvement either. No, I must prepare myself to race in the spring and win."

Jane saw the worry in the set of Elizabeth's shoulders and the furrow of her brow. If she could hasten to London, she knew Mr. Bingley would ask for her hand before too long. Elizabeth would never have to race and risk their mother forbidding her outright instead of the gentle suggestion she had given the day before. "I plan to leave Somersal a week after Christmas. I doubt Lydia will be prevailed upon to accompany me now, but surely Mary and Kitty will come along."

At the mention of their younger sisters, the salon door burst open and the girls entered with Constance on their heels. "Come ladies, gather at the table for your lessons must begin."

Mrs. Bennet entered the room and happily joined her eldest daughters. "What is this I hear from Lady Matlock? She says my Lyddie has become a favorite of the colonel."

Their mother's eyes twinkled with the fervor of a matchmaker and Elizabeth rushed to disabuse her of the notion. "The colonel prefers her company because she is too silly to understand the severity of his injuries. 'Tis nothing more, Mother. He is much too old to be more than a friend to her."

Mrs. Bennet glanced to the other end of the salon and clucked her tongue. "Do not be so sure, Lizzy. Many an older man can become smitten with a much younger woman. Lydia is a happy soul with not a burden or care. That can be quite appealing to some men."

Jane began to discuss her trip to London and Elizabeth rose to quit the salon. Her life had become the stuff of novels and she longed for the simpler days of her youth in Hertfordshire. Somersal had seemed a blessing until only a day ago, yet she did love their new home still.

Wishing to be out of doors to sort her thoughts and feelings, Elizabeth donned her spencer and quietly slipped outside.

At Pemberley, Mr. Darcy sat with his sister in the parlor while James heralded her with tales of the Ton in London. "You will see when your season comes, cousin, there are perils aplenty for lovely young ladies. Do not hurry to leave behind your youth here at Pemberley for the excitement of town."

Darcy nodded his agreement. "Georgiana shall have a wonderful season but yes, to watch the preening and playacting is akin to going to the theatre. I do not miss the frivolity when a season has passed."

Georgiana Darcy was concerned about the coming spring and summer. "Do you think Richard shall be better by then? I cannot imagine going to Town while he is crippled here in the countryside."

Mr. Darcy took her hand. "Richard was in good spirits this morning, poppet. He was charmed by Miss Lydia's company and I am certain he would like for you to visit on the morrow."

The lovely young mistress of Pemberley smiled at the mention of Lydia Bennet. "Miss Lydia is a sweet girl but quite immature. I do not mean to speak ill of her, I am only surprised cousin Richard finds her company desirable. Who would have thought?"

James laughed and caught himself before he said something that would offend his young cousin. "Richard has ever been the flirt, but perhaps her youth and exuberance gives him cause to forget his injuries for a time."

Mr. Darcy had thought as much but he recalled the behavior of Miss Elizabeth's youngest sister from his time at Netherfield. Lydia Bennet was easily swayed by a soldier in a red coat and though his cousin might never wear that coat again, it mattered not to a young lady given attention by a handsome older man.

He would speak with Richard about expectations and such when next he paid a call to Somersal with Georgiana. She would happily join the Bennet sisters after having spent time with Richard and he could broach the delicate subject without interference.

James stood and took Georgiana's hand. "Will you play for me in the salon, cousin? I wish to be elsewhere when Miss Bingley comes downstairs."

Georgiana beamed at him, happy to play for her cousin instead of Mrs. Annesley. "Miss Bingley is harmless where you are concerned, James. You must have noticed how she watches my brother whenever they are in the same room."

Mr. Darcy looked astonished at his sister's tease and then laughed. It was clear to anyone with two eyes that Miss Bingley had set her cap for Fitzwilliam Darcy. However, the woman could not see as clearly as everyone else that the master of Pemberley would never seek her hand.

Alone at last in the parlor, Mr. Darcy paced about the room. He had thought of nothing save Elizabeth Bennet since leaving Somersal earlier in the day.

Richard's accident troubled her terribly and he could not think of a way to ease her mind. Even had she been the one to challenge the colonel and Mr. Bingley to a race, she could not be held accountable for the accident. These things happened and

Richard could have just as easily been hurt on any one of his many military maneuvers.

Sighing as he recalled her sadness and the way she drew away from him, Mr. Darcy resolved to meet her, quite by accident in the early morning and rekindle their mutual admiration. Elizabeth Bennet had won his heart completely and he would make her know his feelings and admit her own.

Happy with his decision, he retired to his study as he was of the same mind as James Fitzwilliam. Encountering Caroline Bingley was not a chance he wished to take before she and Bingley left for London.

Charles Bingley arrived at Somersal with his heart racing in his chest. He had argued with his sister at Pemberley over her letter to Jane Bennet and her disobedience in not leaving Pemberley the morning after the accident as he had ordered. He ought to have known Caroline would not seek a friendship with the woman he now knew he loved.

Riding to Somersal had been his way of showing his sister that she did not speak for him. He meant to tell Jane Bennet in no uncertain terms that he would pursue a courtship though the miles between London and Somersal must separate them for a time.

He was met at the door by the butler and ushered to the parlor. Not wishing to slight the colonel, he smiled at the butler and asked if he might inform Miss Bennet that he had come to see her in particular.

Upon entering the parlor, he greeted the colonel. "Richard, I must say how truly wonderful it is to see you this afternoon."

Richard Fitzwilliam smiled at his cousin's best friend. "From the bits and pieces of my memory, you were dead last in our race Bingley, lucky that."

Charles Bingley crossed the parlor and took a seat beside the colonel's bed. "Indeed! 'Twas a terrible spill you took, old man. I see it hasn't killed you."

The colonel tried not to laugh, but he was never one to become maudlin simply because his body was in pain. It was the life of a soldier to endure pain.

"Not yet, at least. I am worried about Miss Elizabeth though. I assured Miss Bennet that she was without blame before the surgeon arrived that morning. I assume you did the same?"

Bingley nodded and glanced to the door of the parlor. "I most certainly did. My sister, however, laid the charge at her feet before your parents in the breakfast parlor. I told them all it was my idea and sent Caroline back to Pemberley with the threat of returning to London. Sadly, I must leave with her on the morrow. But, yes, everyone does believe I am to blame."

Richard sighed in relief and closed his eyes. "It would never do for anyone to know Miss Elizabeth was the one who offered the challenge."

Jane Bennet had stopped at the parlor door but now her feet carried her quickly across the room. "What is this? Are you saying my sister was the one who wished to race?"

Mr. Bingley stood and took Jane's hands. "Oh dear, you were never meant to know it. And you must not say otherwise now, Miss Bennet. If the colonel holds her blameless that is all that matters."

Jane turned her gaze to Richard Fitzwilliam, the brave and broken soldier who now resided in the parlor of the home that was rightfully his own. "Colonel, I cannot express my thanks in a manner that might convey how truly grateful I am for your consideration of my sister. She believed she was at fault and I convinced her otherwise."

A lone tear spilled down Jane's cheek and she brushed it away as Charles Bingley squeezed her hand.

The colonel glanced to the door and lowered his voice. "There is nothing to be gained by revealing the truth. As much as it pains me, my father is not fond of the stipulation that placed your family here at Somersal. My plan was to soldier on for several more years and when the time came, I would marry and settle here. Now, it seems I shall settle here whether I am ready or not. But I would not see your family put out on my account. So you see, we must work together to thwart my father. He is a good and just man but on this count, he is mistaken."

Jane turned and hurried to the parlor door causing Bingley to call after her, his voice a low hiss to keep from drawing attention to their meeting. "Jane! Jane! Please do not go."

After closing the parlor door, Jane turned and placed a finger to her lips. Returning to Mr. Bingley's side she gave a shy gaze into his eyes. "Lizzy and I have made plans to prepare for the day we might lose our place at Somersal. I cannot reveal her plan, but my own involves going to London to stay with my Aunt and Uncle Gardiner."

Mr. Bingley's smile was as bright as the winter sun reflected on the snow and Jane blushed furiously. "Do you mean to say..."

The colonel cleared his throat. "I believe the two of you might wish to have this conversation without me. As I cannot leave, perhaps you might find privacy in the garden?"

Charles Bingley offered his arm to Jane Bennet and the pair said their farewells to the colonel.

Chapter 19

As they moved slowly across the frozen grounds of the garden, Jane told Mr. Bingley of her plan to follow him to London. "Am I mistaken in thinking there is more than a friendship between us?"

Mortified that she had been so forward, Jane lowered her head and cast her eyes to the ground. Mr. Bingley halted their progress wishing it were not winter so that he might sit with her in a more secluded area of the garden. "You are the woman I have always hoped to marry, Miss Bennet."

When she would not look at him, Mr. Bingley lifted her chin and gazed into the bright blue of her eyes. "Jane Bennet, though we may not declare ourselves at this moment, I shall seek your uncle's permission for a courtship the moment you arrive in London."

Happy tears escaped and Jane's bottom lip quivered. "You must know that I would have followed you to London even if my family's future were secure."

Charles Bingley took the liberty of embracing his love for a moment. "We were the both of us in love that night at the assembly in Meryton, my dear Jane. I ought to have come for you when Lady Catherine arrived with her foolish parson, but with your family in mourning it did not seem proper."

Reluctantly releasing her from his arms, Charles Bingley looked again on his beloved's face. "I leave on the morrow with Caroline, but you must send word to me when you arrive in London. I shall be staying at Darcy House as I will not abide my sister's interference a moment longer than is necessary. Send word to me there and I will come to meet your uncle."

Not believing her good fortune, Jane pushed the sleeve of her spencer up for a moment and pinched herself. Mr. Bingley laughed and assured her she was not dreaming. "It is I who am the dreamer my dear, sweet angel."

In the garden of Somersal, barren and swept by a cold wind, Charles Bingley placed a chaste kiss upon Jane Bennet's forehead before escorting her back inside the warmth of Somersal.

Jane kept her secret from her dearest sister for the remainder of the day until Elizabeth bade her family a good night and left the salon.

Following her sister's lead, Jane kissed their mother on the cheek and said goodnight to her sisters. "Christmas is but a few days hence ladies and we must go to Pemberley for dinner."

Kitty clapped her hands with glee but Lydia only pouted. "How might we leave the colonel here and go make merry at Pemberley? It does not seem right."

Mrs. Bennet waved her handkerchief as she stood, her eyes on her youngest daughter. "Lydia, I am certain his mother will remain at Somersal until we all return from Pemberley. She would not think of leaving him here alone on Christmas Day."

Her mother's assurances were not sufficient and Lydia Bennet crossed her arms and stated her thoughts on the matter. "I shall stay with him as well. It cannot be a happy time to watch everyone go off on a merry sleigh ride to Pemberley."

Jane thought to stay and talk sense to Lydia, but she deferred to her mother as she dearly wished to speak with Elizabeth before she went to bed. "Listen to Mother, Lydia, for she and Lady Matlock have formed a friendship and we must respect the wishes of the Fitzwilliam family in this matter."

Leaving the salon as Lydia's voice rose to object, Jane breathed a sigh of relief. Waiting through the whole of the day to share her news with Elizabeth had been tedious business and her heart sang at the thought of speaking her secret at last.

Hurrying upstairs to her sister's room, Jane knocked only once before opening the door and slipping inside. Elizabeth sat on the bed in her nightgown brushing her hair. Jane could make out the glimmer of tears on her face from across the room.

"Lizzy, whatever is the matter? Is the colonel well?" Jane turned toward the door ready to rush downstairs when Elizabeth hiccuped.

"Oh, 'tis not the colonel Jane, but my own heart that is not well."

Jane was shocked by Elizabeth's admission for her sister was not one to speak easily of her feelings and certainly never as dramatically as Lydia or Kitty.

"Lizzy," she said as she went to sit on the bed beside her favorite sister, "I have never heard you sound so forlorn. Is this about Mr. Darcy?"

Elizabeth nodded and dropped her brush. Jane retrieved it from the carpet and moved to sit behind Elizabeth with her legs crossed as she had in her youth. "Let me brush your hair and you can speak your mind without having to face me."

Touched by the thoughtfulness of her sister, Elizabeth breathed deeply before sharing her woe with Jane. "Mr. Darcy believes that I have not ridden Merrit again since the accident. He thinks I am rambling about on foot and asked that we might continue to meet and walk together. I refused him Jane."

Knowing her sister had become fond of Mr. Darcy in the time since they had come to Somersal, Jane tried to think of a way to help Elizabeth. "Has Mr. Darcy shared the news that he pays the bills for Somersal?"

Elizabeth shook her head no and knew where her sister was headed with this line of conversation. "Why would he share such information with me, Jane? It is not my business as Somersal belongs to his family. I cannot fault him for providing for my family."

Jane sighed and tried to find another way to absolve Elizabeth of her guilt. "If he knew you were planning to race Merrit, what would he say?"

Elizabeth snorted and jumped up from the bed. "He would say it was vulgar and beneath me. He would not understand my reasons. I cannot bear to argue with him about it, Jane. I will race and nothing he says will change it."

There was nothing she could say to calm Elizabeth and so Jane changed the topic of conversation. "Well, you may not need to race in the spring after all."

Elizabeth's mouth fell open and she rushed to sit beside her sister again. "Mr. Bingley came this afternoon. Did he offer for your hand, Jane? Mother has said nothing of the kind and I cannot imagine she would keep it secret."

"Mother does not know, Lizzy, and I shall not tell her until Mr. Bingley has made his offer in a serious manner. But in the garden this afternoon, I told him of my plan to go to London after Christmas. He does love me, Lizzy. He wants me to send word to him at Darcy House when I arrive and he will come to see Uncle Gardiner and seek a courtship!"

Tears of joy and relief flooded Elizabeth's eyes and she grabbed her sister in an enthusiastic hug. "Oh Jane, what wonderful news! You must go as soon as you might after Christmas."

"See, Lizzy? Now you can forget about racing and renew your friendship with Mr. Darcy. You and he can ride the fields again and by the summer, we may have a double wedding."

Elizabeth shook her head and pulled away from Jane. "I cannot Jane. I must race and if I win, put money aside for our family even if you and Mr. Bingley are to wed. He cannot provide for all of us and Miss Bingley."

Jane furrowed her brow, knowing her sister was right. "But the Matlocks and Mr. Darcy would not put our family in the streets. There would be time for us to make arrangements."

Elizabeth knew Jane held good intentions but no matter what happened come spring, the colonel would need a home and the Bennet family would need a way to sustain themselves even if they were taken in by various and sundry family members.

Mr. Bingley could manage providing for their mother and one of the younger girls but Elizabeth and the remaining two would be sent to the Gardiners in London.

"Winning a few races will provide enough money for us to rely upon our relatives until I might find work as a companion or nanny. There is no other way, Jane. I am an excellent racer and Merrit is the best horse."

Wishing Elizabeth was mistaken but knowing she spoke the truth, Jane relented. "Between the two of us, we shall make a way."

The sisters hugged again and Jane left Elizabeth to find her way to bed. As the door to her room closed, Elizabeth Bennet walked to her window that overlooked the garden. How she wished she and Mr. Darcy had been the couple in the garden that afternoon pledging their love and planning a future.

Instead, she was lying to everyone and plotting a future for her family in the event they lost Somersal due to an accident that never should have happened. The feeling of dread and guilt filled her heart and in her mind she saw herself daring the colonel and Mr. Bingley to race.

The memory was so vivid in her mind she could not understand how it was not the truth. She'd seen Mr. Darcy's eyes that morning as he turned to her after watching his cousin be carted off to Somersal, broken and injured.

The thought of losing his good opinion had driven her to run blindly after the colonel, her heart broken in two at the terrible tragedy she had wrought. And then the sharp crack of the pistol as the groom killed the poor injured horse had hit her with a terrible force.

Hugging herself tightly, Elizabeth Bennet stumbled to her bed and cried herself sick. One foolish instant of bravado had cost her family everything. Her father would be so ashamed of her and mother would never speak to her again if the truth were known. And Mr. Darcy, the thought of his reaction if she insisted that she was the one who instigated the race, well, she simply couldn't bear it.

She could keep him at arm's length through spring, until the races were done but afterwards, she hoped to renew their friendship. Her only hope was that Mr. Bingley and the colonel were telling the truth about the accident and that the races would give her family a bit of security when the Matlocks declared Somersal for the colonel.

Thinking of Mr. Darcy's smile, Elizabeth wept softly until she fell asleep sick and exhausted from the stress of the past few weeks.

Chapter 20

When Elizabeth awoke the next morning, after a night filled with restlessness and vague dreams, she hurried to dress and glanced longingly at her riding habit. She could not risk wearing it now and the aggravation of riding in her skirts angered her. With high color in her cheeks, she quietly opened her bedroom door and eased into the hallway, glancing about to be certain there was no one about.

In moments, she reached the bottom of the staircase and halted to listen for the stirrings of the servants. None would think twice of her early morning appearance for they had become accustomed to her comings and goings.

As she passed the parlor, she heard the colonel moaning and stepped to the door wondering whether she should enter. The voice of a footman reached her ears and she scurried to the front door hoping not to be seen.

Of course the colonel would be in pain. The lonely hours of the night were the hardest to pass when a person was injured or ailing. Sending up a silent prayer for his relief, Elizabeth made her way down the broad stone steps of Somersal.

Merrit was waiting for her and she retrieved a few carrots from the groom to offer the horse as was her custom. She would have preferred to bring him an apple but that would have required her to go to the kitchens.

Her heart was heavy from her dreams, the rift with Mr. Darcy, and the colonel's cries that still rang in her ears. She swiftly readied Merrit for their ride and led him outside the stable in time to see the darkness of the night giving way slowly to the dawn. Using a bit of extra effort because of the inconvenience of her skirts, Elizabeth landed in her saddle on Merrit's back and glanced about before urging Merrit into a trot away from Somersal.

The cold mist swirled about them as the horse and his rider navigated the familiar terrain. Elizabeth now wished she had added an extra layer of clothing as a persistent breeze chased them on their way.

What she wouldn't give for a basket of Mrs. Drake's scones right then. The memory of the warm treat brought sadness and regret as she turned without conscious thought in the direction of the Drake cottage.

Mr. Darcy would not be riding so early and she indulged the need to revisit the copse of trees where he had caught her when she stumbled. The memory from when his lips had brushed against her forehead brought tears to her eyes and Elizabeth halted Merrit's progress.

Closing her eyes and recalling that morning with Mr. Darcy was a foolish thing to do but for a moment she only wished to feel the emotions he had stirred in her heart.

His voice drifted across the field to her and Elizabeth startled in her seat. Merrit tossed his head and she soothed him with sweet words and a reassuring rub along his muscular neck. "I am most sorry, sweet boy. 'Tis only Mr. Darcy and though my heart leaps at the chance to see him again, we are found out."

She waited while he approached thinking of what she might say to explain the fact that she was indeed riding the fields on Merrit instead of walking. Her father had always told her that a lie was bound to grow stronger than the truth.

Realizing the trap she'd laid for herself, Elizabeth decided there was nothing to be done but to pretend she did not care what he might think of her deceit. How could she have been honest with him in front of the colonel?

Both men had encouraged her to continue riding but she would never have admitted to doing such when the poor colonel had been through terrible pain and agony because of her childish need to race.

Mr. Darcy pulled his horse alongside Merrit and gazed into Elizabeth's eyes for a long moment before speaking. Though the temptation to lower her lashes and give herself a moment's respite from his quiet judgment tempted her terribly, she held her head up and met his gaze.

Elizabeth did allow her eyes to wander from the curls that lay against the crisp white of his cravat to the angle of his strong jaw to the proud, aquiline nose before her eyes settled on the fullness of his bottom lip.

Mr. Darcy looked away after a time and seemed at a loss for words. Sensing his discomfort, Elizabeth spoke instead. "Mr. Darcy, I did not expect to see you this morning."

Her words brought a low chuckle and a smile to his lips. "I would speak with you, Miss Elizabeth. Shall we walk for a bit?"

Elizabeth had felt able to withstand his questioning while sitting upon Merrit's back and so his request left her suddenly defenseless. She could not refuse to walk with him now that they were out in the fields together and so she nodded and dismounted after he moved his horse away.

Looking up as he dismounted, Elizabeth allowed herself to enjoy his masculine form. The muscles in his legs and backside thrilled her and she was certain the heat that climbed from her neck to her cheeks was powerful enough to warm her entire body.

When he turned to take her hand, Elizabeth dropped her gaze to the ground. Mr. Darcy placed her hand on his arm and they began to walk along as the horses followed behind. Waiting for him to initiate conversation, Elizabeth studied the ground.

Comfortable with their pace, Mr. Darcy finally decided to break the peaceful silence. "I must say I am not the least surprised to find you riding about on Merrit, for I do know you dearly love him. However, I cannot begin to understand why you avoid my company. Am I not as handsome as the beast that follows dutifully behind you?"

Elizabeth stifled a giggle at his words, not because they were not amusing but because she did not wish to give him the advantage. "Merrit follows because I have a carrot in my skirt pocket. As to your question concerning who is handsomer, I would not say as the horse might begin to believe I love him more dearly than I ought."

Mr. Darcy placed his free hand to his chest and arranged his face in a pained expression that caused Elizabeth to laugh in spite of herself. The man smiled to see mirth return to her eyes but let silence descend between them once more.

After a few paces, he paused and Elizabeth knew she could no longer tease him upon hearing his next question.

"Miss Elizabeth, you said yesterday that you could not ride again after what happened to Richard. What has changed since then?"

Knowing there was no use in hiding her intentions and that his reaction would be the same as that night her family had gone for dinner at Pemberley, Elizabeth sighed a deep, unsettled breath and fixed her eyes on Mr. Darcy. It pained her greatly to admit the truth to him.

"Everything has changed, sir. Surely you must know that my family now faces uncertainty once again in but the span of a few months. I shall race Merrit come the spring and hoard my winnings against the day that my family must leave Somersal."

Mr. Darcy listened patiently and seemed to measure his response. "But the Matlocks shall not put your family out of the home, I can assure you of that fact. Richard has no desire to live at Somersal for some time."

Elizabeth shook her head, wishing his words were true. "Mr. Darcy, you do not retain control over Somersal and the earl is not happy that my family resides in the home meant for his second son. Especially now, when the colonel will remain for an indefinite period of time, as he should without concern for my family's needs. I cannot rely upon the kindness of the Matlocks, though they have been nothing but kind in light of this terrible situation. Jane and I are responsible for the well being of our family. I must do my part."

Quite shocked by her words, Mr. Darcy did not trust himself to respond in haste. There was truly not a need for her to worry so over Somersal and he determined to have a conversation with Richard to devise a plan whereby they might reassure Miss Elizabeth without causing her further embarrassment.

Turning again toward Somersal, he walked along in silence with the woman he had come to admire greatly in such a short span of time. Their friendship had become precious to him. Her time at Netherfield while Miss Bennet was ill had shown him a side of the lady he had missed at the assembly.

When her father died, there had not been time to know her better before he had to return to London. And then when her family had come to Somersal, he had begun to believe their friendship was meant to be.

Turning as she sighed and shook her head, Mr. Darcy finally spoke. "I cannot pretend to understand your position, Miss Elizabeth, but I shall make it my duty to find another way to convince you that your family shall live at Somersal for as long as there is a need. I would not see you race after having watched Richard be injured so terribly. I could not bear to see you hurt."

Elizabeth knew he meant well and his concern touched her heart. But Fitzwilliam Darcy was not in control of her future nor his relations. If the Earl of Matlock decreed that Colonel Fitzwilliam was to have use of the house, Mrs. Bennet would have no choice but to arrange for other accommodations.

"Mr. Darcy, I am willing to listen to all that you suggest but I will continue to prepare for the races. I am not afraid upon Merrit's back for he and I have had an understanding since first we met."

She turned and placed a foot in the stirrup and lifted herself easily into the saddle. Mr. Darcy knew she could not race for a few months yet and so he would not argue with her about it. Instead, he mounted his horse and smiled at her. "Shall we keep our habit of riding together every morning, Miss Elizabeth?"

Surprised that he did not seek to change her mind about Merrit and her plans come the springtime, Elizabeth was slow to accept his offer of companionship. Arching a brow, she glanced away and squared her shoulders. Keeping her eyes trained on the copse in the distance, she spoke clearly. "If our habit does not offend the Matlocks then I accept the offer. I cannot abide riding another day in a dress."

Mr. Darcy laughed and let his horse have his head. Merrit ambled alongside his equine friend and Elizabeth glanced at Mr. Darcy hoping to find him distracted. Instead, she found him gazing intently at her skirts. Scandalized by his attention, Elizabeth meant to sound serious but laughter creeped into her voice. "Whatever are you doing, Mr. Darcy?"

Knowing he was caught in his moment of weakness, Fitzwilliam Darcy only gave a devilish grin. "While that is a lovely dress, Miss Elizabeth, I quite agree with your preference in riding attire."

Turning Merrit toward the copse of trees and away from Somersal, Elizabeth called over her shoulder. "Do you think Mrs. Drake might have something to warm us this morning?"

Mr. Darcy laughed at his lady and urged his horse to follow where she went. "There is but one way to know, Miss Elizabeth. Let us visit the Drakes and hope for their kind mercy upon a pair of hungry visitors."

Chapter 21

Mr. Darcy parted with Elizabeth Bennet at the door of the parlor and went in to see his cousin. Richard would know just what he must do to stop Miss Elizabeth from racing.

"Darcy, close the parlor door and come sit beside me if you have a moment. There is something we must discuss."

Obeying Richard's command, Darcy closed the door and took a seat beside his cousin. The man's eyes gave away his fatigue and Darcy wondered if they ought to speak later. "Richard, you appear exhausted. Are you sleeping well? The surgeon surely left laudanum for the evening hours?"

Richard Fitzwilliam was tired, more tired than he could ever remember being in his life. "Tis a part of healing, Darcy, that is all. And yes, the laudanum does help me sleep. Yet, I would seek your counsel on a matter you might find foolish."

Darcy chuckled. "I came to seek yours, cousin, on a matter of the heart, which, I'm sure you would agree, is prone to foolishness."

Richard's shoulders dropped and he gave a low whistle. His body was wracked with injury and pain but he would sleep when Darcy left. For now he meant to speak. "Miss Lydia is a lovely young lady, and much too young to marry. But, I find myself drawn to her Darcy, and it frightens me if I am honest. Yet, I long for her company more each day."

Fitzwilliam Darcy tried to school his face but the shock of his cousin's admission was much too great. "Richard! You cannot possibly be considering that you might have feelings for her!"

The colonel closed his eyes and licked his parched lips. Darcy turned for the pitcher of cold water on the table and poured his cousin a small cup. "Here," he said as Richard opened his eyes, "have a drink."

"I would much prefer whiskey but this will have to do."

Darcy held the cup and after Richard had drunk half of it in halting sips, he placed the cup on the table. "When we have finished our conversation, I shall be happy to pour a draught of whiskey, old man, for if ever there was a need for it, 'tis now."

Richard smiled briefly before relaxing slowly in his bed. "Now, tell me how terribly wrong I am to seek a future with Miss Lydia."

Mr. Darcy resumed his seat and laughed. "There are a thousand reasons why you should not Richard. She is so very young and immature, she has not a bit of money to her name save her dowry, no connections nor a bit of accomplishment to recommend her. Yet, I do admit she is a fair beauty with a happy demeanor. Perhaps the presence of the governess shall aid with her immaturity in time."

Richard listened without interrupting his cousin and thought on each point presented. She was a terribly childish girl, it was true. And yet, when she sat with him there was no pity in her eyes. She had spoken of how he would walk again soon and that she would dance with him come the spring were he in Derbyshire still.

Darcy could not know what her utter lack of morbidity and seriousness did for him. So he tried to explain as best he could. "I have had the honor of dancing with some of the most lovely and accomplished ladies of the Ton, as you well know, and I have traveled extensively in my time as a soldier. So it is not that I am some young man suddenly smitten by a pair of fine eyes."

Darcy sighed and shook his head. Richard was not asking to be talked out of his infatuation for Lydia Bennet, he was simply admitting it to the one person he felt might possibly understand. "I cannot argue those points, Richard, but I must say that your mother and father will not see her the same as you do. They may become angry and send the Bennet family away before you and Miss Lydia might reach an understanding."

Richard knew his cousin spoke the truth. "It is funny you say that, cousin. I imagine father would send them all packing if he paid the slightest bit of attention to your face when Miss Elizabeth enters a room."

A short, sharp bark of laughter greeted the colonel's statement. "Tis that easy to see is it?"

"Indeed. I wondered how long it would take before you forgot I was in the room and gave her the kiss you so desperately wish to bestow," Richard said as a great yawn escaped him.

Darcy's time to devise a plan with his cousin was coming to an end and he launched into his concern before his cousin might fall fast asleep. He rose and retrieved a decanter of whiskey from the sideboard and poured his cousin a healthy dose.

As Richard drank from the cup he held, Mr. Darcy cut to the heart of the matter. "Miss Elizabeth still rides, I met her this morning in the fields, and she wishes to race because she fears your father shall declare Somersal as your home."

Richard allowed the whiskey to do it's work in warming his chest before he answered. The liquid fire was much preferred over laudanum, which left his head fuzzy when he awoke. "If you do not wish for her to race, and it seems you do not, then ask her to marry you. I have seen the two of you together, and it is plain to me that there is a great love in the making. If she is the mistress of Pemberley, her family shall be secure no matter what happens with Somersal. Though I have my own thoughts on that matter."

Mr. Darcy placed the empty cup on the sideboard with the decanter as he considered his cousin's advice. He had thought the same himself as he rode to Somersal with Miss Elizabeth. He did love her and marriage would solve her problems and make him the happiest man in all of the country.

Returning to Richard's side, he thought of the words he might use to persuade her. Meaning to thank his cousin and advise him to proceed with caution when it came to Lydia Bennet, Mr. Darcy bit his tongue as a snore rattled forth from his cousin.

He arranged Richard's bed clothes and smiled. He might have need to advise the maids and footmen charged with Richard's care to make better use of the whiskey when they might.

Elizabeth was in the stables when Mr. Darcy appeared the next morning. She was dressed in her smart, black riding habit with leather boots and when she turned to smile at him, Mr. Darcy tipped his hat. "Good morning, Miss Elizabeth, I am pleased to see you ready to ride with me. I have something of great importance to ask you today."

Leading Merrit to the door of the stable, Elizabeth smiled at the man who had become her best friend. "Ask whatever you wish, Mr. Darcy, and if it is in my power, I shall surely do it."

Thinking she might feel differently once she knew, but hoping against hope that she would accept him, Mr. Darcy attempted to keep his tone light. "You must not commit before you know all that shall follow my dear. It is not something I must have an answer for this day, but I think it will solve a great many problems and bring much happiness."

Elizabeth mounted Merrit with a thrill in her heart that Mr. Darcy had taken her concerns seriously and had spent the rest of his day after they parted considering a way to be of some assistance. Still, she did not know what plan he might have devised that could alter her life so drastically.

They left the stables together, riding in companionable silence with the stable boy bringing up the rear as he had when they first rode together. Mr. Darcy glanced over his shoulder at the young boy and smiled. "Your stable boy seems to think it unwise for us to ride alone together, Miss Elizabeth."

She turned and waved to the young man before addressing Mr. Darcy. "He has hoped he might follow me about each morning since Richard's accident but I would not allow it. Now that you are here, he has taken advantage but I would not be angry with him for it."

Mr. Darcy was pleased with the young man and meant to tell him so when they returned. The concern for a mistress was an admirable trait that ought to be rewarded. "His grandfather taught him well. My mother often had to convince the man to let her ride unhindered though father would have been cross to know the many times he obeyed her wishes."

Elizabeth turned to gaze at Mr. Darcy. "I had not thought of that. I shall be kinder in my reprimands, sir. The Darcy family has taken great care of Somersal through the years. Is that why you provide for everything from the staff to the food? I had hoped that consideration was not only on my family's account."

Sitting straighter in his saddle, Mr. Darcy allowed her remark to settle before giving a hasty answer. Obviously, she had somehow heard of his plan to appease the earl. "Somersal is often seen as an extension of Pemberley and so no one has ever questioned that I should oversee its operations. My steward lived here for many years, Miss Elizabeth, and his father before him. The Darcy family has ever worked with the Fitzwilliam family in the upkeep of this estate."

Not wishing to goad him, and sorry now for her impertinence, Elizabeth turned her gaze to the hills that rose to their right. Steering Merrit toward the summit of one particularly steep hill, she called to Mr. Darcy to follow.

Though the ground was frozen, the horses labored to reach the top amongst the rocks beneath their hooves. Elizabeth's faithful stable boy waited at the bottom for his mistress and she waved to him as Merrit crested the top of the hill. The view was stunning and she sat in silence with Mr. Darcy and breathed deeply, her cares lifting for a time.

Mr. Darcy pulled his horse's reins and moved closer to Miss Elizabeth. Gaining her attention, he pointed out the chimneys of her nearest neighbor. "That is the Morely estate. They are distant cousins of the Fitzwilliam family. Miss Bingley spoke of having tea there the night you first came to dinner at Pemberley, do you recall?"

Unfortunately, Elizabeth did. Caroline Bingley had said that Lady Regina Morely spoke of the races come the spring. "Indeed, I do, Mr. Darcy. It would seem I might invoke disdain from every quarter when it comes to racing. Yet, I am not of that circle which is able to live without a care for tomorrow."

Mr. Darcy thought her words harsh but reminded himself that she alone knew what it was to be without the protection of a father or brother while relying upon the kindness of a family she did not know well at present. "The Morely's have a habit of setting themselves above us all, so it is not surprising that Miss Bingley does enjoy visiting their estate when she comes to Pemberley. However, none of them would dare to speak against a Darcy."

Elizabeth turned in her saddle and smiled. "Tis a good thing Miss Darcy has not yet been corrupted by my vulgar habit of wishing to race, then."

Slipping from her saddle, Elizabeth spied a boulder and carefully picked her way across the rocky slope to sit for a time while Merrit and Mr. Darcy's horse sought what grass might be found amongst the stones.

Mr. Darcy came to stand beside her and remained silent as he enjoyed the view. That Miss Elizabeth enjoyed nature much as his mother had gave the man a deep, abiding happiness. How many times had he ridden these same hills and sat with his mother reciting poetry befitting this vista?

His eyes fell upon the curls that framed her face and a tenderness of heart overtook the man. She must know that he would never see her or her family without a home.

Elizabeth smiled and stretched out her arms, her hands framing the view. "What are men to rocks and mountains, Mr. Darcy? Do they think of us as ants along their backs? Here for a time and then gone like the leaves of autumn, do you think?"

Mr. Darcy took her small hands in his and reveled in the warmth of them safe inside her riding gloves. The firm, yet delicate grasp she returned thrilled him as the scent of lavender drifted from her coat. "Rocks and mountains are hard and unyielding, Miss Elizabeth, much like the hearts of those who would deny a lovely lady her every wish. I would not be of their ilk, though, for I would give you all you might desire if you would only be mine."

Shocked by his passionate speech, Elizabeth furrowed her brow in confusion. "Sir, surely you jest. I do not think your family would agree, though my mother would be most thrilled to answer without delay on my behalf."

His eyes grew darker and he moved closer to the woman he meant to have for his own. "Miss Elizabeth, I assure you this is no jest. Though we have come to know one another better these past weeks, surely you do not think me foolish to seek your hand? I love you most ardently and it is in my power to see that your family shall never want for a home again. Don't you understand? There is no need to open yourself to the censure and scorn of your neighbors. You may always ride Merrit as you please, I shall have him brought to Pemberley after we have wed, but there is no need for you to race."

Elizabeth stood stunned, thinking she must have misunderstood. Had she known Mr. Darcy might love her? She had hoped it, but now to hear him make his offer only after his knowledge of her fears concerning Somersal left her heart in agony while her mind rushed to deliver the words to refuse him.

"Mr. Darcy, I would not marry from necessity, sir. I did not accept the terrible proposal from my cousin that would have saved my family the pain and heartbreak of leaving Longbourn and I shall not accept yours to secure a future where I feel indebted to my husband."

Chapter 22

Mr. Darcy watched as Elizabeth Bennet turned and marched away to mount Merrit. He hurried after her and caught Merrit's reins before she could turn the horse and retreat back down the hill. "Miss Elizabeth, I am not Mr. Collins. I am a man who loves you and wishes only to offer the whole of my self and all that I have in order to ease your burdens. You would refuse me from wounded pride?"

Elizabeth shook her head and looked away, angry tears spilling before she might stop them. "Tis not wounded pride, Mr. Darcy, but a wounded heart. Is it wrong to wish for a love borne of mutual respect and admiration? Racing horses isn't vulgar nor disreputable. I admit that it gives me great pleasure to thunder across a field without censure. My father taught me to ride, to overcome the fears I held as a young girl. We would race home after visiting tenants and when I am in this saddle, I can almost feel him riding beside me."

Her voice broke and Mr. Darcy dropped Merrit's reins. He did not know what he might say to explain himself more clearly. He simply turned and mounted his horse to follow her down the hill.

They rode in silence back to Somersal and Elizabeth turned to look up at him as he remained upon his horse. "Colonel Fitzwilliam would be pleased to see you if you wish to pay him a visit before returning to Pemberley."

Mr. Darcy gave a nod of his head and urged his horse toward the lane in front of Somersal. He did not wish to see Richard at the moment, nor remain in the company of the woman who had cast aside his proposal.

Wiping fresh tears from her eyes, Elizabeth turned and entered the home hoping she might slip upstairs without notice. Laughter from the parlor caused her to slow her steps and approach the open door.

Lydia and the colonel were alone in the parlor and Elizabeth watched as her sister provided a much needed light in the colonel's day. She moved from her chair to perch on the edge of his bed and the colonel took her hand. The laughter ceased and for a time they were simply quiet, staring into one another's eyes.

The colonel was entertaining feelings for her youngest sister! Elizabeth thought to enter the room but waited, hoping to see that Richard Fitzwilliam was merely indulging a young girl's flirtation and nothing more. Instead, she saw him lift Lydia's small hand and place a chaste kiss upon it.

Not waiting a moment longer, she entered the room as though she had not seen what had transpired. The unlikely couple did not rush to break their bond. "Lydia, I would like a moment alone with the colonel."

Richard knew the look on Elizabeth's face meant he must explain himself. He dropped Lydia's hand and gazed into her eyes. "Thank you, Miss Lydia, you will visit with me again on the morrow?"

Lydia stood and straightened her skirts. "I shall, colonel, and I will stay with you on Christmas Day as well. I have seen Pemberley, and while it is like unto a fairytale, I would rather see it another time instead of leave you here alone."

Leaving her sister with the colonel, Lydia veritably skipped from the room no doubt buoyed by the colonel's particular attention.

Elizabeth sat and looked at the man before speaking. His eyes held much more life than they had a week ago and the fatigue that had marked his face before now seemed to have lost its hold. She supposed there was something to be said for the carefree spirit of her sister. "Colonel, I must apologize for coming to see you in my riding habit. I took your advice about living and I see you abide by it yourself with fervor."

The colonel laughed and only gave a small wince as he tried to adjust himself in bed. "Miss Elizabeth, you are yourself a person who lives each day with a fervor as you put it. I will not pretend to be ashamed of the kiss I gave to your sister. She alone has given me such hope and happiness in this otherwise terrible time. Would you have me deny my feelings?"

Elizabeth sighed deeply. "I would say that if my sister is such a tonic in your day, sir, then I am pleased for the both of you. Lydia's demeanor has not often recommended her but I do understand, in this instance, how it might be uplifting. You are a handsome man in need of companionship and she is a lovely young girl. I can only hope you do not give her false hope."

Richard Fitzwilliam thought on the words she spoke. 'Twas true Lydia Bennet was not the woman his mother or father would choose for him for many reasons, chief among them being her childishness. "Miss Elizabeth, I do not think that I would have noticed Miss Lydia's better qualities had I not become injured, that is true. But, I am injured and she has made me long for her company each day. That alone is a most precious gift. Do you know what that is like? To long for the hours you might spend in the company of the person who accepts you for who you are with all your faults?"

The words of Mr. Darcy's proposal echoed in her mind and Elizabeth cast her eyes to the floor. Why could he not see her as the Colonel saw Lydia? She had been wrong to confide her plan to him but it was much too late to remedy that mistake.

Mr. Darcy had made her hope that she could do as she pleased and still hold his friendship. Now that dream was shattered along with any hope of becoming his bride, for she had thought of it after their rides across the fields had brought them much closer.

Raising her head to meet the colonel's eyes, Elizabeth Bennet nodded. "I knew that once, colonel, and hope to know it again. I shall not speak of the kiss I saw this morning if you promise to give my sister time. Wait and see how you feel for her after several months have passed before you build up her hopes and dreams of a future with you."

Richard Fitzwilliam saw the pain in Elizabeth's eyes and wondered what on earth his cousin had said to the lady after their conversation the day before. Surely the man had not mangled a marriage proposal? "You have my word, Miss Elizabeth. I shall never hurt Miss Lydia. You might benefit from taking your own advice, though. My cousin is a good man. In time, perhaps you will judge his heart and not his words as at times, those are in direct opposition to his true feelings."

Elizabeth might have known Mr. Darcy would have spoken with his cousin about their friendship. Not trusting herself to answer the colonel's words, she sat in silent contemplation for moments before Lady Matlock appeared at the parlor door. Elizabeth stood as the woman entered and turned to Richard. "Thank you, colonel. I promise to give due consideration to your advice."

Lady Matlock's eyes swept Elizabeth from head to toe taking in her riding habit. "I say, that coat suits you Miss Elizabeth, even in such a severe color. Do you ride each morning?"

Elizabeth felt the heat flare in her face and nodded, knowing there was no use in pretending now. "I do, your ladyship. Do you ride?"

Richard smiled at his mother and gave a boast on her behalf. "Mother taught me to ride, Miss Elizabeth. A more capable horsewoman I've never seen."

Lady Matlock went to sit beside her son, a smile now upon her face. "Richard exaggerates as usual, but yes, I do ride whenever I have the chance. Would you care to ride with me in the morning, Miss Elizabeth? And in the afternoon we might gather the girls and arrange our dresses for the visit to Pemberley on Christmas Day."

Relieved the lady was not upset at her return to riding Merrit, Elizabeth agreed with the plans. "I would love to ride with you, Lady Matlock, and I will see that the girls are ready for inspection tomorrow afternoon."

Elizabeth left the mother and son to their own visit and given her disagreement with Mr. Darcy, her heart was lighter at having talked with Colonel Fitzwilliam.

Seeking Jane to divulge the terrible proposal Mr. Darcy had given, Elizabeth hurried to the salon before changing from her riding habit. The room was empty but she entered and pulled the cord by the fireplace to summon a maid.

When the maid appeared, Elizabeth sat in one of the chairs facing the fireplace to warm her chilled hands. "Please find Miss Bennet and have her come to me."

The maid curtseyed and went off to find Jane. As she sat quietly by the fire, Elizabeth replayed Mr. Darcy's proposal in her mind. Her heart had been half hope and half agony as he revealed himself to her on that windswept hill.

Were it not for Richard's accident and her foolish admission to Mr. Darcy about the races, would he have been moved to offer a proposal of marriage? She would never know the answer now and yet she hoped that he would have.

Jane entered the salon and went to sit beside Elizabeth. "Why, you are still in your riding habit, Lizzy. What if Mother sees you?"

Elizabeth knew her sister was right. Now that Lady Matlock and the colonel had seen her so dressed, her mother would know soon enough. "She may be angry, but I simply must tell you what happened with Mr. Darcy this morning on our ride. 'Tis terrible Jane, truly terrible."

Clasping her hands and leaning forward, Jane shook her head. "I cannot believe that, Lizzy. Mr. Darcy is a gentleman and most proper."

"He proposed to me Jane. He asked me to marry him so that I might not have to race and so that our family shall have a home at last."

Jane's face was lit with happiness for her sister before she could manage to contain herself. "But that is the best news, Lizzy! Why would you say something terrible happened? Did you refuse him?"

Elizabeth dropped her head and spoke in a whisper. "I did, Jane. I may never find such happiness as we shared in the time before Richard's accident but I cannot accept him when I would not accept the same from our cousin."

Mrs. Bennet had been by the door as Elizabeth spoke and did not hear her answer to Jane. She rushed into the salon, her voice a terrible shriek. "Elizabeth Cassandra Bennet! What have you done?"

Elizabeth rose and backed away as her mother advanced.

"Why are you in that riding habit? What answer did you give Mr. Darcy?"

Jane went to stand beside their mother and calm her but the woman was beyond such help. "No, Janie, she shall answer to me the same as she would if her father were standing here!"

Elizabeth swiped at the tears that stained her cheeks and motioned for Jane to close the salon door. Her mother's voice would certainly bring a crowd to the room once she heard Elizabeth's confession. "Mother, he only wished to marry me to keep me from racing Merrit come the spring. I will not marry a man who would do such."

Mrs. Bennet placed a hand over her heart, her face gone a terrible shade of red. "What is this nonsense about racing horses? You shall not! I told you no more riding after the colonel's awful accident and yet you stand here in a riding habit. And you scorn a man wealthy enough to provide for all of us? Go to your room and return to me with your habit, boots and all."

Elizabeth shook her head no but the word would not cross her lips.

Mrs. Bennet turned to Jane. "Take her upstairs and bring me her clothes after you help her change. There shall be no more riding of horses."

She turned to Elizabeth before sending both daughters from the room. "You will go to Pemberley with us at Christmas and give your apologies to Mr. Darcy and hope that he shall have you still."

Elizabeth had never seen her mother truly angry, and so she left with Jane without another word. While she might surrender her riding habit and boots, her mother could not mean that she was never to ride again, merely never to race.

Mr. Darcy holed up in his library after returning from his awful visit to Somersal and seeing the Bingley's out to their carriage. Mr. Bingley had spoken with him about the use of Darcy House and his plan to seek a courtship with Jane Bennet.

Risking a falling out with his friend, he warned Charles Bingley that Jane Bennet might only be interested in his wealth. He did not speak about their situation at Somersal as the reason for Miss Bennet's feelings for his friend.

Charles Bingley had laughed at him in his irritatingly amiable way and clapped Darcy on the back. "She loves me, Darcy. Whether I was rich or poor, it would not matter to her as her connections do not matter to me. Love conquers all my friend and money only affords me the opportunity to provide for her as an angel from heaven ought to expect."

As he thought of his friend's romantic words, Mr. Darcy chided himself for ever allowing the matter of the races into his proposal. He had been a fool to think he could reason with her at such a moment. No woman wished to be bought and paid for, save one Miss Bingley he supposed, and a proud one like Elizabeth Bennet surely would not accept such an offer.

Christmas Day would see the Bennets and the Matlock family return to Pemberley and so he spent the better part of the afternoon imagining how he might press his case once more without forcing Elizabeth Bennet to give up her plan of racing Merrit come the spring.

He would take her to the hothouse and arrange for a stunning display of blooms as he admitted his error. He would offer her as many horses as she wished just for her use. He might even say that he would support her in her decision to race.

Mr. Darcy laughed at that last thought. There was not a way he would concede that she ought to race with the common folks in Derbyshire. It simply was not done. And not by a mistress of Pemberley.

Stretching his tall form out upon the sofa before the fireplace, he fell asleep and dreamed of Elizabeth Bennet streaking across the fields of Somersal with her curls flying behind her loose and unpinned. The dream changed and he saw her horse stumble and cried out in his sleep as she fell and was crushed beneath the beast.

Waking with a start, he wiped the wetness from his cheeks and took a moment to settle his racing heart. His hands shook with the adrenaline that had filled his body and awoken him. If Elizabeth Bennet would not refuse to race Merrit, he would have the horse moved to Pemberley where she could not ride him again. If it meant that he would lose her forever, at least he might save her from a fate worse than his cousin had suffered.

Chapter 23

After Jane had left her room to deliver the riding habit to their mother, Elizabeth spent the remainder of her day alone refusing even her beloved sister to enter again.

She took her dinner alone and suffered with a terrible headache from hours of crying and distress. Lady Matlock expected her to ride come the morning but she did not think it wise to disobey her mother so soon.

Elizabeth sat at her desk and wrote a note for the lady saying she was unwell and would not ride the next day. It was the truth and she suspected her mother would tell Lady Matlock of the proposal and Elizabeth's banishment from the stables.

After a maid had taken her note and dinner tray away, Elizabeth dressed for bed and hoped she might find peace come the morning.

Dreams of riding with Mr. Darcy and the words he had spoken to her, words full of love and promise, left her restless throughout the night with bouts of wakefulness and more crying.

When morning came, her maid tended the fire before pulling open the heavy drapes of her windows. Elizabeth lifted her head from her pillow and gasped at the pain that made her sink back down again. Certainly she did not feel well and her eyes burned as a chill moved throughout her body.

"Miss, what shall you wear today?" the maid asked as she moved about the room to help her mistress begin the day.

Elizabeth tried to speak, but her throat hurt and her mouth was dry. Only a squeak escaped her as she placed a hand on her forehead. The maid hurried to her side and pulled the counterpane higher.

"Oh dear, Miss Elizabeth, you are not well. We must send for Mr. Arnold, the apothecary in Lambton."

Before Elizabeth might disagree, the young woman had called for another maid and ordered weak tea. "See that the stable boy is sent into Lambton for Mr. Arnold quick like. Our mistress is ailing this morning. Hurry, go on."

Slowly sitting up in case her head decided to explode in pain again, Elizabeth trembled as a draft swept her body. The maid returned to her and arranged the covers of her bed again.

She poured a cup of water for her mistress and held it while she drank. "The stable boy will be on his way, miss. Do not worry. And Polly will bring some tea. I shall tell your mother you will not be down to break your fast."

Elizabeth swallowed the cool water slowly as it gave some relief to her throat and simply nodded at her maid's words. She was almost happy to be ill for it saved her the trouble of facing her mother and pretending all was well.

Easing herself lower in the bed again, for sitting up left her weaker, Elizabeth felt her eyelids flutter as she watched the maid add kindling to the fire. In moments, she was sleeping again and would not wake until Mr. Arnold arrived.

Later in the day, after being given a horrible syrup followed by a cup of weak tea, Elizabeth listened as Jane read to her from a book of poetry retrieved from the library. The words made little sense and the desire to sleep overtook her.

When she awoke again in the early evening, Mrs. Bennet now sat at her bedside with a cup of tea. "Lizzy, my dear, how are you? You've been asleep for some time."

Elizabeth licked her cracked and dry lips and Mrs. Bennet stood to wet them for her with a cool cloth. Afterward she gave her daughter a tepid drink of weak tea. "Shall I call for Jane? She wishes to be sure you have another dose of the concoction Mr. Arnold left for you."

Shaking her head gently in agreement, Elizabeth fought back tears at the pain in her throat. She dared not speak and Mrs. Bennet took her hand. "The girls were lovely today with Lady Matlock. They've chosen their dresses for tomorrow and send you their love. I would not allow them to enter this room for fear they might all fall ill."

At her mother's mention of her sister's dresses, Elizabeth recalled that tomorrow must be Christmas Day. As terribly ill as she was, she was thankful she would not be made to stand before Mr. Darcy and beg his forgiveness. If there was a blessing hidden in her fever and sore throat, that was surely it.

Jane arrived and relieved Mrs. Bennet. "Lizzy, let me help you sit up dear. I would have you take more tea as your fever has not broken. I shall stay the night with you for I have no need to go to Pemberley with mother and the girls, Mr. Bingley has gone with his sister to London."

Elizabeth leaned against the pillows Jane arranged patiently behind her and took halting sips of the tea. When Jane measured out a spoonful of the terrible syrup Mr. Arnold had left, Elizabeth covered her mouth with both hands.

"Come, do not behave as child. I know your throat hurts but this will make you better, love. Open up."

Jane waited until Elizabeth dropped her hands and opened her mouth. "Take it all at once, though I know it hurts, for it will not do to swallow slowly."

After that horrible deed was done, Jane helped Elizabeth to sit up while she washed her face and hands and brushed out her hair. The maid assisted with the chamber pot and by the time Elizabeth was tucked in her bed again, she was exhausted. She meant to tell Jane not to sit with her through the night lest she too fall ill but her eyes grew heavy and she was asleep before another thought could form in her aching head.

In the morning, Elizabeth awoke without the chills that had plagued her the day before but her throat was still sore. Jane had fallen asleep in the chair beside the bed. The fire had been tended in the recent hours and Elizabeth was happy to remain snuggled under her covers.

She wished that she might wake Jane and send her to her own room but she did not think she might capture her sleeping sister's attention with just a whisper and she dared not try her voice just yet.

Thankfully, a maid entered the room moments later and came to relieve Jane. She gently shook the woman's shoulder after laying her hand on Elizabeth's forehead and smiling at the lack of fever.

"Miss, miss," she said as Jane's eyes fluttered open. Jane gave a most unladylike yawn before rising to tend Elizabeth.

"Another dose for you and some tea and I shall leave you for a time. Constance shall surely have the girls in hand but I would see them off to Pemberley before resting myself."

She climbed in bed with Elizabeth and gave her a gentle hug. "Happy Christmas, dear. I am sorry the day has found you ill but perhaps you will be better by evening."

Elizabeth endured her sister's chatter and another dosing before Jane left her for a time. The maid saw to her tea and another washing of her face and hands before Elizabeth asked for the drapes to be drawn aside. Her voice was weak, barely above a whisper and her throat protested at such use.

The maid moved to open the drapes and returned to her side. "I shall be at my home today, miss, but your mother shall come and sit with you for a time while your sister rests. I will see you soon and you will be much better."

After the maid had gone, Elizabeth watched the heavy snowflakes drift by outside her window and wondered if Merrit missed her morning visit. Vowing that she would go to him as soon as she was well, Elizabeth settled herself against her pillows and slept again not caring that her sisters would wake soon and spend the day at Pemberley.

Mr. Darcy stood eagerly at the door to welcome the Bennets and his aunt and uncle. He had visited his tenants earlier in the day and given Georgiana and James their gifts as they ate a breakfast of cold meats, cheeses, and breads.

His eye was trained on the carriage from Somersal and he smiled in satisfaction. Miss Elizabeth would stand before him in but a few moments and before her family returned home, he would offer his deepest apologies at having offended her with his proposal.

As the carriage emptied, he welcomed each guest in turn. Elizabeth Bennet had not appeared and when the driver clucked to the horses to set them in motion toward the stables, Mr. Darcy turned and searched for Mrs. Bennet. Everyone had hurried inside as the snow had grown heavier.

In the entryway, he caught Mrs. Bennet by the arm and waited with her as the rest of her party entered the parlor. She smiled up at him, quite happy to have been invited for an early dinner. "Mr. Darcy, how lovely the house is with all the greenery and pretty ribbons. I must give you my thanks again for the invitation to share such a special time with your family."

Mr. Darcy smiled at the lady and kept a hold on her arm. "Where is Miss Elizabeth? Surely she wished to come today?"

Mrs. Bennet's smile faded and she looked to the parlor door to be certain they were alone. "Lizzy is not well, she fell ill and is abed at Somersal. But Mr. Darcy, before she became so, I caught her in her riding habit after I had asked her not to ride again. I overheard her telling Jane about your proposal..."

Mr. Darcy released his hold on Mrs. Bennet's arm and held up his hands, ready to give his side of the story.

Mrs. Bennet continued on in spite of his need to speak. "I have taken her riding habit, even her boots, sir, and she shall not have them again. I am angry again thinking how she slighted you after you have been nothing but a gentleman and friend to our family."

His stomach felt as though a rock sat firmly lodged in the pit of it and he shook his head at Mrs. Bennet. "But Miss Elizabeth wishes to race Merrit in the spring. She will not be swayed by the loss of a riding habit, I fear."

Thinking for a moment on the man's words, Mrs. Bennet's eyes lit with inspiration. "If Merrit is not there, she may not ride him. My Lizzy is quite fond of that horse but she must learn that her rash decisions without the benefit of my counsel must not be indulged. Remove the horse from Somersal, Mr. Darcy, I beg you. After the colonel's accident, I cannot bear to think of her racing. I will not stand for it."

Mr. Darcy knew he was likely ending any hope of reconciliation with Elizabeth Bennet but he could not refuse her mother's wishes when they so completely fit his own. He would speak with the earl after dinner and see that there was no change in plans for the Bennet family's residence. At least if he knew for certain that Miss Elizabeth's concerns regarding Somersal were completely unfounded, he could see that Merrit was removed from Somersal.

Squeezing Mrs. Bennet's hand and placing it on his arm, he assured her he would do all that he might. "I will send a groom to Somersal come the morning and have Merrit brought here for a time. Once the spring races are done, I shall return him to Miss Elizabeth as I cannot bear to see her lose him forevermore."

Mrs. Bennet was pleased with his decision as they entered the parlor together for an evening of quiet celebration.

Chapter 24

At Somersal, Lydia Bennet sat with Colonel Fitzwilliam in the parlor and dined by candlelight. The maids had been instructed to set up a table at the colonel's bedside and bring their meal there when dinner was served.

Jane remained upstairs with Elizabeth and Lydia had dressed in the prettiest gown she owned to delight the colonel. "Why, Miss Lydia," he said when she first entered the room, "I have never seen you look so lovely."

She had twirled for him as if on a ballroom floor and giggled as he clapped. Now, sitting near him as they waited for dessert, Lydia shared the news of Elizabeth's refusal of his cousin's proposal. "Mother is livid with her, as she ought to be, silly girl. And she calls me the foolish one."

Richard Fitzwilliam shook his head. "My cousin isn't the most romantic man and he often says things in a way that gives offense."

Lydia would not hear a word against Mr. Darcy. "La, Lizzy was always difficult to please, father's favorite and all that. I suspect she will come to regret her refusal sooner rather than later."

As the footman brought their dessert, the couple sat in silence for a time. Sweet smiles for the colonel between bites of a delicious compote caused the man to feel quite romantic himself. "Miss Lydia, what would you think if I told you that I am smitten?"

Lydia dropped her fork and covered her mouth, her eyes gone wide as two saucers. The colonel set his fork down and motioned for her to come sit beside him. She rose from her seat and smoothed her skirts, careful as she moved between his bed and the table.

Her cheeks were tinged a sweet pink and the colonel touched her face lightly with a still bandaged hand. "My sweet girl, I did not mean to love you. But I do. Will you have a man as old as I for your husband?"

As tears shimmered in her eyes, Lydia Bennet simply gave a nod of her head for her mind was overwhelmed with the thought of marrying the second son of an Earl. While her mother would have been pleased that this was the first thought to enter Lydia's mind, the young girl soon passed from that thought to the next. She loved the colonel as much as he loved her.

"Oh Richard," she began but stopped wondering if she ought to use his Christian name.

The colonel waited with a brow raised slightly, hoping against hope he had not made a terrible mistake. Realizing after a moment that she stumbled on his name, he soothed her. "You may call me Richard, love."

Lydia wiped the happy tears that escaped before continuing. She took the hand that still rested on her face and held it gently. "I will have a man as dear as you, as kind and gentle. You have seen the heart of me that others have missed, the girl ever young and happy yet not as foolish as once believed to be. I shall marry you Richard Fitzwilliam, and endeavor to make you as happy as you've made me this Christmas Day."

Pulling the sweet girl close to him, Richard rested his chin on her head and willed his heart to slow its pace. His mother and father would be most displeased, he knew it, but he cared not. Lydia Bennet was his love and they would be married when he was able to stand.

At the sound of maids outside the door, she pulled away but kept his hand in hers. "You shall have to speak with Lizzy and mother, but they will not object. Do you think your mother will be unhappy?"

Richard ignored the maids and longed to kiss away her fears. "Mother shall come to accept you, Lydia, but I will not be parted from you from this day forward in any case."

After their eventful dinner, Lydia called for the footmen to assist Richard before he fell asleep for a time. Their families would soon return from Pemberley and she wished to share her news with Jane and Elizabeth.

In the library at Pemberley after dinner, Mr. Darcy sat with his uncle and cousin before joining the ladies in the parlor. "Richard seems to be doing quite well at Somersal. The Bennets have been most gracious and helpful in his time of need."

Reginald Fitzwilliam gave a snort at Darcy's words. "Likely they are motivated by fear, I'd say."

James Fitzwilliam wisely stood and gave a yawn. "I think I shall bid Mother a good night and retire to my rooms. I have a feeling this discussion does not require my participation."

After his cousin had gone, Mr. Darcy turned to his uncle and considered the man for a moment. Perhaps Elizabeth's fears were founded after all. "Uncle, I should think the ladies are only displaying their natural kindness and generosity for they have no fear of being removed from Somersal."

The earl eased further into his favorite chair by the fire and Mr. Darcy knew he would be the only gentleman to join the ladies in the parlor before it was time to bid his guests a farewell. Thinking his uncle done with their conversation, Darcy rose to quit the room. The man's words gave him much concern as he stood listening at the door.

"Richard has indeed grown quite comfortable at Somersal, too comfortable for my taste. That youngest daughter spends an inordinate amount of time with him. I believe I shall press him to leave there after the New Year and continue his recovery here at

Pemberley. As for the Bennets, if Richard wishes to live at Somersal, they shall have to find other accommodations. Of course, I would not set them out immediately only give them a good notice."

In Elizabeth's room, Jane was pleased that her sister was able to take a bit of bread and broth with her tea. "Lizzy, you'll be well in no time. I won't leave for London until you are, you know."

Elizabeth smiled at her favorite sister. "Then I must rest though I would rather visit Merrit. The sooner you are off to Town, the sooner Mr. Bingley shall ask Uncle Gardiner for your hand."

Jane was relieved at her sister's words. She knew well that Elizabeth would do something as foolish as slip out in her gown and spencer to see her horse. "Merrit will be in the stables still when you are well and if it will ease your mind, I shall go out and see to him myself."

A light knock sounded on the door to Elizabeth's room and a jubilant Lydia entered without awaiting an answer. She capered about the room, her laughter causing her sisters to glance at one another with expressions of curiosity. Jane went to her and took her by the shoulders.

"Lydia, what has gotten into you and how is the colonel?"

Lydia Bennet embraced her oldest sister in an enthusiastic hug before rushing to share her good news. "Richard has proposed Jane! And I have accepted. Isn't it wonderful news?"

Elizabeth gasped and immediately began coughing. Jane rushed to her side, followed by their overjoyed sister. Taking a sip of the tea from the cup her sister held, Elizabeth regained her composure. "Lydia, you must know his parents will be quite surprised. Perhaps we ought to allow him to speak with them before you tell Mother or Kitty and Mary."

"He said they will resist at first but that it will not matter. I shall be the mistress of Somersal, Lizzy. The wife of the second son of an earl."

Lydia resumed her dance around the room and Jane sat at Elizabeth's bedside. "Something tells me we are not to have a quiet Christmas night."

Elizabeth sat on the edge of the bed and rubbed her face. "I would have a bath before the family returns. If Lydia and Richard share their news, I must be present."

Jane called for the maid to bring water before sending Lydia back downstairs. "You must return to the colonel and speak with him about announcing your engagement. Let him lead, Lydia, for he knows his parents well."

Lydia left her sisters, her head still in the clouds, to return to her beloved's bedside. Elizabeth had not expected Colonel Fitzwilliam to act so soon. Jane turned and helped her stand. "Did you know of their relationship, Lizzy?"

Shaking her head and allowing Jane to help her undress before donning her robe to await the maids who would see to her bath, Elizabeth gave an apologetic glance to her sister. "I knew he was attracted to her but I did not think he would seek her hand at this time. Maybe after a few months? Still, all we might do is wait and see the reaction of his parents."

Jane frowned and made Elizabeth sit while they waited. "While I admit I am quite happy for Lydia, do you think the earl will accept the colonel's decision? He hasn't been terribly friendly these few weeks."

Elizabeth doubted very seriously that Reginald Fitzwilliam would welcome Lydia Bennet into his esteemed family, but she knew for certain he would have little choice if his son truly loved her youngest sister. "The colonel is quite old enough to choose his own bride and he is the second son after all. I can't imagine his choice shall please his mother or father but what might they do?"

Jane Bennet thought of many things they might do, chief among them the removal of the Bennets from Somersal as word would spread of the engagement. "I shall leave for London as soon as I might, perhaps tomorrow or the next day, and certainly take Mary and Kitty along. If the worse happens here, then Mother may take Lydia to Meryton to live with Aunt and Uncle Phillips and you come to London."

Not believing that the Matlocks would be so hasty with their son firmly at home at Somersal and in love with her youngest sister, Elizabeth remained hopeful. "I do not think there will be a rush to remove anyone from Somersal. The colonel may be injured, but that alone is a mark in his and Lydia's favor. Lady Matlock will not wish her husband to go against her son while he is recovering but you should leave for London soon. On that we agree."

Jane led Elizabeth to her bath and sat with her while the maids tended her. "In any event, Lizzy, we must go forward with our plans though I do not know how you will accomplish your goals with Mother set completely against you now."

For the first time since she had fallen ill, Elizabeth Bennet smiled and the twinkle in her eyes made her sister know she was truly well. "Mother shall be distracted with Lydia's news and the planning of a wedding. I shall come and go as I always have, Jane."

Chapter 25

Before the carriage returned from Pemberley, Elizabeth and Jane had joined Lydia and the colonel in the parlor. They were having a late tea and listening as Lydia spoke of a wedding come the summer.

"We can marry here, Richard," she said as she sat by his side, her eyes trained on his handsome face, "in the gardens and perhaps take a wedding trip to Brighton! All of Lambton shall come to see us wed. Do you think Mr. Darcy would mind if the wedding breakfast were at Pemberley? How wonderful that would be."

Richard Fitzwilliam smiled and indulged his Lydia's chatter and dreams for their wedding. "My cousin would be honored to open Pemberley for our wedding breakfast, my dear. And we shall go wherever you wish for our wedding trip, and for as long as you wish."

Lydia glanced to her older sisters and gave a happy smile. "Who would have thought I, the youngest sister, would be the first to wed?"

Jane and Elizabeth returned her smile and kept their worries hidden. It would not do to discuss whether their decision would be well met once the Matlocks returned to Somersal.

Elizabeth turned as the parlor door opened and the party from Pemberley entered. Feeling a bit tired and not at all up for an argument, she rose slowly and went to greet her mother and sisters. "How was dinner, ladies? I expect Pemberley was even more lovely than before."

Mrs. Bennet gave her a stern look. "Why are you out of bed, Lizzy? You must return to your room."

Lydia hurried to Mrs. Bennet's side, her face glowing with happiness. "I have wonderful news mother. Come, sit and let us listen to Richard's announcement."

Mrs. Bennet forgot about Elizabeth and wondered at her youngest daughter's use of the colonel's Christian name. Richard waited for his parents to be seated and as the room grew quiet, he spoke. "As you all know, Miss Lydia remained with me instead of going to Pemberley as she ought. Her companionship and good humor have touched my heart and while it will surprise you all to know it, I have asked her to become my wife and she has accepted."

Mrs. Bennet's excited chatter filled the room while Kitty and Lydia joined her merriment. Elizabeth glanced to the Matlocks and was not surprised to find them quiet in the face of their son's announcement.

The earl's face was quickly becoming quite red and before she might warn her mother and sisters, he rose from his chair and paced about the room. Lady Matlock went to stand beside her son and await her husband's words.

"Richard, why have you made such a decision without my counsel?" The earl asked as he paced, his voice so loud it startled the Bennet ladies into silence.

Richard Fitzwilliam remained calm and motioned for Lydia to come stand beside him. "Father, with all respect, I am a grown man and capable of making such a decision without your aid. Kindly welcome Miss Lydia into our family and do not fight me on this. It is what I want after all."

Lady Matlock went to her husband and took his arm. "Reginald, Richard is right. As much as we might disagree, he has made his offer and the young lady has accepted. Let us give them our blessing."

The earl would not be so easily managed and removed his arm from his wife's grasp. "I shall never give my blessing on such a terrible match. Had Richard never been injured, he would not have thought twice about Miss Lydia let alone offered for her hand. This is ridiculous! I shall arrange for him to be moved to Pemberley come the morning."

Richard's laughter boomed throughout the room and the earl's anger doubled. "You may laugh all you please, you foolish man. But I hold control over this estate. Either you leave or the Bennet family leaves. The choice is yours."

Mrs. Bennet fluttered her handkerchief in disbelief. One moment her youngest daughter was set to be the mistress of Somersal and the next the earl had made terrible threats.

Jane and Elizabeth moved to usher the younger girls from the room but Lydia would not join them. She stuck out her chin and took Richard's hand. "I am not afraid of the earl. He is being foolish and unkind."

Richard sat up straighter in his bed and gently pulled Lydia down to sit beside him. "My sweet Lydia is right and displays a sight more sense than you father. I will not leave Somersal and the Bennets shall not either. If you cannot be happy for me, then you must be the one to go. Good night, sir."

The Earl of Matlock stood his ground, furious with his son and glaring at the young lady he had chosen. Mrs. Bennet moved to stand beside her daughter. "Tis late and we might all see things differently come the morn. Come Lydia, let us leave the Matlocks to speak privately."

Lydia looked to Richard and he placed a kiss upon her hand. "Go with your mother, my dear. There is nothing to fear from my father. He is simply angry I did not seek his guidance before following my heart."

Elizabeth and Jane waited by the parlor door for their mother and Lydia. There was nothing to be done but leave the Matlock family and allow them their own discussion of the matter.

Mrs. Bennet followed her girls upstairs hoping the colonel was right. Judging by the loud voices that were barely concealed by the now closed door of the parlor, the Earl of Matlock would likely leave for Pemberley come the morning with or without his headstrong son.

At the top of the stairs, she bid her youngest a good night and shooed Elizabeth back to bed. "I spoke to Mr. Darcy this evening, Lizzy, and he was most gracious considering your refusal. I only hope that you might come to your senses and make your apologies to the man sooner rather than later."

Elizabeth's throat had begun to ache again and instead of arguing with her mother, she made her way to her room leaning on Jane. Once inside, she was grateful for her sister's help and was soon back in her bed and eager for the sweet embrace of sleep.

Yawning fiercely, her eyes already drooping, Elizabeth Bennet could not be worried at the moment for the future of her family. They were safe for a time, at least, and Jane approached with the terrible syrup.

"Open up, Lizzy, I suspect this may be your last dose. Come morning I shall leave you with a maid while I see that trunks are packed to leave for London. It appears that no matter what is settled upon downstairs in the parlor, it shall not be a hindrance if a few of us have flown the coop."

Agreeing with Jane as she swallowed her medicine, Elizabeth took the cup of water her sister offered and drank to the last drop. In moments, she was asleep while Jane sat in a chair near the foot of her bed.

When she was sure Elizabeth was sound asleep a full hour later, Jane Bennet arose and went to her own rooms to rest. She passed a maid in the hallway and instructed her to stay in Elizabeth's room for the night. "If she is sick, come for me and I will sit with her."

Tomorrow she would ready her sisters for their trip to London and leave the day after. Lydia would not accompany her and Mrs. Bennet would not wish for her to go as long as the colonel remained at Somersal. With one daughter having foolishly refused a match with the wealthiest man in all of

Derbyshire, the widow Bennet would not falter in seeing Lydia Bennet secure with Colonel Fitzwilliam.

Lady Matlock stood between her husband and son in the parlor as the rest of the house fell asleep around them. She was tired and cross and her husband was making her head hurt with his railing against the Bennets. "Reginald, for the last time, Richard has made his position clear. He will remain at Somersal and will marry Miss Lydia in the summer if he is able. Now come upstairs with me and rest."

The earl had tried several tacks with his second son, all to no avail, and had been bested. His own wife had not seen fit to support his position and he would not see reason. "I shall not rest here another night. The lot of them has turned my own wife and son against me. I should never have allowed them to take up residence here. 'Tis Darcy's fault they have stayed this long."

Lady Matlock shook her head and covered her ears. "I will hear no more of it. Leave for Pemberley if you must but I am done with your obstinate refusal to see reason."

She went to Richard, who was attempting to hide his mirth at her actions, and kissed his cheek. "You devil," she whispered and winked at him before placing her hands over her ears again and quitting the parlor.

Reginald Fitzwilliam was in a fair temper by this time, incensed by the behavior of his wife. "You will come to regret this, son. I will never accept her and I am tempted to throw you all out of Somersal and damn the consequences!"

Knowing his father was unlikely to change his mind, Richard simply shrugged his shoulders with effort and called for a footman. "Good night Father. I must sleep if I am to be carted out come morning."

Stalking from the room, the earl muttered every curse that came to mind and then bellowed for the butler. Richard was happy to have him gone but felt a small bit of pity for the man. Had his mother taken a stand with his father, the night may have ended much differently for himself and Lydia but Lady Matlock would not abide her son being removed from his own home while he was still injured.

As the footman readied him for bed, he watched the glowing flames in the fireplace and smiled happily though he was most tired. His body was aching from fatigue but his spirit was buoyed by the promise of a future with Miss Lydia Bennet.

Tomorrow they could begin a proper courtship though it would not be as easily accomplished as it would if he were recovered. Still, he would see that she was made to feel as special as she ought. There were flowers to arrange and little notes of love he must write and have a maid deliver to her room when she was away from him through the day.

They would dine together in the parlor and he looked forward to standing by her side in the months to come. Though he would not have wished for the terrible accident that had left him without the dreams he held only weeks ago, he was glad for it now.

Being bedridden at Somersal had changed the course of his life for the better and he whispered a silent prayer as the footman poured a draught of whiskey before leaving him.

Chapter 26

In the morning, Elizabeth awoke with a sense of relief that her throat was not aching and her head was free from pain. Besides a lingering feeling of slight fatigue, she was well again. Rolling over in her bed as a maid tended the fire across the room, her eyes fell upon a riotous display of the most beautiful blooms.

In the midst of winter, the arrangement brought a bright breath of spring and she sat up quickly wondering if the maid had sent for them from the modest hothouse of Somersal.

"These are most lovely but who thought to bring them to me?" she asked as the maid stood and approached the bed.

"They arrived early this morning from Pemberley, miss. There is a letter too." The young maid pulled the missive from her skirt pocket and handed it to Elizabeth.

"Shall I send for hot water for a bath, miss?"

Elizabeth smiled and nodded her head. "I would love that. I believe I am recovered well enough to leave this room for the day, thank you."

The maid curtseyed and hurried to arrange her mistress's morning ritual. Elizabeth leaned against her pillows and stared at the small letter. The crackling of the fire combined with the delightful scent of the bouquet gave her a moment's pleasure as she once again enjoyed the return of good health.

The letter was only a small token but the paper was quite expensive and the hand in which her name was written revealed the sender was of the male persuasion. *Mr. Darcy* her mind suggested and she carefully opened the letter.

My dearest Elizabeth,

I was sorry to pass Christmas Day without your company. I hope these flowers find you truly well this morning. Their beauty brought to mind the sparkle in your eyes as you ride and the fullness of your smile when we share scones from Mrs. Drake's generosity.

I would pay a call to Richard this afternoon and if you are able to visit with us, I would be most pleased. I wish to offer my sincerest apologies for the offense given during our moment together on the hill.

I must say, my heart and mind have not changed and it is my wish that someday you will accept my offer in the manner it was given. Until then, I remain your great, good friend and most ardent admirer.

Fitzwilliam Darcy

Smoothing the letter and biting back the tears that pricked her eyes, Elizabeth gave a deep unsettling sigh. Mr. Darcy loved her and would not be swayed by her refusal. Her heart was hopeful at this news as Lydia and Richard's engagement had caused much upheaval at Somersal.

The earl had not been pleased the night before, and as the head of the Fitzwilliam family he might be pushed into a decision that would separate him from his son and the Bennets from their home.

Elizabeth longed for spring when she might at least do her part to manage a bit of security for her mother and sisters. In her heart she wished desperately to accept Mr. Darcy's proposal. As the mistress of Pemberley, she certainly could provide a constant home for them but how was that different from marrying Mr. Collins?

It was true that she admired and loved Mr. Darcy as she could never have done with her cousin and that they would have a wonderful life together. But she did not wish to marry to see her family settled. She wanted to marry for love and because of a mutual esteem. If Mr. Darcy truly meant the words in the letter she now skimmed again, he would wait for her until the Bennets were secure at Somersal or settled elsewhere.

The aroma of freshly baked bread greeted her when she glanced up at the sound of her maid returning. "Your bath is nearly ready, miss, but I thought you might like a bite to eat first while the water cools."

Refolding her letter, Elizabeth sat on the edge of the bed as the maid placed the tray beside her. Plucking a vibrant red rose from the stunning bouquet on her bedside table, Elizabeth delighted in her private breakfast and Mr. Darcy's romantic gesture. There was still hope for them once the races were done.

Outside in the stable, a groom from Pemberley had come to take Merrit away. He spoke with the head groom of Somersal and relayed Mr. Darcy's wishes. "The young miss who favors Merrit must not know that the master has ordered him removed."

Frowning deeply and regretting the upset this would cause Miss Elizabeth, the groom grunted his assent. In the shadows, the young stable boy remained still and silent. His mistress would be distraught to lose Merrit and he must arrange another horse she might prefer once she knew her favorite was gone.

After going about his morning duties, the stable boy settled on two fine horses he might suggest for his mistress if she came to the stables that morning. He brushed each thoroughly before climbing into the hayloft to eat the bread and cheese his mother had given him earlier in the morning as he followed his father to the stables.

In the parlor, Richard Fitzwilliam sat with his mother listening as she spoke of his father. "I would not be surprised to find he intends to return to London without another word on the matter. While I do not disagree with your choice, I do wish you might have spoken with us privately before making an announcement. You know how your father hates being the last to know anything that affects his family."

"Mother, surely you see that it would not have mattered much. Father has taken offense at my happiness and shall not be persuaded of his own folly. His behavior towards the Bennet family has been less than gracious and now that they shall be his relations, he will not be moved."

Lady Matlock knew her son spoke the truth, but she would go to Pemberley and try to reason with her husband. "Still, he is your father and I shall have him present at your wedding. Though he is in a fine temper now, there has never been a time he has been able to resist my ability to persevere."

Rising and placing a kiss on the colonel's forehead, she quit the parlor and called for a carriage to be brought round. The sooner she attempted to placate her husband and allow him to vent his spleen, the sooner harmony could return to her world.

Mrs. Bennet stepped out of the breakfast parlor and greeted her newest ally. The two women had formed a friendship in the weeks the Matlocks had remained at Somersal. "Margaret, do you have a moment? I wished to speak to you about the engagement. Though I am pleased for my Lydia, I do not wish for my family to become a point of contention for yours."

Lady Matlock took Mrs. Bennet's hands and gave her a warm smile. "Franny, they are to wed as soon as Richard is able and so there is no contention on that point. My husband's objections were to be expected as Richard chose to make an announcement before seeking his father's counsel. I shall tend my husband's bruised ego and all will be well."

Mrs. Bennet nodded her head and offered her own concession. "My Jane shall leave for London in the morning with Mary and Kitty to visit our relations there. It is my hope that with half my family gone, the earl might find a bit more comfort at Somersal."

The women embraced as the butler announced the carriage. "My husband may prefer to leave for London himself after our meeting this morning. Please assure your girls they must not leave on our account."

Elizabeth came down the stairs as her mother stood and watched Lady Matlock quit Somersal. "Mother, where is the lady off to so early this morning?"

Mrs. Bennet turned, surprised to see Elizabeth downstairs. "I think she must be gone to Pemberley to see her husband. It appears he left here late last night."

Elizabeth took her mother's arm and steered her toward the salon. "Do you think he might put us out of Somersal, then?"

Mrs. Bennet forgot her reprimand for Elizabeth and walked with her instead. "I do not think his wife would be happy if he did such. With the colonel being his second son, he might decide to withhold Somersal as his home for a time but once word of the engagement spreads that would become impossible without gossip and unwelcome attention for the Fitzwilliam family."

Breathing a sigh of relief, Elizabeth left her mother at the door of the salon as her sisters rushed past them with Constance following behind. "Good morning, Miss Elizabeth, it is a relief to see you well," the governess said as she passed.

Mrs. Bennet was reminded of her earlier reproval of her daughter. "Do not think of riding again, Lizzy, I have forbidden it. Mr. Darcy mentioned that you planned on racing come spring. You shall not race that horse in the spring nor at any other time. Though your father indulged such behavior when you were younger, I will not."

Elizabeth kept her expression one of calm acceptance while the anger at Mr. Darcy revealing her plan to her mother threatened to erupt. His flowers and the words he'd written to her made her anger double as she watched her mother enter the parlor.

How could he betray her secret plan and pretend he cared for her? She had been right to refuse him before and though her heart shrank in her chest at the thought of never becoming his wife, Elizabeth breathed deeply and hurried to the front door. Visiting Merrit would settle her emotions and riding him, though she ought to wait another day before enduring the chill of a ride, would be a way of thwarting her mother and Mr. Darcy in the most wonderful way she could imagine.

Taking her spencer, she pushed open the doors of Somersal and inhaled the cold, crisp air hoping her throat would not take offense at the assault.

Walking with more calm than she felt, Elizabeth approached the stable and entered without delay. She stopped at the door and retrieved a carrot from the basket wishing she had taken an apple from the bowl on the table in the breakfast parlor before rushing outside. She would bring Merrit two apples in the afternoon to compensate for her thoughtlessness.

Her heart sank as she neared Merrit's stall and there was no welcoming whinny. Thinking the groom or stable boy must have him outside, she turned to quit the stable and join them at the paddock. The stable boy called to her from the hayloft. "Miss, wait for me."

Elizabeth watched as the young boy scampered down from his perch. Perhaps he had news of Merrit. He came to stand before her, his head down, and Elizabeth questioned him. "Where is my horse?"

The stable boy lifted his head and shrugged his shoulders. "He has been taken to Pemberley, miss. The master has said you are not to ride him again."

As the anger at her mother and Mr. Darcy consumed her, Elizabeth took her young friend by the shoulders. "Are you certain? When was Merrit taken away?"

"This morning, miss. The groom from Pemberley came and said you were not to know the master's order. I heard it with my own ears."

Elizabeth considered the young boy before her. He had been her shadow on many of her treks across Somersal, even with Mr. Darcy as her companion. He was faithful to her though his actions today would be seen as traitorous if she marched to Pemberley and kicked Mr. Darcy in the shins. "Thank you for telling me. I know it is a hard thing you have chosen to do and I will not betray your confidence."

The stable boy smiled for her, admiration shining in his dark brown eyes. "Do not lose hope, miss. There are two other horses similar to Merrit, miss. I shall saddle the one you choose."

He led Elizabeth to the first horse and counted off the horse's good traits. Elizabeth listened carefully as she surveyed the animal. Though he was a fine specimen, he was not built like a racing horse and so she asked to the see her second choice.

As soon as she saw the sleek brown Arabian, Elizabeth knew he was much better suited to racing than the previous candidate. "What is his name?" she asked.

Her faithful servant smiled. "Buttercup, miss."

Elizabeth laughed and touched the horse's nose before offering a carrot. "Saddle him up as quickly as you might. I wish to ride for a time alone."

The stable boy did not question his mistress's order but went straight to work preparing the horse. Being made to stay behind at the stable while she rode was against his natural inclination to follow her about but the young miss had been slighted by Mr. Darcy in a most terrible manner. While he did not understand the ways of those he served, the young boy knew what it meant to have others decide your life.

He watched as Miss Elizabeth Bennet mounted the unfamiliar horse with ease, though only in her day dress without riding boots, and waved as she nodded to him.

Chapter 27

Lady Matlock fought her desire to rush through the front doors of Pemberley and take her husband to task. The man had always been opinionated with a quick temper but she did love him so. His anger in the face of Richard's rash proposal to Lydia Bennet was not unexpected and yet she hoped he might see reason.

Her niece, Georgiana, was in the parlor when she entered and stood to accept her embrace. "I am quite proud of you, my dear. You served exceptionally well last evening as your brother's hostess. Is he in the library?"

Georgiana waited for her aunt to be seated before joining her. "He has gone riding as is his morning habit. I believe he intended to stop at Somersal afterwards and see Richard."

Lady Matlock was certain her niece did not know of the marriage proposal, for what sheltered young lady could hear such news and not wish to discuss the romantic details. "I have come to see your uncle. I suppose he is in the library?"

"He is Aunt Margaret but I would speak with you for a while longer," Georgiana said, lowering her voice and glancing about the room.

Without a way to discourage her niece, Lady Matlock simple nodded her head and waited.

"I did not mean to eavesdrop last night, but Uncle Reginald arrived in such a temper that I heard his shouts for my brother all the way upstairs. I crept into the hallway and glanced about before spying upon them in the entryway," here the young girl stopped and lowered her lashes.

"And what did you hear? Come, tell me, for I am certain you wish to know the facts of the matter."

Pleased that her aunt had not scolded her for her behavior, Georgiana looked again to the parlor door. "Uncle Reginald said that Richard had proposed to Miss Lydia!"

Lady Matlock wished they might have broken the news to the impressionable young woman in a more discreet manner but her husband's temper had now insured that their son would do exactly as he chose. "Tis true, my dear. Miss Lydia has been a wonderful help and companion to Richard and they have fallen in love, I think."

Georgiana's smile lit her entire face and she grasped her aunt's hands. "We must help Miss Lydia plan the wedding and host the wedding breakfast. I shall go with you to Somersal after you've seen uncle. What wonderful news!"

The two ladies stood and the younger one hurried from the parlor, eager to return upstairs and prepare to visit the Bennets at Somersal.

Lady Matlock shook her head and steeled herself to face the earl. He could bluster all he wished but by arriving at Pemberley late into the night and causing such a fuss, he'd guaranteed that Miss Lydia Bennet would become Lydia Fitzwilliam.

The earl of Matlock made a displeased sound in the back of his throat as his wife entered the library at Pemberley.

Lady Matlock ignored this warning and went to sit beside him in front of a cheerfully dancing fire. The flames warmed and pleased her at the same time. Glancing at her husband's face, she longed to smooth his worried brow but could not do so until after she settled the rift in her family.

"Reginald, please listen. Richard is marrying Miss Lydia and there is nothing we might do to change it. I am certain the servants both here and at Somersal are well aware of it this morning. The merchants in Lambton are likely overjoyed at the monies we shall spend come the summer for their wedding."

The earl turned his gaze away from the fire reluctantly. "Margaret, I am well aware that Richard will marry that girl but I do not have to lend my support. I am leaving for London later today. You may come with me but I do not expect that you will while he is still recovering."

Lady Matlock was surprised that her husband did not continue his arguments against the couple. "I may return home in a few weeks with Miss Lydia so that we might introduce her to our friends and take her to my favorite modiste for her gown and trousseau. I am certain Georgiana will join us as well."

The earl looked again to the fire and brought his cigar to his lips. The silence between the couple lengthened and Lady Matlock stood to quit the library. She placed a loving hand on her husband's shoulder. "I am pleased you shall no longer fight with Richard, my dear. I can't say I am happy with his choice either but I would rather welcome a daughter than lose a son."

Leaving the room before her husband might say more, Lady Matlock breathed a deep sigh of relief. Now there was only Richard's health to focus upon and preparations for a wedding, two things she could manage quite easily without her husband under foot.

Elizabeth cursed the skirts of her day dress as her horse raced across the fields toward the boundaries of Pemberley. She recalled that Jane owned a habit and riding boots and resolved to borrow them before her sister left for London. Jane rarely rode and had never raced.

Wishing to stay out longer than she ought, Elizabeth instead turned the horse back toward Somersal. Her mother was not likely to notice her absence with Lydia's news to share far and wide but there was nothing to be gained by drawing attention to herself.

The new horse was an excellent racer and she would be able to win come the spring upon its back but she missed Merrit terribly.

He must be wondering where she was and why he had been taken away. The thought of never riding Merrit again caused a sharp pain in her heart and renewed her anger with Mr. Darcy.

She reckoned the acquaintance with Fitzwilliam family had been both a blessing and a curse. Elizabeth would never have ridden Merrit at all had her family not come to Somersal after her father's death and Lydia most certainly would not have become engaged to Richard Fitzwilliam while living in Hertfordshire.

Elizabeth dismounted and held the horse's reins loosely as she walked along wishing with all her heart that it was spring. The cold grip of winter made her shiver as the wind picked up. Even if Richard and Lydia became husband and wife, she would need to make other arrangements. A newly married couple would take a wedding trip before settling down to the business of raising a family so there would be time to decide where to live.

She knew she wished to join Jane in London but if Mr. Bingley proposed, she would not want to live in the same house as Caroline Bingley. Kitty would likely stay at Somersal with mother after Lydia was married and Mary could settle with their Aunt and Uncle Phillips in Meryton.

London was the likely choice for Elizabeth's future. Resigning herself to the fact that she would leave for London after her youngest sister returned from her wedding trip, Elizabeth picked up her pace as the cold wind cut through her clothing.

As she gained the stable with Buttercup, Elizabeth halted her steps as the voice of Mr. Darcy drifted through the open stable door. "Merrit is happy at Pemberley. He may return after the races are done. I would not keep him from Miss Elizabeth indefinitely."

Elizabeth hurried inside and ran straight into a retreating Mr. Darcy. He caught her in his arms as she stumbled backwards. "Miss Elizabeth," he began but she placed her hands against his chest to keep her distance. "I am sorry. Please release me, sir. I did not know you were here."

Mr. Darcy noticed the pained expression she wore and cursed himself for listening to Mrs. Bennet. Of course Miss Elizabeth would not stop riding simply because he had taken her horse. He wondered what she had been told about Merrit. She must have overheard his conversation with the groom just now. "I came to explain and beg your forgiveness."

Elizabeth backed away from him and held up a hand after giving Buttercup's reins to the embarrassed groom. "There is nothing you might say that would cause me to forgive you."

She turned and walked slowly for the stable door biting her lower lip to keep from telling him she knew exactly where Merrit was and why. The stable boy did not deserve to be rebuked for his faithful service.

Mr. Darcy followed her and she hurried to gain the front door of Somersal before he might speak again. Before she could open the door and escape him, he caught her by her arm and turned her around. "Miss Elizabeth, there has been a terrible mistake."

Elizabeth's eyes blazed with the anger she had smothered. "Indeed Mr. Darcy. I am sorry to say I was placated by the flowers you sent and the sweet words of your letter. I believed for a brief moment that we could mend our friendship, that felicity in marriage might be possible."

Here she stopped as her bottom lip trembled and tears welled in her eyes. Mr. Darcy drew her into his arms, his heart breaking for the pain he'd caused her with his selfish, thoughtless actions. "Miss Elizabeth, what might I do?"

The carriage carrying Lady Matlock and Miss Darcy appeared at the end of the long drive to Somersal and Elizabeth moved away from Mr. Darcy. "You might have left Merrit in the stables instead of moving him to Pemberley as you told the groom. You knew such an action would hurt me deeply and I hope to never see you again."

Watching the light leave his eyes, Elizabeth regretted the words as soon as they were spoken but she could not take them back. Instead she turned and fled inside Somersal for her rooms.

Mr. Darcy stood bereft as the breeze lifted the edges of his greatcoat. The arrival of the carriage carrying his sister and aunt did not allow him a moment to regain his composure before the footman helped the ladies down.

Georgiana Darcy rushed to his side and began to discuss the wedding of Richard and Miss Lydia. "We must host the wedding breakfast for them, brother. Aunt Margaret will help me and I shall need to go to London in a few weeks to help introduce Miss Lydia to our friends."

Lady Matlock joined them and took Georgiana's arm. "Come, let us see Richard and speak with Miss Lydia. There is much to be done."

Mr. Darcy watched them disappear inside Somersal. He knew his uncle was leaving for London in the afternoon and after his meeting with Miss Elizabeth, he wished to join the man. Even if he returned Merrit to Somersal, Miss Elizabeth had been terribly hurt by his actions. He had managed not only to remove any trust they had built but to assure her that his presence would only bring her further pain.

Instead of going in to visit with his cousin, he returned to the stable to retrieve his horse and return to Pemberley. There was not much to be done for his return to London as he spent most of his time there at Darcy House rather than at home in Derbyshire.

Remaining at Pemberley would only remind him of what he had lost by his own hand.

Upstairs, Elizabeth gave the maid the bouquet that mocked her misery with its beauty. When she was left alone at last, she took his letter from the table and held it against her heart for a moment before throwing it into the fire.

Chapter 28

Spring 1812

Buttercup's hooves churned the thawed ground that meant winter was well past and Elizabeth breathed deeply of air that was redolent with the scent of freshly turned earth. A morning had not passed, in the months since winter, that she did not think of Mr. Darcy.

He had left Derbyshire with his uncle weeks ago, the day of their last meeting. Still wondering whether she had been rash to turn her back on him, Elizabeth sighed and slowed Buttercup to a walk.

The horse had performed well but she would not admit that he was as proficient as Merrit at racing across the fields. Once she knew Mr. Darcy had gone to London, she thought of visiting her favorite horse at Pemberley's stables but would not dare trespass there with Miss Darcy still in residence.

With Lydia and the colonel to marry soon, Miss Darcy spent a great deal of time at Somersal with Lady Matlock and the effect on Lydia had been profound. Even though the other girls had gone to Town with Jane, mother had insisted that Lydia remain under Constance's tutelage.

The combined effect of the governess and Miss Darcy had wrought a change upon her youngest sister that Elizabeth would not have believed had she not seen it for herself.

The love of Colonel Fitzwilliam, and the patient encouragement of Lady Matlock, had also caused Lydia to blossom into a mature young woman who would make a fine mistress of Somersal.

When Mrs. Bennet discovered that Elizabeth was once again riding each morning, she had complained in front of the colonel and he had shared his thoughts on the matter. "Miss Elizabeth should not be made to stay indoors, Mrs. Bennet. She is a wandering, restless soul who would wither as a flower in a vase were she made to remain indoors. I am still upset over the removal of Merrit from Somersal and have written to my cousin to petition for his return."

Colonel Richard Fitzwilliam was not bound by the same decorum as his father and cousin. Speaking his mind on Elizabeth's part had not been done in a rude manner but he had been firm.

Her soon-to-be brother had even implored her mother to return Elizabeth's riding habit and boots. She brushed her hand across the velvety lapel of her coat at the memory and was thankful once more for his intervention.

Dismounting with ease, Elizabeth gazed at the sun as it rose on the horizon. The sight pleased her and she walked with Buttercup to the boulder in the copse of trees where she and Mr. Darcy had begun to deepen their friendship all those months ago. She sniffed at the tears that threatened to fall and pulled a letter from her pocket.

Jane had written from London every week since her departure and shared news of her courtship with Mr. Bingley. Elizabeth laughed as she read Jane's account of Mr. Bingley's proposal for the second time.

Uncle Gardiner was particularly hard on him, Lizzy, and I felt terrible when they entered uncle's study. I could not follow but I waited by the door with my ear pressed against the wood hoping to overhear some of the conversation.

Aunt Madeline found me there and took me by the shoulders to guide me to the parlor. She said that if Mr. Bingley could not withstand a half hour in Uncle Gardiner's parlor then he was never meant to be my husband.

I sat and tried to keep my mind on my embroidery but my fingers would not settle to the task. When I rose and fumbled an excuse to quit the parlor, Aunt Madeline smirked at me but watched me go anyway.

I tried to walk past the study without pause but Mr. Bingley's voice near the door caused me to once again attempt to eavesdrop. I nearly fainted in surprise and embarrassment when the door flew open. Uncle Gardiner caught me and there was a moment of silence before he erupted in loud, boisterous laughter.

When he stopped, he stepped away from me and addressed Mr. Bingley. He told him he ought to ask me now that he had uncle's blessing.

Lizzy, though I knew he sought my hand, 'tis a very special moment indeed when the man you love speaks the words you have longed to hear.

Of course, I accepted and we shall be married in the summer. I have written mother as well to find if Lydia and the Colonel might say their vows with us at Somersal. Mr. Bingley wishes to marry in the garden where we first admitted our feelings for one another.

Elizabeth was pleased for Jane and quite happy that now two of her sisters would be settled. Colonel Fitzwilliam had declared that all the sisters and Mrs. Bennet were more than welcome to stay on at Somersal after his wedding to Lydia but Elizabeth could not imagine living so close to Pemberley now.

There would be family gatherings and events where she would be forced to be in the company of Mr. Darcy whether she wished it or not. 'Twas not a life she would choose for herself.

Elizabeth had determined that after her sisters were wed, she would go to London and stay with the Gardiners while she considered her future. She would have her dowry still and the money from racing Buttercup through the springtime so as not to be a burden on her family in Town.

There were many wealthy families in London with whom she might find employment as a governess or companion. While it was true that Mr. Darcy had a townhome in London, there was little chance they might meet regularly as they surely would if she remained at Somersal.

Folding the letter again, she hugged herself tightly against the cool breeze of an early spring morning before rising to lead Buttercup home.

The races would begin a week from today and she would go into Lambton in the afternoon to enter herself and Buttercup into the first race. Her heart raced in her chest to think of it but she would not change her mind now. Buttercup was a strong, steady horse and they had become a good team.

If Merrit were still with her, she thought she might not have been so anxious at the prospect of racing in but a few days' time. Shaking off her apprehension, Elizabeth shared her hopes and dreams with Buttercup as they walked along.

By the time she handed his reins to the groom, Elizabeth had calmed her nerves and grown excited for her afternoon trip into Lambton. Once her entry was accepted, she could breathe easier.

Mrs. Bennet and Lydia were in the parlor with Colonel Fitzwilliam and Lady Matlock when she entered. There was much discussion regarding a double wedding ceremony and not a one of them took notice when she entered.

Instead of interrupting, she took a chair behind her mother and waited for their conversation to cease. The colonel winked at her and Elizabeth gave him a smile. Lydia was so fortunate to have caught his eye. Elizabeth was relieved that he would care for her mother and sisters after she had gone to London.

"Miss Elizabeth, do you have any particular wishes for the weddings?" he asked as the other ladies in the room turned her way.

"Only that Lydia must go to London so that she and Jane may arrange for their weddings together. I would think our mothers have already made such plans."

Lydia gave a small sigh at Elizabeth's declaration. "I could not possibly leave Richard now, though I would dearly love to be in London with Jane. Surely there are shops in Lambton I might visit instead?"

Lady Matlock and Mrs. Bennet shook their heads in unison at the young lady's suggestion. "Now, Lydia, you must go to Town and let us present you to our friends and have the very best things made for your wedding. Richard shall be fine for a time alone."

Mrs. Bennet smiled at Lady Matlock. "Margaret knows best, Lydia. Lizzy can stay here with Richard while we are away can't you Lizzy?"

Elizabeth hurried to reassure her sister. "But of course. I promise to keep him company until you return Lydia. I will see that the maids and footmen continue their excellent care."

Richard beckoned Lydia to come sit on the side of his bed. "My dear, you must go to London for I know how dearly you wish to do all that mother has said. I would hate to have you sitting here in the parlor with me when there is much to be done in Town before we wed."

Lydia's face lit up with enthusiasm at her beloved's words. She did wish more than anything to be presented by the Matlocks and to feel as important as Jane since they would wed together. "Are you sure, Richard? I would not go if you need me."

The colonel kissed her hand and leaned back against his pillows. "I am sure, dearest. Now, off with all of you, I need my rest."

The ladies quit the parlor and Elizabeth rose to follow them. Richard waved a hand at her. "Please, wait for just a moment."

Elizabeth moved closer to his bed and sat in the chair her mother had just left. "What may I do for you, colonel?"

"You may call me Richard if it pleases you. I shall soon be your brother after all."

Elizabeth took his hand gently and spoke his name. "Only if you call me Lizzy from now on. What might I do for you Richard?"

He inclined his head toward the table beside her. "There is a letter from my cousin there in the top drawer. Darcy thought I might be persuaded to beg you not to race next week."

Anger rose in Elizabeth's breast and her cheeks grew hot. "Why must he insist upon trying to manage my life?"

Richard held back a laugh at her question for he did not wish to anger her further. Instead, he took a breath and stated the obvious. "He loves you, Lizzy. Can you not see that? My cousin is an obstinate man but even he cannot fight his feelings forever."

Elizabeth rose from her chair and paced at the foot of Richard's bed. "What do you think I ought to do?"

The colonel shrugged his shoulders. "My opinion means nothing, nor does Darcy's for that matter. We would advise you from our fears. Surely you know that?"

Indeed she did know their motives. "I have no fears, Richard, other than the fear that I have pushed away the one man I might have loved with all my heart for pride's sake."

Richard Fitzwilliam knew exactly that fear, he'd felt it when he had considered ignoring his feelings for Lydia Bennet. "Lizzy, will your pride bring you years of joy and contentment? Will it fill a home with children and years of wonderful memories?"

Knowing the colonel was right, Elizabeth buried her face in her hands and turned away. After a moment in which she composed herself, Elizabeth turned again to her friend. "I have never compromised in my life, Richard, and I cannot begin now. It is too late for what might have been had I accepted your cousin's proposal. To think of him now is only torture and my mind must be clear for the races."

Richard wished he could stand and go to her, embrace her and help her to see that she could have her races and his cousin's love. Instead, he watched her quit the parlor.

Calling for a footman, he determined to write his cousin and beg him to put aside his prejudice against Elizabeth Bennet's desires. Darcy must accept all of Elizabeth now before another man entered her life and filled the space his cousin had left.

Chapter 29

Mr. Darcy was in his study after dinner when an express arrived from Somersal. Hoping there was nothing amiss with his cousin's health nor any of the Bennet ladies, he waited until his butler left him before opening the missive.

Mr. Darcy was relieved to see his name written neatly across the front of the paper in Richard's handwriting. His cousin had been recovering well from his accident in the winter and had reported that he had been able to stand for a small amount of time only a week ago.

Sitting again at his desk, Mr. Darcy sipped his port and allowed his eyes to roam the page before beginning to read in earnest.

Darcy,

You must come as soon as you might to Somersal to make amends with Lizzy.

Here Darcy stopped and considered Richard's familiar use of Miss Elizabeth's name. Of course, he would be her brother come the summer and so they must have fallen into a pattern of conversing as though they were already family.

How he longed to use that name for her, to hold her in his arms and forget that any disagreement had befallen them. He sighed and returned to Richard's letter.

She has told me that you are the one man she could love with all her heart but that she will race in a week's time. She believes she could never be your wife, Darcy.

Lizzy will not be managed in the way that you run your business or oversee Pemberley or guide Georgiana. I do not believe you would find yourself so attracted to her if she were to bend so easily to your will.

You must come to understand that love, true love, requires that we accept the good and the bad in those we love. 'Tis true of our parents and siblings, but even more true of those we lose our hearts to and wish to wed.

My Lydia is such an example. I would never have considered her were I not injured. But fate placed me here where I might see her through eyes not weary from the world nor blind to the sweetness of her nature. There are certainly characteristics she owns that I would change did I wish her to be perfect but I now know the same is true for myself.

And so love is what makes the difference when weighed against those things we wish to change in others. If you feel that you may live your life without Lizzy and be truly happy, then I wish you all the best.

But if not, make haste and come mend the rift between you. There may be a man in the crowds when she races who will see her for who she is and not turn away over inconsequential differences.

Mr. Darcy had not thought that Miss Elizabeth might meet another man and his cousin's candor served as a sharp reminder of the emotions he had warred with since returning to London.

There was a knock upon his study door and he folded the letter before placing it into the top drawer of his desk. "Come in," he said and rose from his seat.

Charles Bingley entered, his expression one of eternal optimism. He too held a letter and waved it at his friend. "I am sorry to interrupt your peace, Darcy, but today Jane received a letter from Lady Matlock. She is coming to London with Miss Lydia by the week's end. It seems the Bennet sisters shall prepare for their weddings in town and be presented to friends and relations."

Mr. Darcy pinched the bridge of his nose before offering his friend a seat. "It would seem I am never to be free from the Bennet sisters."

Charles chastised him readily. "Why would you wish for such a thing, Darcy? It is clear to everyone that you are in love with Miss Elizabeth but too obstinate to admit it. It is not the fault of the Bennet sisters you are so unhappy."

Mr. Darcy thought of the words of his cousin still fresh in his mind and here was his best friend, who was also now engaged to a Bennet lady, championing the cause of his reconciliation with Elizabeth Bennet.

"Charles, truly you must know what a scandal it would be were the mistress of Pemberley to race with commoners in Derbyshire. What example would that give Georgiana? Not to mention the damage it might do in securing her an advantageous match when she is presented in Town."

Bingley made himself comfortable in a seat before Mr. Darcy's desk. "Whatever the mistress of Pemberley does should likely become the most fashionable activity to be lauded and imitated by all, I would think. As for your sister, there shall never be trouble finding a suitable match with the wealth of Pemberley seen as her greatest asset."

Mr. Darcy knew his friend spoke the truth but he prided himself on proper behavior and comportment. Though Bingley spoke his mind without reservation, there was still much Mr. Darcy must consider before allowing himself to follow the advice of his best friend. "Do you really believe my servants and the villagers of Lambton and Kempton would not be appalled by Miss Elizabeth's penchant for racing horses?"

"I could not say for certain, Darcy, but what does their opinion matter? She will be their mistress and their thoughts shall not be voiced nor tolerated if they wish to continue in their service to your family. Besides, your name is revered throughout Derbyshire and I doubt the servants are truly the source of your concern," Bingley finished his speech and fixed his friend with a pointed stare.

"Tis true, none from that quarter would stand against her. But what of the families and friends of our circle? They might surely exclude her and make life much more disagreeable. Miss Elizabeth might come to wish she had never met me and certainly never married into such censure."

Darcy paced about after revealing his true concerns and Bingley simply allowed the silence to deepen. Mr. Darcy's thoughts on the matter were related to Miss Elizabeth's feelings and standing in the community.

"But Darcy, she already has won their scorn. Miss Elizabeth and her family are seen as a part of Pemberley and unfortunately my sister was complicit in stirring up gossip and disdain amongst your peers. The damage is done. Marrying her may repair some of that."

Darcy recalled Miss Bingley's conversation regarding Miss Elizabeth and her desire to race that night at Pemberley when the Bennets first came to dinner. She had said then that Lady Morely had heard gossip about the Bennet family.

"I had not thought of that, Charles. Perhaps I ought to consider your advice and that of Richard," Mr. Darcy turned and glanced at his desk.

Mr. Bingley placed his hands on his knees before speaking his next words. "There is something more you must know, though I hate to say it. Miss Elizabeth did challenge Richard and myself to race that terrible morning."

Mr. Darcy remained as still as a stone statue at his friend's admission. Finally, he spoke, his voice low and steady. "Why would you both keep such evidence secret?"

Charles Bingley stood and went to his friend. "Because it was an accident, Darcy, and Miss Elizabeth would have been destroyed by the truth. Nothing we might have said or done would have made any difference. The earl would have likely put the Bennets out of Somersal no matter how strongly Richard opposed him. I could not risk having my Jane without a home and Richard would not be the reason for such harsh punishment."

Turning away from his best friend, Mr. Darcy moved slowly to his desk. "Miss Elizabeth has been certain my uncle would put her family out of Somersal. That is the reason she has pursued this plan to race horses. No matter what I said, she would not see reason. I think deep in her mind she knows she challenged you and Richard. Racing is the only way she may secure her family's future but it is also the reason my cousin's future changed so drastically. I have been a fool."

Charles Bingley merely nodded and bid his friend a good night. "Miss Elizabeth Bennet has borne a great loss, my friend. She feels the burden of caring for her family and the disappointment of jeopardizing their current stability. Please do not hurt her more than she has already been hurt."

"I cannot promise what I may or may not do when I see her again face to face, Charles. But I thank you for your advice and candor. Good night."

Darcy remained in his study a full hour after Mr. Bingley had gone upstairs wondering what he might do about Elizabeth Bennet. Leaving his study to give orders to his butler for the morning, Mr. Darcy considered possible outcomes of a meeting with Elizabeth Bennet.

Was his heart strong enough for the task ahead? Ought he to remain in London and simply leave her to her own plans?

Hoping that morning would bring a clear answer, he entered his rooms and lay awake for many hours more as the plans in his head were made and discarded one by one.

At the end of the week, Elizabeth Bennet waved to the remaining ladies of Somersal as they went on their way in a carriage to London.

She was still in her riding habit from her morning run with Buttercup. They were entered into the first race of the afternoon on a track outside Lambton. The advice of the colonel had been to keep Buttercup warmed up and ready and Elizabeth was pleased she had followed his directive.

Hoping to rest now that the house was empty save for herself and the colonel, Elizabeth stopped by the parlor to see him before she went upstairs to her rooms.

Colonel Fitzwilliam had finished his breakfast and was perfectly groomed and sitting up in a chair by the fireplace. Elizabeth noted that his face was without the tell-tale lines of pain that had marked his countenance for many months.

"Why Richard, you look like your old self this morning! Lydia must have had a terrible time leaving your side."

Richard laughed without wincing and beckoned for Elizabeth to come sit beside him. "Indeed. My Lydia was loath to leave me until I reminded her of mother's modiste. I said I wished to see her in every shade of silk imaginable and that seemed to do the trick."

Elizabeth laughed then too, knowing her youngest sister could never resist such temptations. "You must know she will attempt to have a dress made in every color now so as to please you."

"I have told mother not to spare any expense when it comes to Lydia's desires. I have quite enough money to indulge her and am unable to spoil her myself in Town at the moment," Richard said and gave a disappointed sigh.

Elizabeth felt a pang of sorrow pierce her heart for the man. "I am sorry, Richard, I know you must chafe at the restriction when you wish so desperately to court Lydia in the manner many men might take for granted."

Richard was inclined to agree but there was nothing to be done about it now. "I have a lifetime before me to show my Lydia my adoration and I would not begrudge her the happiness of preparing for our wedding. But, today, I wish to be taken to the races and watch you win, Lizzy."

Elizabeth gasped in surprise. "Surely you must not, Richard. If the carriage ride doesn't fatigue you, I am certain the crowd and the noise will."

The colonel was determined. "I am not a delicate flower, Lizzy. I am able to sit up for hours now and standing is becoming much easier every day. If I must leave after your race, then at least I've had the pleasure of enjoying fresh air and a bit of excitement. Please, a man such as myself grows tired of papered walls and a sick bed."

Knowing she could not dissuade the man, Elizabeth made a bargain. "I shall speak with the footmen and there shall be two maids to accompany you. If there is the hint of discomfort, you must allow them to bring you home, Richard. I shall worry if you will not agree."

Richard sighed and gave his consent. "I would not have you worry on my account, Lizzy. You must do your best in this race. I sent an express to Darcy several days ago after we talked and I am hoping he took my advice. Nevertheless, I shall not have you race without a member of the family present. Now, upstairs and get your rest."

Elizabeth stood and bent to embrace the colonel. She did not know what he might have said to Mr. Darcy in his express but she could only guess he had once again argued with the man on her behalf. Colonel Fitzwilliam had taken the role of brother quite seriously and she loved him dearly for the display.

"You must rest as well, Richard. Buttercup and I may prove to be too much excitement this afternoon."

Elizabeth quit the parlor to the sound of Richard's laughter. She thought how very happy she was to hear it and to know the colonel was regaining his health at Somersal. In the months since her father's death, Elizabeth had never felt at ease nor secure in her family's situation but Richard Fitzwilliam had slowly filled that emptiness with his patience and good humor.

She could not think of Mr. Darcy without a great sadness overcoming her and so Elizabeth simply entered her rooms and retrieved her journal from the desk by the large window that admitted the bright spring sunshine.

Sitting at the foot of her bed, she flipped the pages and relived her family's journey to Somersal and all the wonderful and terrible things that had happened in the months since. Soon, she yawned and kicked off her boots allowing them to clatter to the floor, their soft buttery sheen catching the sunlight from the window as they landed on the green rug beside her bed.

Her eyes fluttered closed and she slept, her dreams of riding Merrit with Mr. Darcy across the fields so vivid she felt as though she were awake the entire time.

Chapter 30

Colonel Fitzwilliam sat on a platform overlooking the racetrack with the mayor of Lambton, his maids from Somersal, and a footman nearby to lend a hand should he require assistance, as Elizabeth glanced at the crowd that had assembled. Her heart raced most alarmingly as the noise of the crowd grew.

It had been years since she had last raced and she wondered what on earth had possessed her to think she might still be able to drive a horse to victory.

Shaking her head and breathing deeply to dispel the nervous jitters that made her limbs twitch, Elizabeth turned and went to soothe herself by brushing Buttercup's glossy coat again.

When she arrived at the stall where Buttercup ought to be, she found Merrit standing there instead. Her jaw dropped open and her hands shook as she approached her old friend.

Merrit gave a whinny at the sight of his mistress and shook his handsome head to and fro. Elizabeth laughed, though tears spilled from her eyes. She glanced about for her stable boy and motioned him to her side. "What has happened? Where is Buttercup?"

The boy smiled at her before turning to look for Mr. Darcy. The gentleman was nowhere to be found. Turning as Elizabeth spoke to him again, the stable boy shrugged his shoulders. "The groom from Pemberley delivered him not more than a moment ago, miss. Buttercup is on his way back to Somersal far as I can tell. The groom said his master gave the order for Merrit to be delivered here before the race."

Elizabeth swiped the tears from her cheeks and looked about the stalls for any sign of Mr. Darcy. Richard had written to tell his cousin she was racing and perhaps the man had sent Merrit to her as a peace offering.

Ordering the stable boy to prepare Merrit for the race, Elizabeth left the stall and went out back to regain her composure. The noise of the crowd was muffled here and she wandered into the high grass of the field behind the racetrack.

Hugging herself and wishing she might thank Mr. Darcy, Elizabeth closed her eyes and breathed deeply. Perhaps there was hope for them after all. Or maybe Mr. Darcy was only being kind once he knew for certain she would not be dissuaded from her plan. He had said he would not keep Merrit from her forever.

A familiar scent tickled Elizabeth's nose and she chided herself. Thinking of Mr. Darcy had brought the memory of his cologne to her in a field outside Lambton. Turning to make her way back to Merrit, Elizabeth let out a surprised cry when she bumped into the very solid presence of Fitzwilliam Darcy.

His eyes were full of love and regret and Elizabeth was very sorry for having left him on the steps of Somersal all those months ago.

Mr. Darcy beheld the beauty of his love for a moment before speaking. The hope in his chest swelled as a small smile appeared on her lovely pink lips. He longed to place a kiss there so that his heart ached at being denied its desire.

"Miss Elizabeth," he began but she placed a finger against his lips.

"Mr. Darcy, I do not know why you have come and brought Merrit. I dare not hope that you love me still for if you do not, I shall find no joy in this meeting save the joy of seeing your face once more."

Mr. Darcy forgot himself and pulled her roughly into his arms, crushing her pliant body against the strength of his own. Overcome with his love for Elizabeth Bennet, he cared not if she hated him forever as long as he could hold her for a moment in time as he had longed to do since meeting her again at Somersal.

They stood in a lover's embrace for what seemed an eternity and yet was such a brief moment. Elizabeth laid her head against his chest searching for the sound of his heart to see if it was racing in time with her own.

Mr. Darcy rested his chin on top of her head. It fit so perfectly there that he swallowed the lump in his throat and simply relished the moment with the woman he loved more than life itself.

When he trusted himself at last to speak to her, Mr. Darcy did not release her from his arms to see her face. Instead, he poured out his heart while she hid her face in the shelter of his shirt front.

"Miss Elizabeth, my Elizabeth, I love you still. I have come to offer my apologies and again beg you to be my wife. I have lived a terrible existence in London knowing how deeply I hurt you. Your pain has been my own through dark, restless nights and days void of peace or joy. Please forgive me, I do not care if you race horses or wear breeches or howl at the full moon like a banshee. I love you, all of you. Please say it is not too late for us."

Elizabeth raised her arms to encircle his body and returned Mr. Darcy's fierce embrace. She could no more deny her love for him than the sun could refuse to rise each morning. Her voice shook as she assured him their future happiness was indeed possible.

"Mr. Darcy, my Darcy, I have loved you always. It is I who must give an apology, sir, for you have been nothing but kind to my family and myself. Even if you had not come today and brought Merrit, I would have left for London come the morrow and thrown myself on your mercy."

Mr. Darcy gazed into Elizabeth's eyes as she lifted her face at last to show him the truth of her words. He gently tilted her chin and kissed her perfect lips with much ardor. Elizabeth's head spun at the fervor of his assault and the rising noise of the crowd barely registered in her ears.

The stable boy came bounding from the stalls, yelling her name. "Miss Elizabeth, Miss Elizabeth! 'Tis time to race!"

Mr. Darcy released her as the boy approached and Elizabeth glanced at her booted feet as the boy skidded to a halt beside the great man. "Pardon me, sir, I did not know you were here."

Elizabeth glanced up at Mr. Darcy as the afternoon sun framed him in its golden glow. "He is here and he has come to see me race."

Taking the stable boy's hand, Elizabeth rushed back to Merrit's stall. As she led Merrit to his place at the staring line, Mr. Darcy stopped her and placed another kiss on her lips for good luck. His whispered words brought a peace and stillness to her once jangled nerves. "Bring home a victory for Pemberley, my love, and I shall have a case made especially for your trophies."

Elizabeth wished to remain at his side and receive more of his tender kisses but the other racers were passing them to line up for the starting gun. "Victory is already ours, my dear Darcy."

She mounted Merrit with ease and her heart sang to be astride her best friend for the race ahead. Elizabeth thought of Pemberley, of the children she and Darcy would have, and how she would teach them to ride and perhaps race across the fields one day. The fields where their father had won her heart.

Mr. Darcy hurried to take a seat near Richard on the platform and gestured towards Elizabeth and Merrit when he addressed the mayor. "She shall soon be the mistress of Pemberley, sir, what do you think of that?"

Elizabeth took her place with Merrit at the starting line and waved to her beloved, her face a study in joyful beauty. When the gun was raised, she leaned over and whispered to Merrit. "Let us win, Merrit, and you shall have a bushel of apples every morning as your prize."

Merrit knickered his agreement and when the gun fired into the air, Elizabeth and her horse dashed away from their competitors and brought the crowd to a rousing, raucous crescendo as they streaked effortlessly around the track.

Mr. Darcy found himself on his feet in moments, cheering his beautiful, beloved Lizzy on to victory. The mayor was shocked by this behavior and the gentleman's earlier words about the lovely beauty now leading the field and looked to Richard to find if his misgivings were shared.

The colonel shrugged his shoulders and motioned for his footman to help him stand. The mayor laughed and jumped to his feet as well, eager to appear supportive of his wealthy neighbors.

Elizabeth turned the last corner into the final stretch to see her future husband and brother-in-law cheering as heartily as those in the crowd below them. Giving Merrit a gentle nudge with her thighs, Elizabeth leaned forward keeping her head down as Merrit's stride lengthened. In a moment, horse and rider were across the finish line to the cheers of the crowd.

After another gallop around the track with a winner's wreath of flowers about Merrit's neck, Elizabeth halted before the platform and took Darcy's hand to dismount and be seated to watch the next race that would begin in moments.

The stable boy retrieved Merrit and assured Elizabeth he would tend her victorious steed with much love and care.

The mayor gave a slight bow before taking her hand. "Miss Bennet, 'twas a truly invigorating win and one I am happy to have witnessed. Will you race again for us this spring?"

Elizabeth looked to Mr. Darcy before answering, for now she did not have a need to race but she did wish to continue to participate for the thrill and excitement the event had brought to her neighbors.

Mr. Darcy gave a slight nod of his head and allowed his beloved to answer the mayor. "Yes sir," she replied with great joy, "I would not miss another opportunity to participate in the Lambton races."

The mayor was quite pleased and left Elizabeth and Mr. Darcy to speak with the colonel. Looking up into the eyes of her true love, Elizabeth moved closer to Mr. Darcy and leaned into him as his arm went around her waist. "Shall we retire to the carriage, Mr. Darcy? There is much I would discuss with you away from the noise of the crowd."

Mr. Darcy needed no further encouragement to be alone with his intended. His eyes darkened with desire as he led Elizabeth down the platform steps and to the carriage Richard had ridden in to the races.

"You may tell me all that is in your heart, Miss Elizabeth, but first I must show you how ardently I love and admire you."

Elizabeth blushed at these words and took his hand as she stepped inside the carriage. Her first lesson in the passionate kisses of a man too long denied began as Fitzwilliam Darcy entered the carriage and pulled the heavy drapes across the windows.

Epilogue

The garden of Somersal was crowded with the townspeople of Lambton as the last of the couples to be married that day stood before the parson.

Elizabeth Bennet gazed steadily into the eyes of Fitzwilliam Darcy as the parson's sonorous voice droned on around them reminding her of the bees that hovered heavily over the surrounding blooms.

The words she needed to speak to become Mrs. Fitzwilliam Darcy and the mistress of Pemberley flew easily from her lips to her husband's ears and she was rewarded with a stunning smile from the man.

A sigh from the gathered crowd greeted the couple as they turned to face their guests as husband and wife. Charles and Jane Bingley stood to Elizabeth's right while Richard and Lydia Fitzwilliam stood to Mr. Darcy's left.

As the musicians gathered beneath a flowering Hawthorn tree, its snow-white petals drifting to the ground to rest in a fragrant carpet, Elizabeth nodded to her eldest sister. The music began and Charles led Jane to the first carriage awaiting the trio of newlyweds. They would all be taken to Pemberley for a sumptuous wedding breakfast before departing on their wedding trips.

Next, Richard led Lydia to the second carriage that arrived, his gait slower than it had been in the days before his accident but still strong and sure as his recovery had been a wonderful success. Some called it a miracle, but Elizabeth knew it was the patient love and care of her youngest sister that had brought the man through his ordeal.

Last of all, Mr. Darcy led Elizabeth forward and to her surprise no carriage appeared. Instead, Merrit and Mr. Darcy's horse were led to stand behind Richard and Lydia's carriage. Around Merrit's neck was a large wreath made from the same flowers of Elizabeth's elaborate wedding bouquet.

She turned to Mr. Darcy, her smile squeezing his heart. "Must we follow behind or shall we cross the fields together? I would like to visit our copse of trees as husband and wife where I might kiss you without the awkwardness of our first meeting there or the prying eyes here."

Mr. Darcy would not deny his Elizabeth a wish that ended with him receiving the sweet fullness of her lips in a secluded rendezvous. He told the footmen of their plan and the party pulled away from Somersal as their guests loaded into their own carriages to descend upon Pemberley for a grand celebration.

Once the party was clear of Somersal and half way to Pemberley, Mr. Darcy led his horse off the lane and into the field pausing to wait while Elizabeth urged Merrit forward.

Together the happy couple waited by the roadside to wave their guests on to Pemberley. Once they were alone, Elizabeth clucked her tongue to Merrit and the horse turned and smartly cantered with his mistress across the field. Mr. Darcy followed behind, admiring the view of his new wife as she sat comfortably in the saddle in spite of the full skirt of her wedding dress.

Never in his life had he been quite so happy and he brushed away a lone tear that escaped in spite of his best effort to retain his composure. Elizabeth Bennet was now Elizabeth Darcy and his heart sang with joy that he had not lost her forever.

The memory of his family's connection to her father gave him pause and he smiled to think that Thomas Bennet's daughter was as brave as her father. Her actions the day Richard Fitzwilliam was injured spoke of that trait more eloquently than words. He hoped a measure of that bravery would pass to their children and the penchant for thrill seeking might skip the next generation.

He caught her up near the copse where she longed to give him their first kiss since they had exchanged vows and smiled as he saw her stable boy standing near the boulder with a small basket in his hands.

Elizabeth saw him too and laughed. She called to the boy as the horses approached. "What have you there in your hands young man?"

The stable boy waited until Mr. Darcy had dismounted and helped his lady down from her seat. When the happy couple approached, he handed the basket to his master. "Tis a gift from Mrs. Drake. She was sorry to miss the wedding, but her twins were too sick to leave for very long."

Elizabeth's brow furrowed and she turned to Mr. Darcy. "Would it be proper for us to send for the apothecary in Lambton?"

Mr. Darcy nodded his approval. He turned to the stable boy and gave him his thanks and a new task. "Thank you for waiting here for us son, now go and do your mistress's bidding and fetch the apothecary to the Drake cottage."

The boy whistled to his little pony but Mr. Darcy thought of a question he hadn't when he followed Elizabeth to the copse. As her faithful servant spurred his pony to action, Mr. Darcy turned to Elizabeth. "Mrs. Darcy," he said, savoring the sound of the title before continuing, "how did he know to meet us here?"

Elizabeth smiled shyly before answering. "Before, when I thought we were to take a carriage like my sisters, I told him we would stop here before continuing on foot to Pemberley. He was to bring the horses and wait for us."

Mr. Darcy took his wife's hand and laughed. His bride had plotted a way to be alone with him while he plotted a way to honor her love of riding with him across the fields. "I am happy for Mrs. Drake that the boy was able to be her messenger and meet us here. Now, shall we enjoy her gift before we make our way to Pemberley?"

Elizabeth agreed and pulled her husband toward the boulder that had been warmed by the summer sun. "I could not have thought of a more wonderful gift. Mrs. Drake may find herself promoted to the kitchens of Pemberley as my personal baker if she wishes."

Removing his coat and spreading it on the boulder for his wife's comfort, Mr. Darcy placed the basket on the ground and helped her to sit. "I know I said I preferred your riding habit when we take the horses out in the morning, but something about this dress stops my heart."

Mrs. Darcy blushed a lovely shade of pink and glanced at her skirts. "It is a beautiful dress and I shall cherish it always but I do long for my riding habit and boots."

Mr. Darcy retrieved the basket and opened it to find two perfect scones and a small crock of jam. He showed Elizabeth the contents and held the basket while she took one and enjoyed the heavenly aroma. Carefully taking the small knife from a napkin inside the basket, she spread the jam with enthusiasm and took a bite.

Her eyes closed in deep appreciation and Mr. Darcy chuckled. "You must not forget your husband, my dear. My stomach demands you share your portion."

Elizabeth opened her eyes and swallowed before taking up the knife to give another generous dollop of jam to the remaining half of the scone. She held it up before Mr. Darcy's lips and smiled. "May our life together be full of sunshine, warm scones, and sweet jam."

Mr. Darcy opened his mouth as she brought the scone near. Taking a heavenly bite, he too closed his eyes as the sweet berry taste of the jam combined with the perfect crumb of the scone. A deep, appreciative rumble sounded in his chest as he chewed.

As his wife eagerly applied more jam to the remaining portion of scone, Mr. Darcy swallowed and licked his lips. "I wonder which is sweeter, your lips or this jam?"

Elizabeth's eyes sparkled with mischief as she pretended to consider his question. "I would say the jam, sir. But, only you may be the judge."

Mr. Darcy moved swiftly and caught her in his embrace not caring that the scone in her hand was now crushed against the pristine white of his shirt front. He gazed into her eyes enjoying the look of longing she could not hide.

Bending his head, he caught her lips softly before deepening their kiss. Elizabeth moaned as the kiss left her breathless and trembling. Her mother had explained a wife's duties to her three engaged daughters days before their triple wedding ceremony and while the details had fascinated her, the execution left her worrying that perhaps she might fail miserably.

If his kiss was any indication, she would be the one left deeply satisfied while he would be the one to exercise patience and understanding. When their lips parted, Mr. Darcy again licked his lips.

Elizabeth watched his tongue with a distracted air thinking how very talented he was with its use. Mr. Darcy smiled a devilish grin and brushed an errant curl behind her ear. "Mrs. Darcy, I am pleased to inform you that your lips are indeed much sweeter than Mrs. Drake's jam."

Laughing at her husband, Elizabeth thought to pay him the same compliment. "I must say that although her scones are the freshest and most delicious I have ever tasted, your lips are still my favorite treat Mr. Darcy."

Proud of his wife's estimation, Mr. Darcy finagled another kiss, this time lifting his happy wife easily from her seat on the rock. Elizabeth gave a startled gasp at his strength and looped her arms around his neck as his lips found hers.

Elizabeth grew still in his arms as a breeze lifted the curls at the nape of her neck. The cooling air was a contrast to the heat that burned through her at her husband's strong embrace and demanding kisses.

Tingling to the tip of her toes, Elizabeth Darcy knew that she and her husband would be late to their wedding breakfast and that tongues would likely gossip for days when their master and mistress arrived flushed and bright-eyed from their bliss in the copse of trees between Pemberley and Somersal.

The End

Made in the USA
Lexington, KY
28 February 2017